MISSING

An LDS Mystery Novel

RONDA GIBB HINRICHSEN

To Rolin, the love of my life.
There's a bit of you in every hero.

And to Dorla Jenkins, my teacher.

This is a work of fiction. The characters and events herein are the product of the author's imagination, and any similarities to real people or situations are purely coincidental.

Walnut Springs Press, LLC
110 South 800 West
Brigham City, Utah 84302
http://walnutspringspress.blogspot.com

ISBN: 978-1-935217-30-5

{ACKNOWLEDGMENTS}

Just as it takes a community to raise a child, so does it take the hearts and talents of many people to create a book. Dozens of friends, fellow writers, and specialists have been instrumental in helping me write *Missing*, but I must specifically recognize a few.

First, a tremendous thank you to my husband and children for both enduring and inspiring my writing endeavors. Their love, support, and familial associations are priceless to me.

Unending thanks to my critique group: Josi Kilpack, Jody Durfee, Becki Clayson, and our beloved, very much "missed" friend, Anne Creager, who recently succumbed to cancer. I could not have brought Stacie's story to fruition without them or their invaluable insights.

Thanks to Walnut Springs Press and my editor, Linda Prince. Their enthusiasm and professionalism throughout the publication process have been invaluable.

Finally, thanks to my parents, Ronald and Kathleen Gibb. I will forever be grateful for their ongoing encouragement and love.

{PROLOGUE}

Thirteen-year-old Stacie Cox walked down the heavily wooded path to the A-frame home where she and her aunt and uncle lived during the summer months. She pulled her bandana from her pocket and wiped the sweat from her neck and forehead before opening the screen door and stepping into the dimly lit living room.

"I won't ask about the hike," Aunt Kathy called from the kitchen, "because I already know you enjoyed it. But what about the Smythes?"

Stacie sank onto the couch. "Mrs. Smythe said the mountains looked the same from there as they do from her store window in Rexburg."

Aunt Kathy laughed. "Some people don't get nature."

"Then why do they go camping?" Stacie loosened the laces on her hiking boots.

"Same reason you like to hike so much. It's a chance to get away from it all and just think." Aunt Kathy, came out of the kitchen, her graying, light brown hair pulled tight in a ponytail, She placed a ham sandwich, baby carrots, and a glass of milk on the table. "Besides, it's cheaper."

Stacie slipped on her flip-flops. "Sorry, I'll have to eat later.

Mrs. Smythe asked me to watch her kids at the pool for a few minutes."

"Don't let them take advantage of you, dear. You work for the campground, not for her."

"I'll try not to. She said I'd only be watching the boys for a few minutes while she and Jessica changed into their swimsuits."

"Okay. But they better not expect you to babysit for free the entire time they're here."

"If it takes too long, I'll tell them you have something you need me to do."

"Like eat your lunch!"

Stacie grinned, stepped out the door, and headed to the pool.

Mrs. Smythe and her children were waiting for her next to the Swim at Your Own Risk sign. She gave Stacie a cool once-over. "I thought you were changing into your suit. You took long enough."

"I—I was going to, but my aunt needs me back soon."

Mrs. Smythe frowned. "The boys are over there. Jessica and I will be back in a few minutes."

Stacie opened the gate to the fence that surrounded the pool and walked to where the boys were swimming. More accurately, they were fighting.

"Let go of Harold's ear!" Stacie yelled to Sam.

"He won't let me have the ball!"

"I had it first!"

Stacie stood to her fullest height. "Let me have the ball. It's mine."

"No it's not. It's the campground's!" Sam had let go of Harold's ear, but now his fingers were entwined in his hair.

"I own the campground!"

"Nuh-uh! On the hike you said your aunt and uncle own it!"

"Yeah, well, I live with them. They're my family, so it's like

I own it too."

Harold screamed and threw the ball to the other side of the pool just as someone tugged at Stacie's shirt. She turned to see Jessica. The young girl's bright, brown eyes shined with excitement.

"Where's your mom?"

"She's in the camper," Jessica said, holding out two pairs of goggles. "These are for the boys."

"Thanks, Jessica. I'll get them in a minute. Right now I've got to get that ball. Wait right there."

Within moments, Stacie had it.

"Hey!" Harold cried.

"If you can figure out how to play without fighting, you can have it back," Stacie said, remembering the babysitting tip her mother had shared with her a few months before she died.

"Tell Harold to let me have it, and we'll stop fighting."

"No, tell Sam to let me have it."

Stacie pushed the long strand of dark brown hair that had fallen from her ponytail back behind her ear. "Uh, who had it first?"

"Me!"

Sam pushed Harold. "You did not. I picked it up as soon as I walked through the gate."

"I had it before you even got there."

"That's enough, boys." Mrs. Smythe had come up behind them, her arms full of towels. "And no more fighting about anything else, either, or it's back inside for a nap."

"A nap?"

Mrs. Smythe smiled briefly, and Stacie.

"Now, where's Jessica?"

Stacie turned. "She's over—"

The goggles were on the side of the pool.

The hint of a grin left Mrs. Smythe's face. "Over where?"

Stacie ran. "Jessica!" She picked up the goggles. "Jessica!"

Mrs. Smythe caught up to her. The boys were close behind. "Weren't you watching her?"

"I was trying to stop the boys from fighting." Stacie scanned the poolside. "She was right here." And then she paled.

Mrs. Smythe looked at the pool too. "Jessica!" she screamed, lunging forward.

Stacie dove in, vaguely aware of Mrs. Smythe's cries for help.

Stroke. Stroke. Reach. Got her!

Stacie lifted Jessica's face out of the water, but the girl didn't sputter. She didn't move at all.

Mrs. Smythe screamed.

Don't listen. Stacie thought. *Just get her out of the pool.*

From the corner of her eye, Stacie saw Aunt Kathy and Uncle Frank rush through the pool gate.

"What's going on?" Uncle Frank rushed to the poolside, took Jessica from Stacie's arms, and laid her on the concrete. He tilted the little girl's head back and began breathing into her mouth.

Please, Heavenly Father, help her breathe!

Stacie climbed out of the pool, her limbs shaking even though it was a hot July day. She saw Aunt Kathy put her arm around Mrs. Smythe, who was now crying hysterically.

"Frank used to be an EMT," Aunt Kathy soothed, trying to lead the woman away from the pool. "Stacie, get the cell phone from the pickup and call 911."

Stacie raced to the gate, but as she pulled it open, Mrs. Smythe began to scream. "Someone do something! She's not responding!"

Tears poured down Stacie's cheeks. *Where is the pickup?*

"Stacie, you were here!" Mrs. Smythe's voice grew venomously shrill. "You were supposed to be watching her!"

Finally, Stacie found the pickup and called 911. Then she

waited for the paramedics to arrive, led them to the pool, and watched their futile efforts to revive Jessica. But it wasn't until they loaded the child's lifeless body into the ambulance that Stacie ran.

She ran and ran and ran.

{ CHAPTER 1 }

EIGHT YEARS LATER

August 12

Adrienne brushed the traitorous tears from her face, wiping away in one quick movement the emptiness that had filled her since the accident. It was as if sudden energy—life—had returned to her veins, telling her she didn't have to feel this way anymore. The agony was over, and that child—soon to be her child, the one she'd watched for nearly an hour now—was right there, running toward her.

Adrienne stepped out from the cover of the pine trees. "Can I help you?" she asked.

The girl stopped running, wiped the tears from her cheeks, and shrugged. Her broken expression reminded Adrienne of when she used to cry herself, especially when her mother left her alone with her first stepfather. It was the greatest of betrayals, but his neglect had given her strength she could share with this child. Her child. Beauty and strength all the world would know she had because she'd raised this Riana. Her new Riana. Her daughter.

"Are you hiding from someone?" she asked soothingly.

Another shrug.

Adrienne glanced through the trees toward the secluded

clearing of the playground. She had seen that other mother arguing with Riana, and Riana had run off in a tantrum, but now the mother had her back to them and was standing at the base of the slide, watching, waiting for another child, a boy, to whisk down to her.

"I bet no one will find you in my car," Adrienne said.

Riana peered at the mother through the trees, and her brow furrowed.

"Did someone make you feel bad?" Adrienne nudged the child toward the road.

Riana nodded.

"Then let's hide, okay?"

The girl didn't answer, but Adrienne took her hand and led her away.

December 15

They say trouble comes in threes, and if this was only number 2, Stacie hated to think what number 3 would be. She closed her cell phone.

"What's wrong?" Janice whispered.

The tour bus turned onto Fort Street.

"Nothing," Stacie replied.

Janice's dark eyes settled on her with that innate, reassuring power Stacie had always believed came from her Sioux ancestry. "Then why are your hands shaking?"

"Read this." Stacie handed her friend her phone and the two of them read the text together.

> Didn't want you to hear from someone else.
> The Smythes have sued the campground
> again. Claim we're financially responsible
> for their daughter's death. Everything

under control. Good luck on your solo.

"You've got to be kidding," Janice said. "I thought that was settled."

"Nothing's ever settled with that woman." Stacie swallowed the bile that always surfaced with thoughts of Mrs. Smythe.

Keep me posted.

She pressed SEND, tucked her phone in the bag she kept in the overhead compartment, and peered out the bus window. The trees and houses flickered by like a slide show on fast-forward, and for a moment Stacie wished the posh Victorian buildings weren't in the middle of a bustling city of almost-green lawns and manicured bushes, but were instead draped with blankets of snow and icicles. That way, it would feel more like Christmas.

Stacie sighed. The choir's Christmas tour was in full swing, and Stacie's accompanist for her solo was ill and unable to play for her. That was trouble number 1. She'd be singing with a substitute accompanist, and the idea made her nervous.

The driver turned into Craigdarroch Castle's driveway, and once the bus came to a stop, Stacie and the other choir members filed off quickly.

"Don't worry," Brother Fillmore, the choir director, said when Stacie stepped onto the wet pavement. "You and Matt will do just fine."

"Did you see where he went? I'd like to at least talk through the solo before we perform it."

"Up near the front. He was one of the first off the bus."

Stacie scanned the crowd ahead of her, trying to ignore her growing anxiety. Then she saw him. He stood at the base of the stone steps beneath the castle's arched entry, and almost as if she'd called his name, he suddenly turned his gaze to hers, held it briefly, then nodded before continuing up to the doorway. Confidence, she suspected, was what he meant to convey, but it didn't comfort her. Sure, Matt was a good pianist, but she and Lara were such a perfect team, always anticipating the other's movements. Stacie had learned to rely on her.

A brisk breeze caught a thick strand of Stacie's hair and plastered it across her eyes, but by the time she'd pushed it away, Matt had stepped inside the castle.

She gathered the skirt of her sapphire formal in both hands and rushed up the steps and through the door. It took a moment for her eyes to adjust to the dim light, but when they did, she saw that she was standing at the front of an open hall. The floors and walls were paneled with a warm white oak and lined with historical displays of Christmas ornaments and children's toys. Ivy adorned the banister of a box-shaped, winding grand staircase, and light filtering through the stained-glass windows added a multicolored luster to the early-twentieth-century Christmas tree display. Across the hall were two widely separated doorways that opened into a large, chandeliered room. And humming through the air were the blended voices of dozens of tourists.

"Are you looking for me?"

Stacie turned and saw Matt standing uncomfortably close to her.

"Yes," she said aloud. "I thought, well, since we haven't practiced together yet, we ought to talk through my solo and—"

He shrugged slightly and looked passed her, or rather he gazed over her head and across the room. "We can if you want, but I've heard it many times." His bass voice was so soft she had to strain to hear him over the crowd's drone. "You sing 'Silent Night' simply enough, Stacie. I shouldn't have any trouble following you."

Stacie tried not to grimace. *Simply enough?* Did he mean that as a compliment or an insult? "This is important to me, Matt. I know the city dignitaries won't be here today, but this is pretty much our dress rehearsal."

He shook his head. "It's too late to do anything about it now. Maybe later we can change things. But I really think we'll be fine."

Stacie suddenly felt nauseous. "What do you mean? Change what?"

Before Matt could answer her, Brother Fillmore, who stood in front of the fireplace between the two doorways, motioned them to the portable risers, and Matt started forward. If Stacie didn't speak now, she'd lose her chance.

"I can change something if I need to," she blurted. "What's wrong with the song?"

Matt stopped, turned, and looked at her beneath lowered eyelids. "The ending's not right. Slow down the last note. Let it float for a second longer, then I'll play the final chord."

Stacie stared at him. Even after all her practicing, she knew he was right about the ending. But before she had a chance to tell him so, he nodded and said, "Like I told you, it's too late now. It's your decision."

"Wait a second. I didn't give you my answer."

Light flashed through his dark brown eyes. "Well?"

Stacie licked her lips, preparing to graciously tell him they'd perform it as he'd suggested, but when a hint of smugness suddenly shaded his expression, she stopped. Was he teasing her or telling her the truth?

Matt shrugged, then headed to the risers where the rest of the choir was waiting. Confused and a bit embarrassed, Stacie followed him.

As soon as they stepped into their positions, Brother Fillmore cleared his throat. "Mr. Underwood, head of the Craigdarroch Historical Society, has asked us to sing our numbers in this hall. However, Stacie and Matt will perform 'Silent Night,'" he motioned to one of the two doors, "at the piano in the drawing room. Stacie, I'd like you to stand on the middle row today, between Tom and Matt, to minimize the distraction."

Stacie dutifully moved to the middle row.

"Have you made up your mind?" Matt whispered as soon as she settled in next to him. He was looking straight ahead as if they were already performing.

Stacie didn't look at him, either. "I don't know. Were you serious?" She gazed at the gathering audience, realizing that many of the tourists would simply be walking by during this concert, somewhat like at an open house, where they could listen to the choir while looking at the displays.

"Of course I was serious. What'd you think?"

"I wasn't sure. I thought you might be joking." Stacie noticed many children in the audience. They were probably on school tours, and their faces seemed so bright with anticipation that it filled Stacie with guilt. How could she even consider giving them less than her best? She turned to Matt. "I'll sing the end the way you suggested. Okay?"

Matt's unexpectedly appreciative gaze held hers so long it sent heat to her cheeks, and she involuntarily inched backward. But still he watched her, wordless.

"Well?" Her voice fluttered uneasily, so she stood even taller than she had before, almost on her tiptoes, hoping it would restore the edge—the self-control—she needed, even though it put her barely at eye level with his shoulder.

"Agreed," he said.

The BYU–Idaho Chorale performed their first few numbers flawlessly, despite the stifling air that smelled of sweat and cinnamon. Out of the corner of her eye, Stacie noticed several children listening so closely that they mouthed the words of the well-known carols. But eventually, it was time for her solo, and Brother Fillmore cued Matt and her forward.

Shoulders back, head poised, Stacie smoothly followed Matt to the elegant, double drawing room. A path of blue carpet led them past period furniture and massive brass chandeliers to a gold-inlaid, nineteenth-century grand piano.

Matt slipped behind the velvet cord that kept visitors from roaming too far into the room and sat on the cushioned bench. Stacie stepped into position next to the piano and looked out at the audience, most of whom were less than twenty feet away from her.

Matt played the introduction.

She sang:

Silent night! Holy night!
All is calm, all is bright.

At the far end of the room, Stacie saw a tall woman in a white hat whispering to one of the tour guides. She seemed upset.

Round yon virgin mother and Child.

The woman turned away from the guide, and Stacie saw a young girl wearing a black coat and green scarf. The girl was wedged between the woman and the wall as if she were hiding.

Holy Infant, so tender and mild.

On closer inspection, Stacie saw that the blonde-haired girl had dark brown eyes and a familiar round face. Stacie's eyes widened. *There's no way it could be Jessica!*

Silent night! Holy night!

Even though she knew it wasn't Jessica—after all, Jessica was dead—Stacie couldn't keep her gaze off the girl. It was almost like she was seeing the ghost that had haunted her nightmares for the last eight years.

Suddenly, the woman folded her arms and stared at the docent with narrowed eyes. Then, with one quick movement, she zipped her tan jacket to her neck, grasped the girl's shoulder, and hurried the child toward the door.

Christ, the Savior, is born!

The girl stumbled to the floor.

Silent night! Holy night!

As the white-hatted woman tugged the girl to her feet, the girl's scarf caught on the woman's jacket sleeve, pulling the scarf from the girl's neck to reveal a large, cauliflower-shaped birthmark that covered most of the skin from the base of the girl's left ear to her throat.

Son of God. Love's pure light.

As Stacie neared the end of "light," a bit of hesitancy crept into her voice, but she pushed through it, trying to focus on the note. *Where have I seen that birthmark?*

Radiant beams from thy holy face . . .

Had she seen it at the university pool where she'd worked as a lifeguard? The campground? Somewhere else in Rexburg?

Sleep in heavenly—

The woman's gaze flitted anxiously round the room, stopping briefly on Stacie, before she finally re-coiled the scarf around the girl's neck and tugged her out the door.

Matt played the last arpeggio.

Stacie took a deep breath and held it, preparing for her final note. And then—

Becka! That's where she'd seen the birthmark. On the "Missing" posters for Becka Hollingsworth—a little girl missing from Rexburg for several months. Stacie and half of Rexburg had searched for poor Becka.

Stacie's throat strangled around "peace" as an empty roar filled her ears. And then, no longer thinking about the song or Matt or even Jessica Smythe, she charged into the audience and raced toward the door through which the woman had disappeared. She had to catch that girl.

Breathing fast, Stacie ran past the choir and through the hall. She frantically scanned every face, not caring whom she bumped into and almost knocking over several Christmas displays. When she finally reached the exit, she raced outside, but no one was there.

Trouble number 3.

{CHAPTER 2}

ecka!" Stacie yelled. Only the rain and the wind and the distant, sporadic cry of car tires on wet asphalt answered her.

"Stacie?" It was Janice's voice, Janice's hand on her shoulder.

Stacie whirled. "Did you see her?"

"Who?"

"Becka Hollingsworth!"

"Becka Hol—the girl who's missing?"

"Yes!" Stacie tugged Janice toward the long driveway. "We've got to find her. You try that side of the castle, and I'll go this way."

Janice stumbled after her. "Are you sure it was Becka? Here— in Canada?" She motioned to the small parking lot that circled the castle. There were several cars but very few people.

"Yes, I'm sure!" Stacie gulped. "She had a birthmark like the one on the poster."

Janice's eyes widened. "Not many people have birthmarks like that."

"And not many people would have let her disappear again!" Stacie jerked from her grasp, but Janice caught her before she'd crossed the driveway.

"I know what you're telling yourself, Stacie, and it isn't true."

Stacie lifted her face to the thunder.

"Did you hear me? Even if it was Becka, and we don't know for certain that it was, no one can blame you for this—not even Mrs. Smythe. Let's go back and talk to Brother Fillmore. Maybe he can help us figure out what to do. Uh, does that sound okay?"

"No! If I quit looking now, I'll lose her for sure."

"Listen to me," Janice said, her voice louder. "If Becka is still in the castle, she and that woman will have to leave sometime, right? So, why don't you wait here and watch for them while I go find Brother Fillmore?"

Stacie nodded numbly. She could do that. She could stay and keep looking. And she wouldn't give up.

Janice peered into her face. "You'll be all right?"

Stacie nodded again, but she knew Janice wasn't convinced. Even so, Janice gathered the skirts of her long formal and ran back to the castle.

When she was gone, Stacie wrapped her arms tightly around her shoulders, shielding herself from the wind, then walked across the drive and down the concrete steps that led to the expansive castle grounds. She paced back and forth, scanning the surroundings, hardly noticing the water seeping from the soggy, green-brown grass into her black dress shoes.

"Stacie?"

She turned and saw Janice running toward her from the gift shop. Brother Fillmore, his posture rigid and formal as always, followed her, as did several choir members.

"Are you ill?" Brother Fillmore demanded when he caught up to her.

"No."

"He was almost here when I found him," Janice interrupted

with a whisper. "I didn't have a chance—"

"Then what was the emergency?"

A soprano named Ivana flipped her wavy, red hair over her shoulders and sidled up next to Stacie's friend Zach. "Maybe the solo was too much for her."

Ignoring her, Stacie said, "I saw Becka Hollingsworth!"

Ivana's jaw dropped open. So did Brother Fillmore's.

"You saw her?" Zach rushed forward and grabbed her hands. "Where'd she go?"

"I don't know." Emotion crept into Stacie's voice. "She practically dragged her off."

"She?" Zach exclaimed.

Stacie understood his surprise. The news reporters had never mentioned a woman in connection with Becka's disappearance— only a man, one of Becka's neighbors. "Yes, it was a woman! And yes, it was Becka. I saw her birthmark!"

The other choir members began talking at once, but Stacie felt like screaming. They needed to find the girl! "Maybe one of you saw them?" she blurted to Mr. Fillmore and the others. "Becka was wearing a black coat and green scarf, and the woman had a white hat."

They shook their heads.

Brother Fillmore took his cell phone from the inside pocket of his tux and handed it to her. "You'd better call the police."

Stacie gaped at the phone, struggling to bury her sudden memories of little Jessica's body in the swimming pool, of how she'd had to retell the tragedy over and over again to the police.

"Go ahead," Brother Fillmore urged. "If my child was missing, I'd want anyone who saw her," his voice softened, "or thought she saw her, to report it."

Stacie hesitantly took the phone.

"As for the rest of you, please go back to the bus. I'll be there right after I discuss this with Mr. Underwood."

Stacie flipped open the phone and looked down at the numbers, wondering how one called for help in Canada.

"Dial 911, like in the U.S.," Matt said, filing past her with the others.

"Just do it," Zach whispered into her ear. "He's always right."

No one's always right, Stacie thought, but she punched in the numbers.

"Nine–one–one, what is your emergency?" the dispatcher said.

Stacie glanced at Matt. He'd only gone a short distance before stopping and looking back at her with a faint smile.

{CHAPTER 3}

Except for Janice and Zach, everyone was safely on the bus by the time Stacie hung up. "A constable will meet me at the castle entrance in a few minutes," she told her friends as a raindrop splattered against her cheek. "What should I tell him? Everything happened so quickly that I don't know how helpful I'll be."

Zach rubbed his chin, reminding her of the fourteen-year-old boy he'd been when they'd first met. "I bet you recalled more than you think you do. You're a lifeguard, remember? You've trained yourself to notice things."

At the word "lifeguard," Stacie turned away from her friends, trying to reclaim her composure. She'd received her lifeguard training soon after Jessica's drowning, hoping to prevent such a tragedy from happening again, at least on her watch. But here she was again, feeling responsible for the loss of a child.

"Come on," Janice urged, glancing anxiously at the waiting bus. "Name one thing you remember."

"I . . . like I told you before, I remember what the woman was wearing. And I think she had brown hair, but I'm not sure because most of it was covered by her hat. But really, you guys, I appreciate your help, but you better go back with the rest of the choir. You have to get on to the next performance. I'll take care of this."

Janice held up two fingers, ignoring Stacie's last comment. "Good. That's two things—clothing and hair. What was her build?"

Stacie half smiled. She never had been able to get away from Janice or Zach very easily, but it was one of the characteristics she most loved about them. "Thin. And tall."

"Age?"

"I don't know. About thirty, I guess."

"Eye color?" Zach asked.

Stacie hesitated, remembering that the woman had looked right at her. "I don't know," she finally said, "but her face seemed, well, pointed."

Both friends looked at her quizzically but said nothing.

"I mean, she had a long nose, a triangular chin, and sharp bone structure, kind of like, well, a witch."

Zach chuckled and hugged her around the shoulders. "That's good! See, you noticed more than you thought."

Stacie leaned against him. "Thanks. But please go—both of you. I don't want to be responsible for another messed-up performance." She smiled cheerlessly. "Janice, do you think the Garners would pick me up later?"

Janice tilted her head to one side. "I think they'd be upset if we didn't ask them. Here, let me call, okay?"

"Tell them to bring my purse too, please. I left it on the nightstand."

As Stacie handed Brother Fillmore's cell phone to Janice, her friend's innocent expression reminded her of when Janice had come to Rexburg to live with the Garners. The Garners had lived next door to where Stacie and her aunt and uncle had lived during the school year, and both girls were thirteen at the time. That day,

Sister Garner had found Stacie sitting on their back steps, her face buried in her hands.

"I'm sure Janice won't be that long," Sister Garner had said, sitting next to her.

Stacie didn't look up. "They don't know what they're talking about!"

"Who doesn't?" Sister Garner wrapped her arm around Stacie's shoulders.

"Those women. They're wrong! Mom never would have purposely left me alone like this." Stacie's lips quivered. "Not with Dad dead too!"

Minutes later, the choir's tour bus left, and Stacie, poring over every passing face, retraced her steps back to the front foyer where she was supposed to meet the constable. When she got there, instead of the constable, she found an elderly docent standing near the door. He looked up and Stacie instantly recognized him.

"You were in the drawing room during my solo!"

"Yes." The man nodded in a way that was almost a bow. "Your song was magnificent until" —he cleared his throat and smiled pleasantly— "the disturbance. I look forward to hearing the rest of it on Friday." He held out his hand. "I'm Cecil Underwood. And your name again?"

She took his hand, grateful he'd glossed so smoothly over her faux pas. "I'm Stacie Cox. You talked to a woman who was wearing a white hat."

He furrowed his eyebrows. "Oh?"

"In the drawing room, remember? She had a child with her—a *missing* child."

"Ahh . . . that's right. Your director talked to me about that. It's why you ran—" Mr. Underwood looked across the top of her shoulder, apparently distracted by the tourists behind her.

Stacie looked too and saw that except for a couple of elderly women, they were all male, so she turned back to him. "A constable will be here any minute. I thought I'd have to talk to him alone, but now that I've found you . . ."

"I'm sorry, Miss Cox. We have many patrons today, you see." He stepped sideways and skirted round her, clearly headed toward the entrance hall. "And it's my responsibility to make their visit as pleasant as possible. I will, of course, talk to the constable at a later time." Then Mr. Underwood walked away.

Stacie stared after him in frustration. Then she crossed to the podium and looked down the list of names on the guest register.

"Are you Stacie Cox?"

Stacie jumped. She hadn't seen the officer step inside with the last group of tourists. "Yes," she answered.

"I'm Sergeant Price. I understand you saw a missing child?" The middle-aged man's words clicked rapidly, like an old-fashioned typewriter, and there was a hint of French Canadian in his accent.

Stacie quickly recounted how she'd seen Becka in the drawing room, recognized the birthmark, and ran after her and the woman. She also told him about the woman's conversation with Mr. Underwood and her own background in relation to Becka's search.

Eventually, the officer seemed satisfied. "I'll report this to the command center in Idaho," he said, "but please call the Child Find hotline—here's the number—and tell them what you've told me."

His gaze seemed so sincere, so instinctively wise, that Stacie felt a surge of optimism. "What if I remember something else about Becka, or the woman?"

"Call me at the station, especially if you remember more about the woman." He looked up from his notes. "The best way to find a missing child is to find the adult she's with. Adults can be traced. They own homes, drive cars, pay bills. Children don't. Children disappear."

Suddenly, a familiar desperation washed over Stacie. It was the same feeling she'd had while combing the hillside those first days after Becka had disappeared. A few of her friends thought it strange that she'd felt so much grief for a girl she had never met. But Becka was lost, away from her home, and her mother—everything and everyone that was important to her. And Stacie knew exactly how *that* felt. "What's your next step?"

Sergeant Price closed his notepad. "I'd like you to come down to the station tomorrow and work up something with our sketch artist. After that, the officials in Idaho will take over."

"They'll take over? But Becka's here."

He lifted one graying eyebrow but responded patiently. "The command center has all the information about the child's disappearance, Miss Cox, so they can best analyze this report. However, we'll work as closely with them as we can. Missing children are a high priority."

Stacie nodded, trying to accept the finality in his voice. "Thank you."

After the sergeant left, Stacie moved to the staircase and leaned against the railing for several minutes, thinking about Becka. She knew she'd done all she could—that Becka's rescue was now in someone else's hands. She also knew she needed to turn her attention back to the choir's five-day tour, to try to forget about the little girl until she was found.

But if she isn't found? Stacie looked up at the ceiling. *No!* She wouldn't even consider that possibility.

"We close in half an hour, miss."

Startled by the voice, Stacie looked at her watch. It was four o'clock. "I'm sorry," she faltered. "I had to talk to the police."

The brown-wigged docent smiled thinly. "Then you must be

Stacie Cox. The Garners are waiting for you in the gift shop."
She urged Stacie to the exit.

"Another moment, Miss Cox." It was Sergeant Price's voice
she heard behind her.

"Yes?"

"You did say it was Cecil Underwood you saw talking to the
woman?"

"Yes."

"It wasn't someone else, one of the other docents, perhaps?"

"No. It was him. Why?"

He pursed his lips. "He says he remembers your solo, and he
remembers several people asked him questions during it, but he
doesn't remember anything about a woman like you described."
His eyes narrowed, studying her face. "I haven't found anyone
else who saw her, either."

For one horrible moment, Stacie doubted herself, but in the
next second, when Becka's face flashed through her mind, her
uncertainty vanished. "I know what I saw, Sergeant."

"Those were Mr. Underwood's words, too." He turned to the
docent standing next to her. "I'd like to talk with you in a few
minutes too, please." Then he headed back to the main hall.

Stacie clenched her fingers around the folds of her formal,
trying to still her trembling hands and swallow the butterflies that
churned inside her. Could Mr. Underwood really have forgotten
that woman?

She grabbed the woman's arm. "Do you know where Mr.
Underwood is now?"

"Sorry. I believe he left."

"Is there any way I can reach him?"

"We don't give out that information. Would you like me to
leave him a message?"

"No, thank you. But I'd like to know when his next shift is."

The woman smiled patiently. "He'll be here tomorrow afternoon around 1:00."

Stacie nodded, quickly running the next day's performance schedule through her mind. One o'clock should work. And somehow she'd make Mr. Underwood remember. And tell the police.

While she waited for Janice to get back to the Garners' house after the senior center performance, Stacie searched the internet for information on Becka. Most of the facts she already knew, but one small detail triggered another memory she could tell the police, something that might give them a clue to work with. Even though it was chilly outside, Becka had been wearing sandals, and they were so small that her toes hung over the edge. It might not be a big deal, but if the woman had to get Becka different shoes, couldn't she have found her some that fit?

Stacie was still sitting at the computer when Janice returned from the choir performance with good news. Brother Fillmore, she'd said, did *not* let Ivana sing Stacie's solo even though she'd almost begged him to let her. "You and Matt had performed it together so beautifully, before you ran out, that he doesn't want anyone else to sing it," Janice told her. "He also told Matt he wanted him to play for you even after Lara gets well."

Stacie almost choked. "I hope you're kidding."

"Nope. I think his exact words were, 'Matt, you and Stacie really connected on that song. If you have any other ideas, make sure you share them with her.'"

The same apprehension Stacie had felt when Lara first became ill twisted inside her again. She and Lara had spent months together working on that song, tweaking every note and phrase until it was perfect—well, except for that last note Matt had noticed—so how could he possibly be better than Lara? Stacie would have to talk to Brother Fillmore about that.

That night, Stacie dreamed Becka was running down a long, yellow corridor, past doors that didn't open. And though Stacie raced after her, faster and faster, calling her name, she wouldn't stop.

Finally, a door opened to a dark stairwell. Becka hesitated, and Stacie caught her arm.

"Let me go!" Becka screamed.

Stacie held tighter.

"Mommy!"

Becka yanked her arm from Stacie's grasp and ran again— almost flew—level after level, down the dimly lit stairs.

At the bottom, Stacie saw a heavy, metal door with a window that led to the outside. When she reached it, Stacie looked through the window at the beam of light that shone from a lamppost, but she saw only her reflection.

A second later, the view changed, and she saw a woman with harsh, pointed features.

"Come back to me," she said to Stacie, who was calm now. "You'll get lost out there."

Both Stacie and Becka reached for the door, but just before Stacie opened it, she stopped and waited for the woman to take Becka's hand and lead her into the night.

The dream flashed black.

Stacie awoke with her heart pounding so hard against her chest that she could hardly breathe. She opened her eyes, but the blankness of the ceiling only compounded her desperate emptiness, so she turned onto her stomach and slipped the top of her head under her pillow. Why had her mind conjured such a horrible sequence? And why had she seen herself as Becka?

At 7:50 a.m., Stacie and Janice entered the rough-hewn granite church and headed for the Relief Society room, where she and Matt—and later, the entire choir—were to practice.

"I've been waiting for you," a male voice said just behind Stacie as she stopped to hang her coat in the foyer. "Here, let me help you with your jacket."

Both girls turned around.

"Hey, why does she get all the attention?" Janice teased.

Zach grinned lopsidedly, hung Stacie's jacket on the rack, and offered her his arm. "Just trying to be a gentleman."

An uncomfortable warmth crept into Stacie's cheeks. Was he teasing her?

"Yeah, right. Stacie's not the only girl around here, you know." Janice bumped his arm playfully, but he seemed to barely notice her. His attention, to Stacie's dismay, was entirely on her. She shot Janice a silent plea for help.

Thankfully, Janice caught the hint. "I need to visit the restroom," she said. "Uh, Zach, your hair's sticking up in back. Maybe you ought to check it."

Zach ran his hand over his hair. "It's fine for now. Go ahead."

Stacie frowned. *What's up with him this morning? He is always worried about his hair!*

Janice shrugged. *I tried,* she mouthed to Stacie before walking away.

Stacie frowned. "See ya in a minute."

When Janice left, Zach again offered Stacie his right arm, more insistently this time. She hesitantly took it, and he slipped his left hand over hers.

Stacie gulped. *He's just concerned about me because of last night, like any good friend would be.*

Zach opened the door to the Relief Society room. "After you."

From the hall, Stacie had heard Matt playing a jovial, dancing-around-the-Christmas-tree sort of melody on the piano, but just before they entered the room, the music shifted to a melancholy refrain with phrases reminiscent of "I'll Be Home for Christmas."

Zach urged Stacie forward, but she held back. Matt hadn't noticed them yet, and while she was disappointed that Lara couldn't accompany her, Stacie couldn't deny Matt's skill at the piano. *It's almost like magic,* she thought as she listened to him play a gentle tune, one she'd never heard before. And yet something about it brought back a memory she'd forced from her mind years ago: the last Christmas she'd spent with both her parents. Mom emptying her stocking. Dad kissing Mom under the mistletoe. The three of them sitting together, making up stories about the figurines in their Christmas village. It was the way Stacie wished things could have continued with her family. The way they should still be for Becka . . . Becka . . . *Please, Heavenly Father, help someone find that little girl.*

A few minutes later, Matt, his posture tall and strong, played the last note and looked up at her. "How'd it go with the police yesterday?"

"Okay, but I'd rather not talk about it." She took a deep breath, pretending she hadn't noticed how close Zach had moved in behind her, and stepped purposefully ahead of him. "Sit there," she told him. "You can be our audience." Then she moved quickly to the piano. "Ready, Matt?"

"Whenever you are." Matt placed his hands on the keyboard but didn't play.

"What's wrong?"

"Um, yesterday at the castle, I noticed I played louder while you sang softer. Right here at measure thirty-eight. Not long before you . . . ran off."

Stacie stiffened. She knew the place he was talking about well, for she and Lara had experimented with it dozens of times. "That's okay," she said, "next time you'll know to play it soft."

He raised his eyebrows. "Wouldn't it be better if you sang it forte? This is the song's climax."

"I've tried that, and it turns out okay, but a softer effect is better." She placed her hand on the piano and tilted her head slightly. "You know, sotto voce—half voice."

Matt glanced at her hand then back up into her eyes. "Okay. Have it your way."

Stacie bristled. "Listen, Matt, like I told you, I've already practiced it that way, and a lot of other ways too, and softer is best."

"Suit yourself."

Just then, Janice walked into the room and sat next to Zach. Stacie immediately felt calmer.

"All right, Matt. Let's go ahead and run through it your way once. As an experiment."

He shook his head. "No, it doesn't matter, Stacie. We'll do it your way."

Both his voice and expression seemed condescending, but Stacie held her tongue. Allowing him to bother her just wasn't worth it, plus she wouldn't sing well if she was angry.

"Looks like Ivana was right," he muttered under his breath.

Stacie froze. "What are you talking about?"

He shrugged, and though she could tell she'd caught him off guard—like he hadn't meant to say what he'd said—he answered her. "Why won't you listen to someone else's opinions once in a while?"

Stacie looked at Janice for backup, but she seemed just as shocked as Stacie by Matt's words.

"Oh, come on, Stacie!" Matt said. "Don't hold on to things so long."

"I wouldn't put too much stock into what Ivana says, Matt," Zach cut in.

Stacie nodded at her friend, grateful for his support. But because she'd dealt with Mrs. Smythe for so many years, she knew the best way to meet an accusation—especially an unfounded one—was to face it squarely, without emotion. "Like what, for instance?"

"Like your own opinions, and—" A shadow of emotion—was it remorse?—momentarily swept over his face.

"And?"

"Forget about it." Matt lowered his voice. "Keeping the ending pianissimo is fine as long as we both know that's how we're doing it." He looked away from her, took a deep breath, and then played the introduction as if nothing had happened, except that he pressed the keys too harshly.

Stacie responded in kind, belting out, "Silent night! Holy night!"

Both Zach and Janice jumped to their feet.

"I hope you two work this out before tonight," Zach said.

Almost instantly, Stacie felt sorry—and mortified. What had got into her? Why had she let Matt get under her skin like that?

"Come on," Janice urged, "call a truce."

Matt remained stoic, and Stacie, restraining her irritation at his stubbornness, put on her experienced "the-campground-customer-is-always-right" expression and held out her hand. "Truce?" She knew her request sounded more like a dare than an apology, but it was the best she could muster.

Matt glanced from Zach to Janice and finally settled on Stacie before finally taking her hand. "Truce."

His face was slightly flushed, but other than that, Matt seemed calm. Stacie hoped that reserve would carry him through her next statement. "Sotto voce?"

Matt held onto her hand for several seconds. But then, without so much as a nod and almost as if her touch had become a hot iron, he released her and turned back to the piano. He played the piece her way—all three times—until Brother Fillmore and the rest of the choir arrived.

When they'd finished, Stacie touched his arm. "Thanks, Matt."

He looked up at her, but then she saw him glance past her to Ivana, who'd just entered the room. Ivana looked at Matt and Stacie, then headed straight for Zach, but he didn't notice her and moved next to Stacie. Ivana glared at her.

"Why don't you come with us back to the hotel after rehearsal?" Zach asked. "We can walk around town for a little while, maybe go down to the harbor and get a bite to eat before we help at the community center."

"Thanks, Zach," Stacie answered, "but I have to go to the police station as soon as we're finished here. After that, Janice and I are going back to the castle." Matt was watching her, listening, so she lowered her voice. "I need to talk to Mr. Underwood about Becka."

"Shouldn't the police do that?"

"They already have. He told them he didn't notice anything, but I saw him talk to that woman. I've got to make him remember."

"Why?"

"He talked to her!" she repeated. "Saw her up close!"

Zach sighed. "All right. Then how about after the Garners' ward party? We could walk around and see the Christmas lights."

What's going on with him? "I don't know. I might be—" As usual, she turned to Janice for help.

Zach looked at Janice too. "Tell her to come. It would do her good. Help her get her mind off, well, everything."

"Yes, it would be good for her. Me too, actually." Janice glanced at Stacie. "I've been dying to go look at the lights."

Stacie frowned. Janice had caught the hint, all right, but it wasn't quite what she'd hoped for. Couldn't she have just said she'd needed Stacie's help with something back at the Garners'?

"What do you say, Matt? Should we make it a foursome?" Zach asked.

"Sure." And to Stacie's complete amazement, Matt stepped next to her—so close she could feel the heat from his body—and muttered, "You were right about measure thirty-eight." Then he walked briskly away.

{CHAPTER 4}

Leah Hollingsworth placed one foot on the floor, then the other. Her gray terry-cloth bathrobe hung on a hook next to the closet. All she had to do was walk from the bed and put it on. But what was the point? Ethan, she knew, had already made the boys' lunches and driven them to school on his way to work, and Becka, her daughter, was . . . missing. Leah squeezed her eyes against the rising pain. She might as well go back to bed.

For a long moment, she seriously considered doing just that, but the image of her husband trying to run both his business and the household stopped her. Ethan. Strong, sturdy Ethan. He'd been carrying so much of this load alone, and she knew it was time for her to change that. Only two nights ago she'd promised him she'd try to pull herself out of this depression, and she was going to do it. Now. This morning.

Leah made her way to the closet, fumbled her arms into her bathrobe, then went to the window and pulled aside the long, taupe curtains. The sky was still overcast, but that, along with several inches of new, windswept snow, was all that remained of last night's snowstorm. She shivered. She'd always hated snowstorms, especially windy ones.

When she was a child and there was a bad snowstorm, she

would hide in a corner of her bedroom, piled under a mound of thick patchwork blankets, believing the outside howl was a pack of hungry wolves waiting to eat her as soon as she stepped out of the house. Now the wind was something worse: a terrible, mocking, demon that incessantly screamed, *"It's your fault your daughter's gone."*

Leah sunk back onto the bed and sobbed again. Sobbing was something she didn't try to stop anymore; it was almost part of her routine. Climb out of bed late in the evening. Cry. Put the children to bed. Cry. Ask Ethan for the day's police update before he went to bed. Cry some more. She'd once thought a person could only cry until the tears were gone, but now she knew better. Becka had been missing for nearly four months, and Leah had never run out of tears. Maybe she never would.

"Dear Heavenly Father," she whispered, "please help us find her alive or—"

Leah couldn't make herself finish that sentence. Becka had to be alive. It was impossible to think of her in any other way.

The telephone rang.

Leah brushed away new tears on her bathrobe sleeve and rushed to the kitchen. "Hello? Oh, hi, Grace . . . No, I'm not doing well today." Leah covered her mouth with her hand to stop it from quivering. "No, we don't need to reschedule your hair appointment. I'll be fine. Yes, I'm sure . . . Good. See you in an hour."

Dear Grace. It seemed strange to Leah, now that Grace was so much a part of her life, that they'd never met before that first horrible night. Grace had simply shown up on her doorstep, dressed in a carefully tailored business suit and carrying a briefcase full of sample "Missing" posters and other ideas for getting the word out to the media. Leah had seen Grace around town before but hadn't realized she was the local president of a support group for women who'd lost children. She also hadn't known Grace was directly involved in the safe return of two missing children from Idaho.

"I'm here to help," was all Grace had said, taking Leah's hands and comforting her with a confident smile.

And she had helped. Besides staying awake with her and Ethan through several sleepless nights and acting as a family spokesperson before Leah's parents and in-laws had arrived, Grace had instigated the Hollingsworths' first media blitz.

"The police should have put out an AMBER Alert and contacted the media first thing!" she'd said when Leah told her about the officer's response. "Those first few hours are critical. If they'd done their job properly, they'd have likely found her by now."

Found her by now. The words still haunted Leah, and yet they gave her hope, too. *Found her by now.* Didn't the words themselves indicate that Becka was alive somewhere, only waiting to be found?

Still hoping, still holding the receiver, Leah quickly punched in the police department's number. It was a new day. She could take over this responsibility for Ethan. "Detective Boyle, please . . . Hello, I'm calling to check . . ."

"Yes. Mrs. Hollingsworth. As I told your husband this morning, we've received two new leads."

Leah braced herself against the counter. In the beginning, dozens of leads had come in daily, but in the end, each had been eliminated from the investigation for lack of substantial evidence. Did she dare hope? "Go ahead."

"First, Ted Delano, the registered sex offender we've had our sights on, has been connected with a child molestation case in Idaho Falls two weeks prior to Becka's disappearance. The second is a report from a local girl who's currently in British

Columbia on a college choir trip. She believes she saw Becka there with a woman during a castle tour."

Leah caught her breath.

"There isn't much to go on with this one, Mrs. Hollingsworth," he continued, "but we are releasing Becka's picture to the provincial media, just in case there is something to the story."

"What about a description of the woman? Can the girl help with a sketch?"

"They're working with her on that."

"Thank you." Leah hung up and tilted her head toward the ceiling. She had no new words to pray, only desperate feelings she could throw into the heavens and trust God would hear. "Please, Heavenly Father . . ."

A long moment later, she picked up the day planner she kept by the phone. Ethan had said Grace wasn't the only hair appointment he'd scheduled for her today, but she couldn't remember who they were and what times they were coming.

At the bottom of the list was Mrs. Ewing, 12:00. Sarah Bradly, 10:30. And at the top—Leah smiled to herself, thinking of how pleased her friend would be to hear there was another lead—was written the name Grace Smythe.

{CHAPTER 5}

Watching. Patiently watching. It was one of Adrienne's most sought-after skills, and it was something she could do forever if that's what it took to get what—or whom—she wanted. Like Underwood. *The liar.* She could smell his falsehood as strongly as if it were alcohol on his breath, and now she was going to get at the truth.

"I told you to stay down," Adrienne said, watching the girl in her rearview mirror. Maybe she'd spoken a little harsher than she needed to, but Riana was becoming much too impulsive these days. Adrienne had to regain control immediately.

"My legs hurt."

"We've been through this before, Riana. You can't get up until I say you can. It's one of the rules."

Riana slid back onto the floor behind the driver's seat, and this time she didn't whimper.

Adrienne smiled. Patience, like watching, paid great dividends. Like now, for instance. Not many people could wait as long and as contentedly in a car across from Craigdarroch Castle with only the hope that Mr. Underwood would show up today.

"I'm thirsty." Riana's voice was muffled by the seat between them.

Adrienne took a water bottle out of her cooler and dropped it over the back of her seat. It made a soft thwack as it hit Riana's flesh, but again, Riana didn't complain or cry. *Very, very good.* "Riana? Since you've been such a good girl today, let's play our game, okay?"

No answer.

"Riana?"

"I'm drinking."

Adrienne clenched her fist, resisting her sudden urge to turn around and slap the child. It had been several weeks since she'd had to use such force, and she wasn't opposed to doing so again, but she really wanted to find out if her hypothesis had been correct: the idea that one, strong, never-to-be-forgotten punishment was enough to thwart all future disobedience. Besides, maybe, just maybe, the child didn't know the rule. "Answer when I speak to you, Riana."

"Yes, ma'am."

The girl's reply came almost before Adrienne had finished her statement, and Adrienne wished she could see the contrition in the child's face. She always learned so much from watching people's reactions.

"Let's play our game for a few minutes, okay?" Adrienne repeated.

"Yes, ma'am."

Adrienne relaxed. "Question one. What's your name?"

"Beck—Riana—Doyle."

"Good girl. You caught your mistake. Keep practicing."

"Riana Doyle. Riana Doyle. Riana Doyle. Can I please sit up now? My back hurts."

"Not yet, dear. Maybe after one more question, if you get it right. Hmm . . ."

The child squirmed against the back of Adrienne's seat.

"Hmm," Adrienne repeated. "I know. What's rule number one?"

"Obey."

"Very good, dear."

"Can I sit up now?"

Adrienne scanned their surroundings. No one was around, and she knew a little positive reinforcement, no matter how small, could go a long way in gaining further control of the child. "Yes, for now. But get back down as soon as I tell you. Understand?"

"Yes, ma'am."

Adrienne smiled. Her parenting skills were so much better than that other mother's, for Riana, *her* Riana, would always do exactly what she told her to do, because if she didn't, well, let's just say Adrienne would always be watching.

"Can we go in the castle again?" Riana asked hesitantly. "Maybe I'll see Santa this time."

"No. Sitting up is enough fun for today."

Riana's frown crept from her eyes to her chin.

"Where are your glasses?" Adrienne asked.

"They hurt my ears."

"Where *are* they?" Adrienne repeated as patiently as she could.

"In Riana's—my suitcase."

"Put them on as soon as we get back. You don't want to lose what little eyesight you have, do you?"

"No, ma'am." Riana closed her eyes.

Adrienne's iPhone sounded.

"Hello? Yes, Mrs. Rees . . . No, not yet, but I'm getting close . . . Of course, I'll let you know when I find him . . . Yes, I completely agree with you. He must pay for his mistakes."

She disconnected the call, then retrieved her client account ledger from beneath the passenger seat. "And so will you, Mrs.

Rees, with money. Very, very soon." She methodically ticked her pencil from her projected income column over to her list of projected expenses. "You see, Riana and I are headed for England."

{CHAPTER 6}

Stacie pressed the manila envelope against her chest as if it were a security blanket. Inside were the picture of Becka she'd printed from the internet the night before and a photocopy of the drawing she'd helped the sketch artist put together. "We shouldn't be long," she told Janice as they climbed the steps up to the castle entrance. "We'll simply go in, get what information we can from Mr. Underwood, and leave."

"Good." Janice reached for the door. "I'd really hoped to do some Christmas shopping before the service project." But just as she'd taken hold of the handle, a young man opened it from the inside.

"Hello again."

Janice startled backward. "Have we met?"

Stacie stepped past him into the castle. "Is Mr. Underwood here?"

"No, not yet. He should be here anytime, though."

There was a distracted tone to his voice, like he was barely aware of her question, and Stacie turned sharply. "This is really important, um" —she looked at his name tag— "Quinton. We're members of the choir who performed here last night. I saw a missing child and . . ."

"Yes, I know. I remember—both of you." He pried his gaze away from Janice. "What can I help you with today, eh? Would you like to tour the castle?"

"Yes," Janice said, a pink tint coloring her cheeks.

Stacie frowned. "Then you must have talked to the police?"

"No, actually I didn't. My shift ended before your performance." Quinton's gaze again settled on Janice, who blushed a deeper red.

Stacie sighed, then quickly took the pictures from the envelope and handed them to Quinton. "I saw this girl while I was performing in the drawing room, and this is the woman she was with. Do they look familiar?"

"Let me see." He switched between the photographs. "What was the kid wearing?"

"A black coat and green scarf."

"Was it wrapped tightly, eh? The scarf, I mean?"

"Yes! You do you remember her!"

"A little. I felt sorry for the kid. She looked pretty warm."

Tingles ran up Stacie's spine. Finally, she'd found someone else who'd seen Becka. "Do you remember anything about the woman?"

He crinkled his thick black eyebrows into one undivided line. "Not much. Only that she had blue eyes. Pale blue, I think."

Stacie yanked a small notebook from her jacket pocket. Last night, she'd recorded everything she could remember about that moment when she'd locked gazes with the woman, and now she crossed out "light-colored eyes" and wrote "blue eyes."

The tour guide cleared his throat. "They were the same color that's in that stained glass window up there. Actually, that's why I noticed them. I was telling a tourist where—" He stopped, looking sheepishly at Janice. "I'm rambling, eh?"

Janice laughed gently.

His face reddened this time. "I'm sorry. I know I'm acting kind of, well, it's just that I—I'm writing a thesis on native nationalism, and I was hoping to talk to you about your experiences in the States. You're a First National, right?" He touched her arm, and she demurely lowered her eyelids.

Trying to ignore the obvious attraction between her friend and Quinton, Stacie asked him, "Um, do you remember anything else about the woman?"

Quinton glanced at Stacie. "Only that she asked about a docent who used to volunteer here."

"What was his name?"

"What's a First National?" Janice asked at the same time.

"First Peoples," Quinton explained to her. "Aboriginal groups. Native Americans, eh?"

Janice frowned slightly.

"Don't get me wrong," Quinton went on. "That's not the only reason I want to talk to you."

Stacie fiddled with her notebook. "What was the docent's name?" she repeated.

"I didn't recognize the name, so I referred her to Mr. Underwood. He's volunteered here longer than anyone else."

She gave Janice a meaningful look before writing the information in her notebook. "Is that all?"

"No, I mean, yes, that's all I remember about her, but—what do you say, Janice? Can I talk to you sometime?"

"It depends on when. Our performance schedule's pretty tight, and we leave Friday."

Stacie stepped further into the castle. "Do you mind if I look around a bit, Quinton, while I'm waiting for Mr. Underwood?"

"No. Actually, why don't you let me show you both around? We could start in the drawing room, eh?"

"Sure. Maybe seeing it again will trigger another memory."

Stacie glanced at Janice. "But only 'til Mr. Underwood gets here, okay?"

"We'll see," Janice said.

{CHAPTER 7}

If this had been any other time, Matt would have reveled in the chance to perform his Christmas song for a large audience, at least by way of recording. But neither his fingers nor his brain would respond as they should, making the whole experience feel awkward.

Sister Garner clicked the STOP button. "Perfect," she said "What a great talent you have, Matt, being able to write your own music."

"Thanks," he muttered. "Let's record it again."

"Are you sure? I don't think it's necessary."

"Yes, it is."

She seemed puzzled but reset the recorder anyway. "Go," she mouthed, lowering herself into a nearby chair and smoothing her blue skirt across her lap.

Matt started the song again. He forced thoughts of snow and stars and holy mangers through his mind, trying to re-create the necessary emotion, but the timbre was still wrong. Why couldn't he bring out the music's warmth, its reverence?

Actually, he knew why. Stacie.

He scrunched his eyebrows together. *Focus!*

Still, the image of her hazel eyes flashed into his thoughts.

They were as brilliant as they'd been the previous October when a group of choir members had stopped for lunch at the food court in the Manwaring Center. Stacie and Zach had claimed a round table in the center of the room after getting their food, and Ivana, arriving a bit later, had asked to sit with them. She left her books on the table and then went for her food.

Before she returned, however, a young man with a plateful of nachos sat in one of the seats across from Stacie and Zach. He was skinny and gangly, and though he had to be in his late twenties, he looked as awkward as a fifteen-year-old.

"Um, I just remembered I told someone else I'd sit with them," Ivana had loudly said when she returned.

She avoided the young man's gaze, set her plate of salad on top of her books, and carried the entire stack across the aisle to a table close to where Matt sat. On the other hand, Stacie was friendly to the young man and included him in her conversation with Zach.

Matt felt himself blush hot with embarrassment. Why had he been such a jerk about measure thirty-eight? He'd known as soon as he'd heard her sing it the first time that morning that she'd been right, and while it goaded him to think he could be so wrong, that wasn't what most bothered him now. It was the words he'd repeated. Ivana's words.

Matt stood. "This isn't working, Sister Garner. You'll have to get someone else."

The elderly woman placed her hands on his shoulders and pressed him back onto the bench. "Oh, no, we won't. The Nativity pageant needs your song. Now try again, please."

Not wanting to disappoint her, Matt did try again, and again, but each time he played the song, something went wrong.

This is ridiculous, he thought. His girlfriend, Holly, was at home in St. George, waiting for him, trusting him. Why was he thinking about someone else?

His right hand stumbled through a difficult passage.

Think about Holly.

Gradually, his arpeggios rippled beneath the melody, highlighting his mild allusion to "I'll Be Home for Christmas." When he finished, he released a long, slow breath.

Sister Garner clicked off the recording system. "Perfect. Right?"

Matt gave her a half smile. "It'll do."

"The whole town's in for a treat this year," she went on, fussing with the electrical chords. "First the university chorale, and now you. I wouldn't be surprised if next year's music director keeps the same recording."

Just then, Brother Garner entered the Relief Society room carrying a box labeled Lost and Found Costumes. He scooted it under one of the chairs at the back of the room, and as he rose, readjusting his winter coat, he said, "Let's get Matt back to the hotel, eh? We've kept him long enough."

Still trying to think of Holly rather than Stacie, Matt followed Brother and Sister Garner outside the church, but as he looked across the parking lot and then at the expanse of Topaz Park where the choir would perform at the pageant the following night, he relived his practice with Stacie that morning. How could he have been so rude to her?

"I know it's out of the way," Matt said, "but could you take me to the castle instead of the hotel?"

"Certainly." Sister Garner smiled slyly. "The girls are there, aren't they?"

Brother Garner lifted his collar against the cold, wet wind. "If we hurry, you can catch a ride to the shelter with them." He winked.

There was no use pretending he didn't catch the hint. "Uh—I

already have a girlfriend."

"What a pity," Sister Garner said.

Brother Garner helped his wife into the car and walked around to the driver's side, but before climbing in, he winked at Matt again. "But all's fair in love and war, eh?"

Matt smiled to cover his exasperation. Why did older people always try to play matchmaker? Didn't they know how humiliating it was? Besides, all he wanted to do was apologize to Stacie.

The drive down Quadra Street was particularly slow that morning with all the holiday traffic, but the worst thing was that all Brother and Sister Garner talked about, other than pointing out some of the places Brother Garner used to hang out at when he was a kid, was Janice. And Stacie.

"The two of them were as different as corn and radishes," Sister Garner added, "but they soon became fast friends." She looked over her shoulder at Matt. "In a way, they were both motherless, you know."

Matt felt the guilt twisting inside him. His only consolation was that he hadn't repeated Ivana's other accusation: that Stacie wore her mother's death on her shirtsleeve. It was so obviously untrue.

Brother Garner turned left onto Fort Street and shortly thereafter steered into the castle's driveway. He pointed to one of the three vehicles parked there: his own Cadillac. "You're a lucky guy, Matt. The girls are still here. And remember, neither of them has a boyfriend."

Matt hurried out of the car. "Thanks for the ride." Before he'd closed the door, however, a short, round man, wearing a charcoal-colored suit and oval, silver-rimmed glasses, stepped in front of them. He waved at Brother and Sister Garner.

Brother Garner rolled down his window.

"Hello, John, Karen," the man said. "I didn't know the two of you were scheduled this morning."

"We aren't. Just dropping off a friend of ours. Matt, this is Mr. Underwood."

Matt raised his eyebrows. *So this is the man Stacie is looking for.*

Mr. Underwood nodded a greeting.

"Take care of him, will you, Cecil?"

"Of course."

After the Garners said good-bye and drove away, Mr. Underwood turned to Matt. "If you'd care to follow me to the other side of the castle?"

Surprisingly, his short-legged pace was as quick as Matt's long strides. As he walked, the docent's head moved slowly back and forth as he inspected the grounds.

"How long have you volunteered here?" Matt asked him.

Mr. Underwood paused to collect several brown leaves from beneath a partially green hedge. "I've given tours at Craigdarroch Castle for the past ten years."

Almost as if he'd been watching for them to appear, a tall, wiry man with large ears shuffled awkwardly toward them. "Be careful, Mr. Underwood! She's delicate."

"The bush is fine, Alton."

Alton knelt next to it, bending his face close to the earth and scraping several more dead leaves from its base. "There. Good as new." He stood. "Last night's cold hit her hard. Hit some of the others, too."

"Don't worry about it, Alton." Mr. Underwood patted his shoulder. "No one expects you to control the weather."

"I wish I could control it. Then my plants would bloom all year and never die." Alton headed toward a large cedar several yards away.

Mr. Underwood's face momentarily contorted into a painful

frown. "Yes, Alton. Very good." He turned away from Matt's scrutiny and motioned him inside the gift shop. "Would you like a tour of the castle? Either myself or Miss Merrill would be happy to oblige." He nodded to the girl at the counter.

"Thanks, but I'm looking for—" Matt hesitated. Should he tell Mr. Underwood that Stacie wanted to talk to him? He looked closer at the older man, who was still waiting for his answer, and decided he'd better not. Stacie had mentioned that the man hadn't been very cooperative. "I'd like to look around on my own, if you don't mind."

"As you wish." Mr. Underwood pulled a brochure and map from his inside suit-coat pocket. "This will help you find your way around."

Matt eventually found the girls on the fourth floor, in the circular glass tower.

Janice was the first to see him. "Matt! What are you doing here? Brother Fillmore isn't looking for us, is he?"

"No." Matt looked at Stacie, but when he opened his mouth, the words stuck in his throat. "The Garners brought me," he finally stammered.

Stacie watched him with those deep, hazel eyes, and his pulse raced. He turned to the wall and brushed his palm against the paneling. "The oak's beautiful."

"Yes," Quinton answered. "Are you a carpenter, Matt?"

"He's involved in his father's woodworking business," Stacie said.

Matt turned to her. "How'd you know that?"

She shrugged. "Zach."

"You aren't a student?" Quinton asked him.

"I graduated last week. I'll be going home after our tour here to take over my father's business." He glanced at Stacie again. Her expression seemed so unguarded. He cleared his throat. "It's been in the works for some time now."

"And from what I hear, you're also going back to get married," Janice said with a smile.

"Oh. I hadn't heard that," Stacie stated.

Matt turned back to the windows, gazing at the gray-blue water and the thickly evergreen mountainsides. "Have you found out any more about that girl?"

"A little," Janice answered. "Quinton, here, remembered a few things, but we're still waiting for Mr. Underwood to show up."

Matt gulped. "Um, he just let me in through the back way."

Stacie charged for the door. "Where is he now?"

"Wait a second, will you?"

Stacie flinched beneath his grasp of her arm. "Why?"

He stared at her, opening then closing his lips, telling himself to just apologize and get it over with. But as he saw how anxious she was to leave, he said instead, "At least let us help you."

Stacie crinkled her eyebrows in apparent confusion. "Okay, sure."

A few minutes later, they found Mr. Underwood at the front entrance. "How was your tour?" he asked Matt, ignoring Stacie.

"Fine, thank you."

Stacie moved directly in front of Mr. Underwood. "You told Sergeant Price you didn't remember talking to a woman during my solo."

"Oh, yes, Miss Cox. The beautiful owner of the beautiful voice. We met last night."

"Yes, we did, but you left—prematurely."

Remarkable! Matt thought. He'd heard only a trace of accusation in her voice even though he knew how upset she'd been with the docent.

Stacie handed the photograph of Becka and the artist's sketch of the kidnapper to Mr. Underwood. "Do you recognize either of these people?"

"I've already spoken to the police about this."

Stacie lifted her chin slightly. "Please look closely at the pictures. It's important."

Mr. Underwood brushed them aside. "How many times do I have to say I don't remember the woman?" He picked up a clipboard. "Now, if you'll excuse me."

Matt could tell that Stacie was not going to be dismissed so easily, and in spite of himself, he smiled.

"Last night," Stacie pressed, "John Garner told me you have an excellent memory."

Mr. Underwood's step slowed.

"And I remember," Quinton suddenly put in, "sending the woman to talk to you."

"You—uh—I—you did?"

"Yes. She asked me about a volunteer who used to work here. It was before my time, so I referred her to you."

Mr. Underwood paled considerably.

"Please tell me what you remember," Stacie said.

To Matt's surprise, Mr. Underwood didn't walk away. Instead, he pulled a handkerchief from his pocket and furiously wiped at an invisible blemish on the paneling.

Stacie pushed her hair behind her ears and moved to within a couple feet of him. "Mr. Underwood?" Her voice was low. "Brother Garner mentioned how much he trusts you. He looks up to you as a man who takes impeccable care of this castle."

"I've admired it since I was a child."

"I—" Her voice caught, and she glanced at Janice. "I admire the castle too." She pulled a tissue from her pocket and wiped it along the window ledge, carefully eliminating a trail of dust from a tiny crevice in the wood. "It's a tremendous gift to this city. I'm grateful you've taken such good care of it, but more than that,

I'm grateful no one has tried to destroy it."

"If anyone even attempted to mar this building I'd do everything I could to protect it!"

Matt stared at Stacie, suspecting where her train of thought was headed.

"I saw Mrs. Hollingsworth, the missing girl's mother, on a television news broadcast," Stacie continued, "and that's exactly what she said." She turned, and though Mr. Underwood was a head taller than she was, she faced him squarely. "Only someone had already marred—stolen—the one she cared so deeply for." Stacie slipped the tissue back in her pocket.

Mr. Underwood turned red, eyed her for several tense seconds, and opened and shut his mouth three times before finally giving in. "I can't, with certainty, say I remember the woman. Like I told the police last night, I was listening to your solo. But now that you and Quinton mention it, I do remember someone asking me about a lady who used to work here."

He hesitated, his mouth still open, and Stacie inched slightly closer to him. "What was her name?"

Matt, Janice, and Quinton leaned closer too.

"Elsie Yates. She left the castle about three years ago."

Stacie wrote the information in her notebook. "Why did the woman leave so quickly after you told her about Elsie?"

"When she didn't find Mrs. Yates, she left. That's all." He tucked his clipboard under his arm, nodding dismissively at the three visitors. "Quinton, will you please take this post?"

Matt offered Mr. Underwood his hand. "Thank you for your help."

Stacie followed suit. "Let us know if there's anything we can help you with."

Mr. Underwood didn't shake their hands, but Stacie must have taken his smile as a good sign, because rather than leaving, she added, "Does Elsie Yates still live in this area?"

The smile disappeared. "There's nothing I can tell you about that."

"Would you mind calling the police and telling them—"

He walked away before Stacie could finish her request.

Quinton touched Janice's elbow. "I suppose you have to leave now too?"

A silent communication Matt had seen before but didn't understand passed between the two girls.

"Ten minutes?" Stacie asked.

"I'll take whatever I can get," Quinton answered. "Thanks."

Seeing his chance to finally get Stacie alone, Matt motioned her to the door. "There's something I need to talk to you about, Stacie. Do you mind?"

Her expression grew cautious. "Okay."

He closed the door behind them, and they started down the steps. "You were amazing in there."

"Thanks. Mr. Underwood seemed so caught up in the castle, like it's the only thing he cares about, that I thought it was worth a try." A gust of wind blew over them, and Stacie shivered.

Matt moved to put his arm around her, but stopped himself. "I wanted to tell you—"

She looked up, giving him her full attention.

His breath stopped. "Uh, I need a ride to the community center."

"Okay." She shrugged, then walked away from the castle ahead of Matt and peered across the drive into the grove of trees. "I wonder if Becka's kidnapper parked on the street instead of in the parking lot. Maybe that's why I didn't see where she went."

Matt swallowed hard, but somehow, with her back to him, the words came easier. "I brought you out here because I—I want to apologize for what I said this morning."

She stopped and turned.

"I was out of line."

Several silent, agonizing seconds later, Stacie looked at him, wide-eyed. "No, Matt, I was the one out of line. You were right about the end of my solo," she glanced away, "and I had a hard time accepting that."

"I was talking about that idiotic comment I made about you not listening to other people's opinions. It was inconsiderate of me to say it."

"Oh."

Were those tears in her eyes? Matt peered closer, but whatever he'd noticed had disappeared. "Anyway, I wanted to clear the air between us. Start fresh. Maybe we can be friends." He held out his hand. "You know, a truce, for real this time?"

Stacie stared at his hand but didn't take it.

He waited several seconds before self-consciously stuffing his hand in his coat pocket. "I'm also sorry I criticized your performance. You're an experienced, well-trained musician. I should have respected that."

Her expression softened briefly, as if perhaps she believed his apology, but all she said was, "I think I better call the police."

{CHAPTER 8}

Keeping her eyes averted from Matt's, Stacie withdrew her phone from her pocket and clicked "phone book." Last night, before researching Becka's case online, she'd programmed the Victoria Mounted Police's phone number into her phone, so now she selected it and pressed CALL.

"Stacie, did I say—do—something wrong?"

"No . . . uh . . ." She glanced up at Matt. He was still watching her, so she turned her back to him and walked faster toward the castle. "Sergeant Price, please," she said into the phone when the dispatcher answered. "It's not you, Matt," she said over her shoulder.

"Then what is it?"

"It's—complicated. Believe me, we're better off leaving our relationship with 'Silent Night,' and that's all."

He touched her elbow, and she stopped and turned to him.

"Why?" he asked.

Thankfully, the dispatcher came back on the line. "Sergeant Price isn't in. Would you like to leave him a message?"

"This is Stacie Cox. Tell him I've learned more about the woman I saw last night."

Matt followed her to the entry steps, and though she'd hoped

Janice would be there waiting, all she saw was a tall, gangly man kneeling between a wheelbarrow and the dormant flower bed that surrounded the castle. He glanced up at them briefly then turned back to his work.

"Go ahead," the dispatcher said.

Matt moved in front of Stacie and sat on the steps, blocking her ascent. The sun had crept out from behind the clouds, and the wind stopped, so Stacie wasn't surprised when he unzipped his jacket. But her pulse tripped as she caught a glimpse of the well-defined, muscular chest that his black T-shirt couldn't hide.

She whirled away from him. "Please tell Sergeant Price that the woman who had Becka Hollingsworth asked Cecil Underwood about a lady who used to volunteer at Craigdarroch Castle. Her name is Elsie—" She paused as the dispatcher wrote down the information. "—Yates."

The dispatcher thanked her for the information, and when she disconnected, a quiet voice said, "I liked Elsie."

Stacie looked toward the voice. It was the wheelbarrow man.

Matt edged closer to him, like he was approaching a frightened child. "Alton? Did you know Elsie Yates?"

He still hadn't looked up. "She always said, 'Hello, Alton.'"

"Do you know where she went after she stopped working here?" Stacie asked.

"I was sad. I took her my favorite yellow rose bush. Said it was a present from me. Said, 'Elsie Tang, I'll miss you.'"

"You mean Elsie Yates, don't you?" she asked gently.

"No. Divorced already."

Stacie glanced at Matt. "Are Elsie Yates and Elsie Tang the same person?"

"Yes." Alton gathered several dead leaves into the wheelbarrow. "She was nice. Pretty, too. Like you, miss."

"Where'd she live?"

He shook his head, picked up his wheelbarrow, and pushed it toward the trees.

Stacie followed him, anxious to learn what he knew, but at the same time trying not to move so quickly that she'd scare him away. "Please tell me where she lived, Alton. I really need to talk to her."

Alton stopped. He towered over both her and Matt. "Elsie's at Tang's Trading Company in Chinatown."

"Thank you, Alton." She squeezed his hand. "You've helped us a lot."

He grinned. "If you see her, tell her Alton says hi."

When he was gone, Stacie hurried up the stairs. "Yes!" she said.

Matt reached around from behind her and opened the door. "Are you gonna call the police back?"

She turned, still within the crook of his open arm. "Of course." The warmth of him next to her . . . the rhythm of his breath . . . "Janice! There you are."

"Sorry we took so long. Quinton and I couldn't figure out when to get together. I finally promised him I'd call if I found some spare time."

The three of them headed to the parking lot. "Janice! You'll never guess what we just found out." Stacie then repeated the information Alton had given them, but as she finished, an unfamiliar nervousness crept over her.

When they reached the Cadillac, Stacie moved to the passenger door and Janice unlocked the driver's side, but all the while, her gaze remained focused on Stacie's face.

"All right. What is it?" Janice asked.

Stacie pulled out her phone. "I've got to call the police."

"And?"

"It's nothing. Really. I'll just call and get it over with."

Matt and Janice shrugged at each other as the three climbed into the car. But soon after Stacie had reported the rest of her information to the police, Matt leaned forward from the back seat. He placed his hand on her shoulder. "Something's bothering you, isn't it?"

Stacie glanced at Janice.

"Don't look at me," she said. "I'm with Matt on this."

Stacie sighed. "Okay. Here it is. Tell me what you think." She fidgeted with the seat belt. "Logically, I know I've done everything I can for Becka, and it's time for me to let the police do their job."

"But?" Janice asked when Stacie didn't continue.

"But whenever I think of quitting, I feel sick inside. Really sick. You know, like that conscience thing. Like I'm doing something wrong. Yet, when I think . . ."

"It's okay. You're among friends." Matt emphasized the last word.

"Yet when I think about going to Chinatown to talk to Elsie myself, I feel better."

Silence.

Stacie leaned against her window, staring at the road ahead of them. If only someone would say something that could make sense of her feelings. But instead, Matt only cleared his throat a few times, and Janice gave her a furtive glance.

Finally, Janice pulled into the community center's driveway. "Matt, I'm going with Stacie. It won't be easy, but please try to smooth it over with Brother Fillmore."

{ CHAPTER 9 }

Adrenaline surged through Adrienne's veins as she glanced first through her windshield at the singers standing outside the castle and then back at the castle's entertainment schedule on her iPhone screen: "Brigham Young University–Idaho Chorale." She'd seen signs for that school all over Rexburg.

"Get on the floor, Riana!"

Adrienne raked her hands through her hair and then snatched her white hat from the seat beside her. *No!* She'd worn that one last night when that soloist had stared at her. She flung it to the floor and grabbed the black hat instead.

Those singers couldn't possibly have recognized the girl, could they? Adrienne had taken such pains to hide Riana's identity, and she had wrapped that scarf around her neck. She gasped. The scarf. It had caught in her zipper. They could have seen the birthmark!

Riana started to whimper.

"What's your problem now?"

"I want to see Santa."

"You had your chance last night." Adrienne slumped eye-level with the steering wheel and peered over the bottom edge of the window. The singers were getting in the Cadillac.

"But I didn't see him!"

Adrienne turned on the car's engine and inhaled slowly. She was in control again. "What's the big deal, anyway? You saw him when we passed by the shopping center this morning."

The Cadillac exited the driveway.

"I know, but" —Riana's voice dropped so low Adrienne wondered if the girl had started crying again— "I wanted to ask him something."

Oh, yeah. Christmas presents. "I'm sorry, dear. You should have paid more attention when you were in the castle. It doesn't look like we'll be going back after all." She pulled onto the road a short distance behind the singers.

"Why?"

"Don't whine, Riana. This isn't my fault. The people in that car ahead of us—at least that guy—talked to Underwood already. Made it too risky for me to talk to him again." Then under her breath she added, "Looks like I'll have to call the station."

Riana bumped twice against the back of Adrienne's seat, readjusting herself, Adrienne assumed.

"Can I get back up on the seat? I'll lie down."

"No, not yet."

Adrienne picked up her phone and dialed. "Hi, Carol? It's Adrienne. Yes, it's been a while. Listen, I need you to locate someone for me."

The Cadillac turned onto Yates Street.

"The name? Genevieve Yates. She lived in Victoria three years ago and volunteered at Craigdarroch Castle. I don't know if she's still in Victoria or not."

The Cadillac maintained a steady, comfortable speed as it approached Pandora Avenue. *Poor things. They don't even know they're being followed.*

"Date of birth?" Adrienne opened her notebook. That

information, at least, she'd already located. "March 5, 1938. Let me know when you find something."

Suddenly, the Cadillac pulled into the parking lot of the community center. As Adrienne parked across the street, her phone rang.

"Hello? Yes, Carol . . . Genevieve Yates Tang?"

The back door of the Cadillac opened. Only the male singer climbed out. *Uh-oh.*

"Gift shop. Fan Tan Alley. Right."

Even more suspicious now, Adrienne headed after the Cadillac again, but it wasn't until the singers turned onto Fisgard Street that she felt the blood leave her cheeks. She grabbed her phone again and punched in Eric's number.

"It's me." She cringed, picturing his greasy brown hair and his "Baby, I'm Yours" necklace. "I need your help . . . The details? They're headed into Chinatown."

{CHAPTER 10}

Seagulls as gray-white as the clouds that now hovered over the entry into Chinatown circled above Stacie and Janice.

Janice stepped next to one of the two stone lions that guarded the gate. "What do ya think? Check that restaurant across the street or try this side first?"

Whether it was due to nervousness or to the unfamiliar smells that wafted through the air, Stacie didn't know, but her stomach churned. "Let's try the restaurant. It looks busy. Maybe someone there will know Elsie."

"Hey!" A short oriental man Stacie had seen watching them from the doorway of his nearby shop waved them to his store. "You come here. I have Anglo sandwiches. I give good price."

Stacie glanced at Janice, who shrugged. "It's worth a try."

The man grinned when they reached his doorway. "Come in, come in. See my wind chimes. All handmade. Good Christmas gifts."

"Yes, they're very beautiful," Stacie said, "but we don't want to buy anything. We're just trying to find a woman who might live around here. Her name's Elsie Tang. Do you know her?"

The man frowned. "Tangs not have wind chimes."

"So you do know where she lives?"

He shrugged.

Watching him, Stacie fished her wallet from her coat pocket. Her blue winter headband fell out with it. "Sandwiches would be nice," she said, picking up her headband and stuffing it back in her pocket. "Can we get them to go?"

"Yes, yes. To go is my specialty." He led Stacie and Janice past shelves crammed with beach mats, lacquered boxes, and incense, to a small delicatessen counter along the back wall. "What sandwich you like? Ham and Swiss? Turkey? Roast beef?"

"Roast beef," Janice said.

"I'll take the turkey." Stacie took out a Canadian ten, the biggest bill she had. "Can you tell me where Elsie Tang lives?"

The man's gaze flitted from her wallet to her face before taking the bill. "Tang in Fan Tan Alley. Not everyone find her. Most not want find her."

"Why?"

He handed them their sandwiches. "Tongue sharp as dragon tail."

Stacie had dealt with lots of "sharp tongues" while working at the campground, so she wasn't too concerned. "Where's Fan Tan Alley?"

"Halfway down block. Or through Trading Company."

"Thank you." Stacie's phone vibrated as they headed back to the entrance, so she pulled it from her pocket.

"Nice! When did it start raining?" Janice asked as they stepped outside.

Stacie paused beneath the red and white awning to read her message as Janice unwrapped her sandwich.

Hurry. Bro. F. MAD. Everything ok?

"Who's the text from?" Janice's mouth was so full of sandwich that Stacie could barely make out her words.

"Matt. I wonder how he got my number."

Janice's right eyebrow lurched upward meaningfully.

"Don't read anything into it! He just said to hurry." Stacie wiped a large raindrop from her top lip and lifted her hand in front of her face to protect it from the blowing rain. She still didn't feel like eating.

"Uh-huh," Janice said with a grin. She gulped down the last of her sandwich, and Stacie stuffed hers inside her coat pocket.

When they reached the Trading Company, they found a young Chinese woman standing behind the checkout counter. Her hair was pulled into a long, sleek braid, and her expression was cordial. "Ni-hao," she said to them. "May I help you?"

Stacie wiped the rain from her face with her free hand. "Ni-hao." She'd heard the greeting a few times while they were standing next to the entry gate, and she hoped she'd said it correctly. "Is this the way to Fan Tan Alley?"

"Through the back."

Stacie and Janice moved through the maze of rooms and mounds of merchandise until they located the back door near a collection of Chinese artifacts. The alley, they discovered, was packed with tourists.

"The rain's stopped, so everyone's coming out of their holes," said a gruff voice close behind Stacie's ear. "It's not usually this crowded."

Stacie turned. The man's face wasn't more than a few inches from hers. His brown hair was greased straight back into a ponytail, and he wore a mostly open, button-down beige shirt beneath his brown jacket with a gold neck chain draped down his bare chest. The large, rectangular pendant on the chain read "Baby, I'm Yours."

"Is this Fan Tan Alley?" Stacie's voice quavered.

"Cozy, ain't it? Not much wider than four feet in some places." He stepped even closer to her, brushing the length of his left arm against hers.

"Really?" Stacie backed against the wall.

He nodded, then after giving both girls a slow once-over, stepped around them and out the door into the throng of people.

"That's one guy I wouldn't want to meet on a dark night," Janice whispered when he was out of sight.

Stacie's phone vibrated with another text message from Matt.

U didn't answer.

She texted him back.

Sorry. We r ok.

On first inspection, Fan Tan Alley seemed nothing more than a narrow gap between two brick buildings, but as Stacie and Janice weaved their way through the crowd, they soon discovered that a few of the buildings actually housed small boutiques on the ground floor with tenements above. Some of the shops and most of the tenements were boarded over.

"I'm not sure, but I think that triangular sign up ahead says Tang's Gift Emporium," Janice said over her shoulder as they passed an old-fashioned barbershop.

She was right.

The first thing Stacie noticed when they stepped inside the boutique was that no one was at the cash register. In fact, she and Janice were the only people in the store. "Hello?" Stacie called.

Silence.

The store was crammed full of goods, some similar to those they'd seen earlier, like baskets and teapots and papier-mâché. What set this business apart from the others, however, was its lavish assortment of home décor.

Janice stepped around a shelf overloaded with madras bedspreads. "Where is everybody?"

Stacie motioned to the slightly open door at the back of the room.

The two made their way through the furnishings to the door, which seemed squashed between stacks of pillows and handcrafted rugs. A gray cat sat on top of one stack. When they approached, it jumped to the floor and scurried out the door.

Stacie glanced over her shoulder. Still no one. "Hello?" she called again. She nudged the door open until she could see that it led to an empty, square room. At the far end was a metal staircase. Stacie walked to the base of it and called up. "Is anyone there?"

At first, Stacie wasn't sure she'd really heard the frail voice, but after a second, louder call, she caught her breath.

"Help me! Please."

She and Janice stared at each other briefly, then mounted the stairs.

"Where are you?" Stacie called.

"Manda?" The voice sounded almost frantic.

Stacie rushed to the upper landing, Janice at her heels, and seconds later, they went through another open door only to find a bulky white stove, matching refrigerator, and gray-speckled dining table.

"Let's get out of here," Janice whispered. "We're in someone's kitchen."

"Shh!" Stacie's heart was beating so loudly in her ears, her nerves so tightly wound around her breath, that she barely heard the voice again.

"Manda?"

She motioned Janice to follow her through yet another door that led into a dim, incense-filled living room. Near the far wall,

Stacie saw a petite Chinese woman lying on a black vinyl couch. Her head was propped up by several multi-colored silk pillows, and when she saw the girls, she shrunk beneath her bright, red blanket.

"Who are you?" she demanded feebly.

"We were in the store and heard you calling for help," Janice said in her most taciturn voice.

"Get out."

Janice inched toward her. "Please, let me help you. I'm a nurse."

Or soon will be, Stacie thought.

The old woman's skin hung loose and frail from her face, but her hollow black eyes flashed fiercely. "I said get out!" Then, without warning, her body stiffened, and a deep, frowning moan came from her mouth.

A young Chinese woman burst into the room behind them. "Grandmother! I have it."

The older woman relaxed visibly at the sight of her, but still her groan punched the air. "Help me, Manda!"

Glancing warily at Stacie and Janice, the young woman hurried to her grandmother's side, placed some pills in her mouth, and helped her with a glass of water. Only then did the young woman turn her full attention to Stacie and Janice. "What are you doing in my grandmother's house?" she demanded.

"She cried for help," Stacie answered.

Manda was clearly not impressed, so Stacie tried again. "We were at Craigdarroch Castle yesterday, and Mr. Underwood mentioned Elsie Yates, uh, Tang, and no one was in the store and—"

"My grandmother's not seeing visitors. Please leave."

"Your grandmother? You mean she's Elsie Tang?" Stacie swallowed hard, fighting a sudden urge to force the older woman to tell her anything—everything—she knew about Becka, or about the woman in the castle.

"Manda, please!"

"It's all right now, Grandmother. They're leaving."

Manda then ushered them from the room, down the stairs, and back into the store. "Leave now or I'll call the police."

It was storming outside again, and the emporium was now packed with wet tourists, all staring at the three young women.

Stacie pushed her damp hair behind her ear. "Maybe we could come back at a later time?"

"She's too ill today," Manda said with forced pleasantness, her hands trembling as she glanced toward the tourists.

"How about tomorrow, then?"

The girl's eyes narrowed with the same fierceness Stacie had seen in Elsie's eyes. "Why do you want to see her?"

"I think she might have information that will help us find a missing child."

Manda squirmed, looking again at the tourists, then replied, "Very well. Tomorrow."

"Thank you," Stacie said with a sigh, then nudged Janice's arm and headed for the entrance. As the two girls stepped outside, a blast of glacial wind and rain pelted them. Zipping her jacket to the neck, Stacie stuffed her hands into her pockets. "Oh, no!"

"What?" Janice asked.

Stacie yanked out her phone, her sandwich, and her headband. "My wallet's gone!"

"You're kidding!"

"I only took it out to pay for the sandwiches." She felt along the crevices of her empty pockets. Then she remembered. She gasped. "You don't suppose that man . . . ?"

The blood left Janice's cheeks. "Was there much money in it?"

"No, but it had my driver's license, my ATM card, and the . . ." Stacie moaned.

"The what?"

"The Garners' house key."

{ CHAPTER 11 }

Matt removed his tux jacket from the motel room closet and draped it neatly over a chair.

"I really need your help," Zach said, stepping out of the bathroom.

Matt pulled the ironing board from the closet. "I'd rather you left me out of it."

"But I've tried everything I can think of. She just doesn't notice me."

Matt laid his dress shirt across the board, remembering how Stacie had tried to avoid Zach during rehearsal that morning. "Stacie notices you."

"Yeah, as a friend. But I want to move beyond that." Zach raised his collar and fastened the top button. "So what do you say?"

You ought to feel lucky to have her as a friend, Matt thought, keeping his eyes on his ironing. "I don't know what I can do."

"Come on. You must have some idea. You've never had trouble getting girls to notice you."

"One girl, Zach. It's only been Holly since I started high school. You know that."

"You're lucky you found the girl that fit your list so early."

Matt laughed, but when Zach didn't join him, he turned away until he'd regained control of his expression. "You really have a list? Can I see it, or don't you keep it with you?"

"Get out of here! I bet you have one, too."

"No. I don't. What's on it?"

Zach dropped his shoe and retrieved it, then studied Matt's face. "Okay. Number for number. You tell me yours and I'll tell you mine."

"I told you, I don't have a list."

"Yeah, right. Everyone has one, even if they don't write it down."

Matt shrugged.

"All right. Then just tell me about your perfect Holly."

"She's not perfect, Zach. And neither is Stacie, if that's what you're trying to say. But we like them—"

"—*love* them—"

"—because they're close to what we want. Both my parents told me if I'm too picky, I'll never get married. Holly fits pretty closely, so why not?"

"Ah, who're you foolin'? Holly's the one 'cause you're head over heels, like I am for Stacie. Only Stacie also fits my list. Perfectly. See?" Zach lifted a stack of neatly folded shirts from his suitcase, put them on the bed, and then pulled out a brown leather journal. He removed a folded piece of notebook paper from it and began to read. "Beautiful . . ."

Grinning, Matt folded his arms across his chest. "That's first, huh?"

Zach ignored him. "Dependable, thrifty—"

"—Brave, clean . . . Stacie could be a Scout."

"Appreciates music. Enjoys the outdoors. Is great with kids . . ."

Matt inhaled, picturing Holly snuggling against his arm as they walked along the Lake Powell shoreline several summers earlier at a family reunion. Her seven-year-old nephew had tagged along. Holly usually seemed fine with that, but not this time. And Matt hadn't thought anything of her behavior until the boy had slipped in a pile of rocks, wailed for help, and Holly, rolling her eyes, had told him to get up and quit crying. He wasn't hurt, she'd told the boy. Later, they discovered he had a deep gash on his knee.

Zach looked up. "What?"

Matt, no longer laughing, looked him straight in the eyes. "Don't try to start something with her now, Zach. Wait 'til we get home. All Stacie's got on her mind is that missing girl. Throwing anything else into the pot will only bug her."

"You're wrong. I can't believe I just said that. 'Matt is wrong.' Huh!"

"I'm serious, Zach."

"So am I." Zach slipped his left foot into his dress shoe. "You don't know Stacie like I do. She's always got something on her mind. Keeps to herself a lot, too. But even so, I know very well that she feels a lot more for the people around her than she usually lets on, and I intend to make sure there's a lot more in there for me." He put on his other shoe and smirked. "Besides, I already know what bugs her, and I'm not it."

Matt looked away with forced disinterest, pretending to tighten his bowtie. "All right, I'll bite. What does bug her?"

"You."

Normally, Matt would have thrown a similar insult back at Zach, but this time, to Matt's chagrin, Zach's comment stung. Matt untied his tie.

"Which is why you're the only one who can help me tonight," Zach continued, running the lint brush over his slacks. "She'll never see what's coming."

Matt gulped, retied his tie, and then loosened it again. There had to be some way out of this. "It sounds like you already have a plan?"

Zach shrugged. "All I can think of is—"

"Begging?"

Zach punched him in the shoulder.

"Oh, I see," Matt said, "you're gonna beat it into her!"

Zach jokingly clenched his arm around Matt's neck. "No, I'm not gonna beat it into her. I'm gonna tell her, straight out, that I want to date her seriously."

All emotion drained from Matt's face, and he felt strangely numb. "That's not something you need me around for."

Zach let go of Matt's neck. "No, what I need you to do is get Stacie away from Janice long enough so I can talk to her."

Matt avoided his gaze. "You really should wait 'til . . . Christmas Eve. Or how about New Year's?"

Zach ran a comb through his hair. "Nope. It's gotta be tonight. Have any ideas yet?"

"No. I can't do—"

"That's okay. I'm sure you'll think of something." Zach slid his comb into his inside jacket pocket and moved quickly to the door. "You won't be much longer, will ya? The others are probably already in the lobby." He looked meaningfully at Matt. "Stacie too." Then he shut the door.

Matt stormed into the bathroom. He took his electric razor from the drawer and ran it quickly over the black stubble along his jaw line. But the longer he stared into the mirror, the more he saw Stacie's face—her mesmerizing eyes, her upturned chin, her reserved expression—and the more he realized what a fool he'd been not to absolutely refuse Zach's request for help. There was no way he could help him win Stacie over. Stacie was much too perceptive for such a game.

He slapped aftershave on his cheeks.

What's more, he didn't know anyone who'd like being set up like that.

Maybe I could just tell Zach I've changed my mind, Matt thought. But even as he thought the words, he knew he couldn't follow through with them. Zach, for all his bravado, would feel betrayed if Matt didn't do this. And yet, if he did do this, Stacie would feel betrayed. Matt was in the middle of the classic rock and a hard place.

Matt slammed the bathroom door behind him. "I guess Stacie was right in not wanting to be my friend."

CHAPTER 12

I need to talk.

The tour bus stopped outside the stake center just as Stacie pressed SEND.

"I hope your aunt answers this time," Janice said, moving into the aisle. "You're looking pretty stressed."

Stacie's stomach hadn't stopped churning since she'd discovered her wallet was missing. "So are you ready?" she asked, changing the subject. That afternoon Brother Fillmore had asked Janice to give a "My Favorite Christmas Memories" talk during the program that night in Lara's place.

Janice scowled. "I was trying not to think about it, thank you very much."

"Sorry."

"You don't feel sorry for me at all, do you?"

"Nope," Stacie teased. She removed her coat from the luggage compartment and was about to slide her arms into the sleeves when someone ran into her from behind.

"Excuse me! Some of us want to get off the bus before tomorrow." It was Ivana.

"Oh. I didn't know I was blocking you." As Stacie headed

down the aisle, she glanced at Zach and Matt, who stood at the front of the bus. Zach was watching her—or maybe Ivana—but Matt stared at the floor.

When Stacie reached the exit, she put on her hood. "It's sprinkling."

Ivana impatiently brushed past her and stopped next to Zach out on the wet pavement. "I hope the weatherman was right about the rain not turning to snow. I hate snow."

Matt, who'd been standing on the asphalt in front of the bus, moved next to Stacie. "Makes you wonder why she chose to go to school in Rexburg," he said under his breath.

Stacie laughed, then turned to him, noticing that he looked pale. "Is something wrong? You're not getting sick, are you?"

He swallowed and looked at Zach. "It's probably just the moonlight."

Ivana, glancing at Matt when he said "moonlight," stepped closer to Zach and then looked triumphantly over her shoulder at Stacie. But as she slowly lifted her hand, reaching, Stacie assumed, for Zach's elbow, Zach moved away from her and took Stacie's elbow instead.

"Can I talk to you privately before the warm-up?" he asked her.

Ivana glared. Stacie bit her lip.

"Sorry, Zach," Janice said, squeezing between them. "You'll have to wait your turn. Stacie promised to critique my talk." She wiped the rain off her nose and wrapped her arm through Stacie's. "Actually, why don't you come too? I need all the help I can get."

Zach frowned, but it was the surreptitious look he suddenly gave Matt that shot a shiver of suspicion through Stacie.

"Actually, Stacie," Matt said quietly, "I think we ought to run through your solo before we perform it tonight. Why don't you let Zach critique Janice's talk?"

"Why?" She stepped into the warmth of the building. The smell of cooked ham permeated the air. "Is there something else wrong with the song?" She hadn't meant to sound so sarcastic, but on second thought, if sarcasm helped her figure out what they were up to . . .

"No. I just want to make sure we're ready—that we're together." Matt glanced at Zach. "So to speak."

Stacie tried to read Matt's expression, but he only stared blankly back at her.

"Okay, go ahead." Janice tugged firmly on Zach's arm, leading him toward the kitchen. "I'm sure Zach will do."

Ivana looked from Zach to Janice, to Matt, and then to Stacie before finally stomping into the cultural hall. At the same time, Stacie noticed Zach nod meaningfully at Matt before sauntering away with Janice.

"Well," Matt said.

Narrowing her eyes, Stacie cocked her head to one side. "Well, what?"

He cleared his throat. "Let's see if we can find the Primary room. It should have a piano, don't you think?" He started down the long hallway.

Stacie didn't follow. "What's going on with you and Zach? And don't tell me nothing, because I've known Zach long enough to recognize when he's up to something."

Matt opened a door, looked inside, and closed it again. He tried another but closed that one, too.

"Matt!"

Matt's jaw muscles tightened, but all he said was, "I haven't told you yet how nice you looked last night in that white dress. Makes me doubly glad you girls are wearing white tonight."

Stacie felt herself blush. "Hollow praise won't get you off the hook!"

Matt glanced around anxiously, as if he was trying to find some way out of answering her, and then, apparently, he found it. "Hey!" He waved at someone behind her.

Stacie turned.

A boy around eight or nine years old rushed toward them. "Hi!" He reached up to shake Matt's hand. "I'm Josh. Are you guys coming to our Christmas party?"

"Yes. We're singing," Matt glanced at his watch, then gazed down the hallway.

"Singing?" Josh scrunched his nose. "I hope it's not boring. If it's boring, Alecia will poke me, and I hate it when she pokes me, so I'll poke her, and Mom will get mad. Last time, Mom got so mad at me for poking Alecia I had to miss dessert, and tonight they're having pumpkin pie. Do you like pumpkin? Some people don't. If you don't, can I have yours? It's my fav—"

"Josh, do you know where the Primary room is?" Matt interrupted.

"Sure! It's this way." He moved in the direction Janice and Zach had gone. "Around the corner. It's the big room in the middle of the hall. I'll show you."

"No, thanks. We can find it from here." Matt, glancing at his watch again, turned away from the boy. "Why don't you go on back to your family and tell them about the pie?"

Stacie bristled. What was that about? Matt had no reason to be irritated with the boy. *He'd* been the one who'd first called him to them. "That wasn't nice, Matt," she whispered.

Josh's eyes rounded, turned watery. He clapped his hand over his mouth. "Ha–I–ak–too–uch?"

Stacie rested her hand on his shoulder. "What did you say?"

"Have I talked too much? My schoolteacher, last year's, not this year's, said—"

Stacie smiled reassuringly. "No, you haven't talked too much."

Out of the corner of her eye, she saw Matt looking at her, so intensely that she blushed. Her fingers trembled, too.

"Mmm. Smell that ham," she went on to Josh, forcing steadiness into her voice. "Must be about time to eat."

"Oh, no! Mom said I had to be back before they started serving or . . . Are you sure you can find the Primary room? If you wait while I ask my mom, I'll—"

"No, thank you, Josh. Really," Matt said, his gaze still on Stacie. "We're fine. You've been very helpful."

"See ya in a few minutes," Stacie added.

Josh grinned and shook Stacie's hand. "Don't forget about that pumpkin pie, I mean, if you don't want it." Then he was gone.

Stacie turned back to Matt. He still stared at her, and for a long second, she couldn't breathe.

Matt brushed his hand past hers. "Josh said the Primary room's this way, around the corner, right?"

She swallowed hard, avoided his eyes. Finally, they found a room labeled PRIMARY.

Stacie reached for the doorknob, but Matt leaned past her and opened it. "You're really good with kids," he whispered.

She stepped inside, away from him, and clicked on the light, revealing a wide room with stacks of large and small chairs in one corner, a piano in the other, and several children's drawings of families taped to the walls. "So?"

He shrugged. "It just surprised me, that's all. Zach told me you were an only child."

Stacie frowned. "Gossiping, huh? What else has Zach said?"

"That you're strong and smart. And compliments aren't gossip."

Stacie blushed again, but this time she didn't look away. "Stop it, will you? You're starting to sound like Zach."

"I'm not Zach."

"Matt, what's going on?"

He pulled out the piano bench. "Are you ready for the intro?"

"I expect an answer."

He looked at the ground, took a slow, deep breath, then gazed steadily into her eyes. "Zach wants to talk to you."

"I already know that. What about?"

"That's between you and him." He sat on the bench and played an introductory chord. "Let's just practice, okay? While there's still time."

Stacie moved beside him. She studied his expression for a long moment. "You can't tell me, can you?"

"No."

Aggravated, she pressed her lips together into a straight line. No matter how much she wanted Matt to answer her questions, she couldn't ask him to betray a confidence. "Go ahead with the song," she finally told him with a sigh.

Matt nodded and played the introduction, and Stacie began to sing. To her relief, her voice lilted lightly over the high notes, and her vibrato rippled softly.

When they'd finally come to the end, neither spoke for several silent heartbeats.

"That was almost perfect," Matt said.

"Almost?"

"Yes. At measure sixty-five, my accompaniment didn't quite match the beauty of your voice."

She glared straight at him, assuming he was trying to flatter her again, but this time, his eyes were unguarded, and his expression seemed sincere.

"Can we try it again?" he asked.

"Sure."

The second time through was better, Stacie thought.

"Perfect," Matt said.

Stacie turned away, pretending her pulse hadn't accelerated when Matt looked into her eyes. In truth, she was almost grateful to see Zach enter the room and move toward them.

He clamped his hand down on Matt's shoulder. "You can leave now. Thanks, buddy."

His mischievous—or was it nervous?—gaze remained on Stacie's face, and suddenly, she knew what Zach wanted to talk about. She nearly choked. "Don't go, Matt. Please."

He hesitated. "I'd rather leave."

"Let him go, Stacie." Zach put his hands on her shoulders. "I really need to talk to you. Alone."

As Stacie turned to face him, her resolve wavered. Zach was her friend, and in many ways, more like her brother. She owed him a chance to voice his feelings, even if she didn't share them. "You can go, Matt," she said at length.

But before Matt had opened the door, her cell phone rang. Stacie tugged it from her coat pocket. *Finally!* Her aunt Kathy. "Hello?"

"Stacie! Are you okay?" Her voice sounded agitated.

"Yes. I'm sorry if my text worried you."

"Heavens, no! The text was nothing. It was that call from the police."

"The police called you?"

Both Matt and Zach turned to her.

Aunt Kathy paused. "The woman said someone found your wallet and turned it in. It seemed to be intact, she said, but she wanted to know where you're staying so she can return it to you."

"Stacie!" Zach grabbed her arm. "You're pale. Are you sick?"

"I'm all right." Stacie stepped away from him. "That doesn't make sense," she said into the phone. "I gave them that information almost two hours ago, just as soon as I realized my wallet had been stolen."

Zach grabbed her arm again. "Were you hurt?"

"No," she mouthed, "just wait, please?" And that was when it hit her. "Aunt Kathy! You didn't give her the Garners' address, did you?"

"Of course I did, dear. It was the police, after all . . . Stacie? Are you still there?"

Stacie tried to swallow. "I don't think it was the police."

"Of course it was, dear. Someone probably misplaced the report, that's all." Aunt Kathy laughed nervously. "Call them back. I'm sure they'll straighten everything out."

"Uh—I hope so."

"And afterwards, text me so I won't worry, okay?"

"I will." Stacie hung up.

"What is it?" Matt asked, laying his hand on her arm. His touch, she noticed, settled her trembling, but instead of answering his question, she quickly dialed the police department. "My wallet was stolen today and—yes, I'll wait . . . hello? This is Stacie Cox. My aunt received a call from someone there who says she found my wallet . . . Yes, I'll wait. . . Yes? Oh, I see. Are you sure it . . . Okay, thank you."

"Now you definitely look sick," Matt said. "I'm going to find Janice."

Suddenly lightheaded, Stacie dropped onto the piano bench. "Aunt Kathy told her where I'm staying."

"Told who?" Matt and Zach asked simultaneously.

"I don't know. Some woman. But it wasn't the police." She pressed her fingertips to her temples, trying to clear her growing panic. "Maybe it was the person who stole my wallet. But if so, how did she get my home number? I don't keep it with me . . ."

"Stacie, you're not making sense. Tell us what happened," Zach demanded. "From the beginning."

The retelling didn't take long.

"Maybe it wasn't the thief who called," Zach said when she'd finished, but he seemed doubtful.

"Maybe." Stacie wished she sounded less nervous than she felt. "But if not . . . don't you see? The Garners' house keys were in my wallet! What's to stop the thief from breaking into their home? He could be there right now." She dropped her head in her hands. "How could I have been so foolish?"

Zach sat next to her and slid his arm around her shoulders. "You're not foolish!"

"Zach's right." Matt sat on a chair across from them. "Don't be so hard on yourself."

Zach pulled her closer into the crook of his arm, so close she could feel the warmth of his breath against the base of her neck, and she shrunk back.

"Don't worry about the Garners. They'll be fine."

"The Garners!" Stacie jumped to her feet. "I've got to tell them about this."

A few moments later, Stacie walked through the double doors that led into the cultural hall. It was a festive scene, with dozens of laughing, chatting people sitting at long rows of rectangular folding tables, matched end to end and decorated with white paper and colorful Christmas ornaments. Stacie saw the Garners sitting in the middle row.

When she reached them, Brother Garner stood and took Stacie's hand. He tugged her to the table. "Do you have time to sit with us?"

"No, thanks. I have to get back to the choir just as soon as I—I have to tell you—" Her news about the phone call—she'd already told them about the theft—came out in a flood of words, but even so, Brother Garner had his coat on before she'd finished.

"I'll call the police and ask them to check out the house before we go in" he reassured her.

Sister Garner grabbed her coat from the back of her folding chair.

"No." Brother Garner gently pushed his wife back into her seat. "You stay. Everything will be fine, I'm sure of it."

Sister Garner stood back up. "I'd rather go with you."

She hurried into her coat, and Stacie followed them from the cultural hall and to the outside door. But as she watched them walk out into the misty night, facing the possibility of a nightmarish loss, she couldn't help but think of another couple who had walked slowly away from a swimming pool, their heads low, their shoulders shaking.

{ CHAPTER 13 }

Leah's gaze swept across her living room, taking in the faces of the people who had showed up that night at a moment's notice: Broulim's manager, a waitress from Me 'n Stan's, a farmer who was also a small-plane pilot, a local high school teacher, and several men and women she hadn't met yet. So many times over the past months, good-hearted people just like these had sacrificed their time and means to help locate Leah and Ethan's daughter. In fact, though Leah barely knew most of them, she couldn't help but think of them as almost an extension of her own family.

"This woman was recently sighted with a child who looks like Becka," Ethan said, handing out the photocopied sketches. "Tonight's goal is to canvas these six blocks on the south side of Main Street. Please ask everyone if they remember seeing her in our area, especially at or near Porter Park, the day Becka disappeared."

"We've divided the neighborhood into several small zones," Leah added. "When you finish searching along your assigned route, please report back to Detective Boyle at the police station."

Ethan motioned to the broad-shouldered officer standing behind them. "Contact him immediately if you learn anything—

anything at all. And please know how much we appreciate your efforts. We know it's not easy to come out" —his voice caught— "on such a cold night."

Fighting her own emotions, Leah clasped her husband's hand in both of her own. The searchers zipped their coats, tightened their scarves, and shoved their hands into gloves.

"Where's Grace?" Ethan asked.

"She said she'd be a little late. Her sons were involved in a couple of Christmas programs today."

A stream of light from a vehicle's headlights flashed across the living room wall.

"I bet that's her." Leah followed the crowd to the door, but as she opened it wide, allowing the others to step through, she gasped. "Ethan! The porch—Becka's light—it's out!"

"Thomas, son," Ethan called over his shoulder, "please get a lightbulb from the hall closet."

Leah grabbed the white pine bench from their dining table and dragged it to the door.

"Wait, sweetheart. Let me get a ladder."

"No, I'll do it. We can't let Becka think she's forgotten!" She climbed onto the bench. "Thomas, where's that bulb?"

The seven year old, brushing his too-long, sandy-colored bangs from his eyes, appeared in the doorway. "There's only an empty box on the shelf."

"That can't be. I bought several of them." Leah looked at her husband. "I know I did."

Ethan urged her from the bench. "That was two months ago."

"No, it was . . ." Leah stared then blinked as comprehension dawned. "Has it really been two months since I—" Tears filled her eyes. "Since I—"

"Since you've—slept at night?" Ethan led her back into the

living room. "Yes, sweetheart, but you're improving. You slept four hours last night, and tonight you'll do even better. I'm sure of it."

Just as he'd done from the beginning, Ethan was comforting her, shielding her from the pain. "We have to get more bulbs," she said, scanning the room for her purse. "Go ahead and take the boys around the neighborhood, Ethan. I'll do my route when I get back from the store."

"I know," Ethan said. "Why don't we take a bulb from the hall light fixture for now and—"

"You don't have to do anything of the sort!"

Both Leah and Ethan whirled. "Grace!"

The middle-aged woman limped heavily up the porch stairs and leaned against the doorframe.

"What happened to your foot?" Leah asked, reaching out to her.

"I'm afraid my driveway's icy," she sighed. "I fell and twisted my ankle this morning."

"You should be home with your foot up."

"I'm needed here." Grace slipped the purse from Leah's shoulder and handed it to Ethan. "And I'm sure one of your neighbors will let you borrow a lightbulb."

A neighbor! Why hadn't Leah thought of that? "Thank you, Grace. You're heaven-sent."

Grace, her face crinkling into a smile, patted Leah's hand. "Why don't we try the neighbor across the street? They're bound to have an extra bulb or two."

"Yes, of course." Leah put on her coat and grabbed a copy of the police sketch from the kitchen counter. "Ethan, we'll take the route across the street, okay? That way I can get the bulb at the same time."

"Sure, honey. Thomas, get your brother. It's time to go."

"Let me help you down the stairs, Grace." Leah took hold of her friend's elbow.

When they stepped off the last concrete step, Grace turned until she faced Leah. "That's a good husband you have there. You're a blessed woman." She placed her free hand atop the one Leah held her arm with. "I know you don't feel blessed," she continued. "I didn't when I lost my daughter. But later, especially after I helped those two families find their children, I realized how blessed I really was. I wasn't alone."

Leah bit her quivering lip, wanting to say, "I'm sorry for your loss," but when the words wouldn't break through her emotions, she simply clung tighter to Grace's arm, and they walked across the street and up the walk of a Christmas-lit home. She rang the doorbell.

A woman with graying red hair answered the door.

"Hello, Sister Stokes," Leah blurted. "Do you have a lightbulb I could borrow?"

"A lightbulb? Yes, I'm sure we do. Come in out of the cold." Sister Stokes led them into the large entry. "Marty!" she called to her husband. "Get a lightbulb from the pantry, will you, please?" She turned back to them. "He'll only be a minute."

"I also have another favor." Leah held out the sketch. "The police are looking for this woman in connection with my daughter's disappearance. Do you recognize her?"

"Oh, yes. I saw the report on the television." Sister Stokes took the flyer, scrutinized the picture, and then handed it back. "I'm sorry. I don't recognize her."

Masking her disappointment, Leah gazed out the Stokes' large, arched front window at their elaborately decorated yard: Santa and his sleigh, blue lights illuminating plastic milk containers along the driveway, spotlighted cartoon characters playing hide-and-seek behind the bushes.

"Look at that darling blonde mouse," Grace said gently. "The one sitting in the tree swing. Even her ponytail bobs up and down."

A sob choked inside Leah's throat.

"Oh, dear!" Grace put her arm around Leah. "You told me, and I forgot. Becka liked to swing too, didn't she?"

Leah nodded, trying not to think of how she'd thought it best to leave Becka alone while she got over her tantrum. She'd only turned her back on her for a moment while she watched Thomas, but when she went into the trees to check on her, Becka was gone. The police had thought she was probably hiding, and at first, Leah had too.

"So someone's seen Becka?" Sister Stokes asked, leading them to the sofa.

Leah brushed a stray tear from her cheek. "Yes. It was a girl from here, actually. Stacie Cox, Detective Boyle said."

"*Stacie Cox!*" Grace's chest rose and fell as if she were taking in great gulps of air. "I wish you would have told me this sooner, Leah!"

"Why?" Leah wrapped her arm around the woman's shoulder, trying to calm her. "Are you all right? Do I need to get help?"

"No, no. I'll be fine." She twisted out from under Leah's arm.

"Here are the bulbs." Brother Stokes, his hair, nose, and fingertips smudged with white paint, stepped into the room and handed the box to Leah. "Don't worry about replacing them."

"Thank you." Leah reached for Grace again, but the woman hobbled quickly ahead of her.

Then, after Sister Stokes closed the front door behind them, Grace said, "Let's go home and replace your bulb. When the others return, we'll tell them we made a mistake and apologize for wasting their time."

Leah froze. "What are you talking about?"

Grace's trembling fingers flew to her mouth for a second, but when she removed them, her composure had returned. "I'm so sorry, Leah. If I'd have known, I never would have encouraged you to . . ." She paused, caught her breath, and went on. "Listen to me. Stacie's the girl who killed my Jessica."

Leah's frozen gasp fogged in front of her.

"I know it's hard to believe. It took me a while to see it too, but I eventually realized Stacie had lied to me. She'd said she'd watch my children, but—you know the rest." Her eyes grew moist and weary. "Stacie's a liar, Leah. Her report must be a hoax."

Like an arctic breeze, Grace's voice sent a shiver down Leah's spine. She stepped backwards. "Are you sure?"

"Isn't it obvious?"

"But what if it's not a lie?"

"Leah, you have to ignore this report."

They started down the stone steps, and though Grace clung to Leah's arm, she somehow managed to pat it, too. "I know it's hard to let go of something you put so much hope into, but it's got to be done. That way we can focus our energy and money in the right direction."

"But if Stacie really saw Becka, and I—oh, Grace, I couldn't live with myself if I was wrong!"

Grace rested her warm hands on Leah's quavering shoulders. "Trust me."

Leah looked hard into her eyes, and for several seconds, the older woman appeared to study Leah's expression.

Finally, she dropped her hands. "If you can't see the truth, then I can't help you."

Leah wanted to speak, to tell her that she of course believed her—to beg her not to leave, not to give up on Becka—but Grace's gaze restrained her.

"What a pity. The media attention was just starting to take off." Grace limped toward her car.

"Grace!"

"Call me if you change your mind."

{CHAPTER 14}

After returning with the choir to the motel, Stacie, Janice, Zach, and Matt took the Cadillac straight to the Garners' house. When they arrived, instead of finding the Garners comfortably safe in their home, they found two policemen in their living room. The younger officer was standing next to an overnight suitcase and speaking into a police radio.

"I'm so glad you made it before we left," Sister Garner said to Janice and Stacie. She was carrying a toiletry bag from her bedroom. "These officers say everything checks out fine, but we're staying with some neighbors tonight, just in case. As for the two of you, I'm still trying to get hold of our Relief Society president. She has a large house. Most of her children are married now, and we're pretty good friends. I don't think she'll mind letting you stay with her for a night or two."

Janice frowned. "We'd hate to impose on anyone."

Brother Garner, walking closely behind his wife, balanced a large jewelry box against the end table. "The only locksmith we could reach said he couldn't come until tomorrow, so until then, we thought it best, just in case someone does try to break in, to take our most important valuables with us."

"We tried to get a couple of motel rooms, one for us and one for the two of you," Sister Garner went on apologetically, "but with the Christmas season, there was nothing available." Setting her bag on the floor, she bustled from the room again, and a moment later returned with a stereo, which she promptly handed to Matt. "Take this out to the car, please. The trunk's open."

Matt nodded but didn't leave. "There's room for two more in Ivana and Sharon's motel room," he told Stacie. "Why don't you ask if you can stay with them?"

"That's a great idea." Zach took the jewelry box from Brother Garner. "You'll be closer to—the choir that way."

Stacie tried not to grimace. Ivana? It was hard enough coping with her from a distance.

Janice cocked her head to one side. "What do ya say?"

"I don't think we have much of a choice."

Sister Garner clasped Janice's hands as if everything was already settled. "That's perfect! What a relief!"

Stacie glumly took her cell phone from her coat pocket and handed it to Matt. "Will you call Ivana? At least you get along with her."

"Scared?" he teased, shrugging at her offered cell phone. "I'll use mine. Actually, I think I'll have Zach call her."

"Zach—?"

Matt grinned.

Stacie chuckled. "Good idea."

"Excuse me, ladies," the younger officer said after Stacie closed the door behind Matt. "The sooner everyone's out, the sooner we can secure the house and get back to our beat."

"Right. Come on, Stacie." Janice led the way to the Garners' guest room, where they helped each other out of their formals, dressed in blue jeans and sweaters, and filled their suitcases. About five minutes later, Stacie returned to the living room, pulling her luggage. She found Zach on Matt's cell phone, probably talking to Ivana, and Matt was talking to—

"Sergeant Price?"

"Hello, Miss Cox."

What's he doing here? Stacie wondered. Earlier that day, when she'd gone to the police station to report that her wallet had been stolen, an officer at the front desk had made it perfectly clear that pickpocketing cases weren't Sergeant Price's responsibility. He dealt with more serious crimes, like drug dealing. And kidnapping.

"Have you learned more about Becka?" she asked anxiously.

"No." He narrowed his eyes, obviously studying her reaction. "I'm here to check into a report made by a Manda Tang. She said you entered her grandmother's home without permission this afternoon. Is this true?"

Stacie blinked. "We went there, yes, but I thought we'd worked that all out with her."

"Tell me about it, please."

"I wanted to talk to Elsie Yates. Mr. Underwood told me that Becka's kidnapper had asked about her, so I—"

"Broke into her house? There are laws against that, you know."

"Stacie's not a criminal!" Zach said defiantly.

Stacie took hold of his arm. "It's all right, Zach." Then she turned back to the sergeant. "We didn't break in. The back door was open and no one was in the store."

"Living quarters look different than stores," Sergeant Price reminded her.

Janice had entered the room and quietly put her suitcases on the floor next to Zach's feet. "Elsie was calling for help," she interjected. "We couldn't just walk away."

"She was in a lot of pain," Stacie added.

Sergeant Price's eyes widened, but a second later they narrowed again. "Tell me about that too, please."

As Janice rehearsed the events that had transpired at the emporium, Matt edged closer to Stacie. "Don't tell him about your feeling," he muttered.

"Why?"

"He won't get it. He'll think you've become emotionally involved."

"But I am emotionally—" Janice had finished her description, and now both she and Sergeant Price were watching her. "Sorry." Stacie glanced at Matt.

Sergeant Price frowned. "I'll talk to Miss Tang again and see if she can corroborate any of your story, but take this as a warning. Both of you. Do not involve yourself in this case again." He turned to leave then stopped. His voice was softer now, but no less grave. "You've already done your duty, Miss Cox. Now let us do ours."

"Sergeant Price?"

Matt touched the back of her hand. "Careful."

"Look, Miss Cox, after you contacted us about Ms. Yates, I personally went and talked with her and her granddaughter. They know nothing about the woman you described nor about Becka."

"But maybe if I talk to her, she'll remember something. It worked with Mr. Underwood, and—"

Sergeant Price shook his finger at her. "Don't you realize you might be hurting that child more than helping her? If the kidnapper really is in Victoria, you nosing around could push her into doing something desperate."

The sick feeling Stacie had felt earlier that day twisted inside her again. "I can't abandon Becka!"

"Letting someone else do what they're trained to do is not abandoning her." He opened the door, stepped outside, and paused. His voice softened. "When I interviewed you last night, you told me you were a lifeguard. Correct?"

"Yes."

"Then answer me this. If you and perhaps the parents see a child drowning, who should swim out to the victim? You or one of the others with good intentions but less skill?"

Stacie stared at him. "We'd probably both go."

He sighed. "You're right. They're emotionally involved, so they might. But who *should* go?"

"Me. The others could wind up—" Stacie fidgeted—"in similar trouble."

"Exactly."

{CHAPTER 15}

Adrienne flicked Cox's driver's license into the black metal wastebasket that stood next to the double bed. *"One petty theft and a stupid phone call,"* Eric had said. *"That's all it took to send that girl and her friends packing. Should keep them busy for a while, don't you think?"*

At the time, Adrienne had agreed with him. But now, remembering how Cox had returned to the castle and somehow gotten the truth out of Underwood when she hadn't been able to, Adrienne started to wonder if she'd discounted the girl too quickly.

With a sigh, she reluctantly retrieved the license. "Guess I better come up with plan B," she grumbled, "just in case."

Sitting on the forest-green fleece blanket the campground staff kept folded at the foot of the bed, she studied the girl's photo. "Hmm. What else could throw a girl like you for a loop, Stacie Cox?"

She flipped the card over and then turned it back to the front. "Rexburg . . . BYU–Idaho—*Mormon!* Of course. Cox has to be one of those self-righteous goody-goodies, which means almost anything could slow her up." Adrienne laughed. "Maybe Eric could get her drunk. Now that would be fun to watch!"

Still chuckling over her mental image of the intoxicated girl passed out next to a toilet, Adrienne returned the license to the lamp table and grabbed her copy of the *Victoria Times Colonist*. Alcohol was a fun idea, but not practical. From what Adrienne had heard, Mormons were pretty stubborn about such things. What she really needed was something more subtle.

She read the front-page headline: "Recent Storms, Dangerous Rivers." Not much to work with there. Page 2 featured an article titled "Homelessness at All-time High." Ugh! Wasn't anything more alarming going on in this city? All Adrienne needed was something small, something petty, like the pickpocket— something that would turn Cox's inconsequential world upside down again.

And then she saw a color photo of a constable she didn't recognize. Above it, the caption read: "Still No Suspect in Estate Jewelry Heist."

Adrienne grinned. *A crime.* What a perfect Plan B. She licked her lips. Implicating Cox in a crime could provide a bit of entertainment, too. Maybe not as much as the girl heaving over the toilet would have, but the image still had merit.

Riana whimpered from the other room.

Adrienne rolled her eyes. "What's wrong, Riana?" *As if I don't already know.*

No answer.

Adrienne sighed, returned the newspaper to the nightstand, and walked barefoot across the cabin floor from the bedroom she slept in to the small couch she made into Riana's bed every night.

"I asked you what was wrong," she repeated as sweetly as she could.

"It's dark in here."

"We've talked about this before."

"I know."

Adrienne pursed her lips. This had to be the hundredth time Riana had wakened, scared of the dark, and so far nothing she'd said had helped. Time to try a new tactic.

She knelt beside her. "You're a smart girl. What do you think will help you not to be afraid?"

"A story?" Riana swallowed hard. "Daddy always told me a story when I was scared at night. It helped me fall asleep. And when I woke up, it was light again."

Adrienne forced her frown into a smile. "You're lucky you don't have a daddy anymore. He and that woman got mad and sent you away, remember?"

Riana's lower lip quivered.

Adrienne ruffled the top of the child's freshly cut, newly black-dyed hair. "You've got me, though, and we'll be just fine. We don't need any of those kinds of daddies, do we?"

Riana lowered her eyelids.

"Do we, Riana?"

"No, ma'am."

"That's my big girl." Adrienne tugged the patchwork quilt up around Riana's neck. "Now close your eyes and tell yourself a story. A happy one about you and me. When you wake up, it will be daylight again. And just as you'd hoped, I'll be here too, and we'll start searching for our Paul treasure again."

Riana turned onto her side, her back to Adrienne, and tucked her knees toward her chin.

Content, Adrienne walked back to her room and closed the thin door. *Poor girl,* she thought. *The sooner she realizes she's better off without a man to mess things up, or to tell her stories, the happier she'll be.*

She sat on the bed, picked up Cox's license, and glanced at the open newspaper. Looking at the photo from this angle, the officer's build and hair coloring displayed a striking resemblance to Price when he was younger.

"I believe that's why the perps start with—practice on—the small stuff," he'd once told her in frustration after releasing from custody an obnoxious drunk who'd impersonated a diplomat in order to get more alcohol. *"Because they know we don't have the time or the budget to deal with them."*

Suddenly, an idea took root. Adrienne grinned exultantly. That's what she needed! It was a crime big enough to upset that Mormon girl, yet small enough that the RCMP wouldn't take the time to investigate it back to its source.

She placed the license in the nightstand drawer, but before she'd closed it, she took out the open notebook in which she'd written tomorrow's plans. Number 1, call Eric to find out if anything's changed with Cox. Number 2, visit Tangs. Number 3, locate N. Yates. And number 4?

"It all depends on how big a fool you really are, Stacie Cox."

{CHAPTER 16}

When Stacie and Janice arrived at the motel room after ten o'clock that night, Ivana gave them a key and Sharon asked them to please be quiet so they could sleep. Other than that, her new roommates didn't speak, and that was perfectly fine with Stacie. All she wanted to do was try to forget all that had happened that day.

"How 'bout a late-night swim?" she whispered to Janice, pulling her swimsuit from her luggage.

Janice slipped into the bathroom and Stacie followed her, clicking the door closed behind them.

Leaning over the counter to wash her face in the sink, Janice asked, "Too wound up?"

"I guess. I can't stop thinking about what Sergeant Price said about the kidnapper getting desperate, though." She rubbed her hand along the right side of her neck, trying to ease the tension in the muscles.

"Does that mean you're gonna let this go?"

"I'd have expected that kind of a response from Zach, or even Matt," she whispered, fighting the wave of discouragement that washed over her. "But not you. You were the one who convinced me to do something in the first place."

Janice pressed a clean white towel to her face. "That was before you started trying to actually search for Becka. I thought, and still think, you needed to report what you saw and even help with that police sketch, but beyond that, well, Sergeant Price is right. We're in over our heads."

"I didn't know you felt that way." Managing to avoid bumping into Janice within the confined space, Stacie dabbed eye-makeup remover on a folded piece of toilet paper. "I'll try not to bother you about it anymore."

"You don't need to get defensive. You know I want that little girl found as much as you do, but I think—" Janice smeared a glob of green-striped toothpaste onto her toothbrush. "Look, we almost got in a lot of trouble today, and for what?"

"Who knows?" Stacie asked at length. "Maybe after we talk to Elsie in the morning we'll find out."

Janice nearly choked on a mouthful of toothpaste. "You can't be serious!"

Stacie shrugged. "Manda did invite us back."

"Yeah, but she also reported us to the police!" Janice wiped her mouth then faced Stacie squarely. "Why risk it? Sergeant Price already told you the Tangs don't know anything. There's nothing more you can do."

Stacie stared at the floor, avoiding Janice's gaze.

"Right?" Janice pressed.

"That's just it," Stacie faltered. "I'm not sure there isn't more I can do."

"But Officer Price said . . ." Janice crinkled her eyebrows into an uneasy line. She grabbed Stacie's arm. "You have to stay out of trouble."

"Believe me, I want to, but remember how Manda squirmed when I mentioned we were looking for a missing child? What if she lied to the police?"

"I'm sure Sergeant Price knows when someone's lying to him."

Stacie shrugged. "Maybe. But what if he didn't talk to Elsie? What if Manda didn't let him?" Exasperated, she leaned against the bathroom door. "Have you ever had a feeling, a thought—" She shook her head, knowing that wasn't quite the right word, but not knowing what else to call it. "—or something that bugged you so much you couldn't let it go until you did something about it?"

"Like the way you felt sick earlier?"

"Yeah. Only worse."

Janice cocked her head to one side. "It's that bad, huh?"

Stacie nodded.

Frowning, Janice lifted her hairbrush from the counter and ran it down the length of her black hair. "Do you have a plan? I mean, no matter what Manda said, she won't welcome our visit. What would you say to her, anyway?" She flipped her hair slightly at the end, sweeping it into a curl, before starting again at the top.

"I don't know. Apologize, I guess. But mostly I've got to convince her to let us talk to Elsie."

Janice yawned. "Why don't we sleep on it? Maybe something will come to us in the morning."

"I wish I could sleep, but I'm still too wound up. Which reminds me. You never answered my first question. How about a swim?"

Janice yawned again, but this time her eyes closed, too. "Sure. For a little while." She inched open the bathroom door and headed for her bed. "I'll get my suit," she mouthed. "You change first."

Several minutes later, Stacie left the bathroom wearing a black, one-piece swimsuit underneath an extra-large T-shirt. She found Janice sound asleep on top of the bed with her own swimsuit cradled beneath her head.

Not having the heart to wake her, Stacie wrapped a towel around her waist and stepped into the hall. It was empty and quiet. If she was lucky, she thought, the pool would be empty too.

When she entered the pool area, she saw several people in the water—all men. A couple of them gawked at her as she walked past them, and one even let out a low whistle. Feeling vulnerable, she turned to leave.

"Couldn't sleep?"

She whirled. "Matt!" He was so close that she bumped into him, and when she felt the wet skin from his bare abdomen against the back of her hand, she stepped back self-consciously.

He dried his face with a towel. "Where's Janice? Shouldn't she be here, you know, for protection?"

"Don't worry about me. I can take care of myself." Then, grinning to hide her nervousness, she placed her towel, key, and shoes on a bench, hastily slipped off her T-shirt, and dove straight into the deep end of the pool.

When she came up for air on the far side, she saw Matt swimming toward her with seemingly effortless strokes.

"I can see why you decided to become a lifeguard," he said, slightly out of breath. "You're fast."

"That's not why I became a lifeguard."

"Oh?" He watched her so closely it made her senses swirl.

"But that's a long story." She thrust her body through the water and headed for the other side of the pool again.

Matt stayed right beside her until they reached the edge. "I have time."

"It's nothing, really."

Still, Matt watched her, only now there was a depth in his gaze that urged her to trust him, the same way his touch on her arm earlier that evening had settled her anxiety over the "police" call to her aunt. It would probably be okay to answer his question, at least briefly, and she did so.

When she finished, Matt said, "So Jessica's drowning is the reason you became a lifeguard." Then, lowering his eyes to look directly into hers, he asked, "Is it also the reason you've been trying to help save Becka?"

Stacie shrugged. "I've asked myself that question several times, and I've always come up with the same answer. *Maybe.* But I also know it's not the only reason. Jessica died. I wish she hadn't. I wish I'd been more prepared, more watchful, so it wouldn't have happened. But now, with Becka—she's out there somewhere, Matt. Alive." Her voice caught. "And without her parents. No one should have to live like that."

His gaze held hers for so long that she finally had to remind herself to breathe. "You're gonna keep searching for her, aren't you?"

"Yes."

"That's what I thought." He pushed himself out of the pool, turned, and sat on the edge, still dangling his feet in the water. "I've been thinking about your search too, and I've had an idea." He patted the concrete beside him. "Want to hear it?"

Feeling nervous beneath the dancing light in his eyes, Stacie pulled herself up onto the edge next to him. "So what is it?"

Several rivulets of water dribbled down his bicep. He stared out across the pool. "Once, back home in our shop, my Dad told me the trick to wealth is figuring out what the customer wants before he knows it himself. To get ahead of the game."

Stacie shivered.

He turned to her, glanced at her arms and her neck. "Goosebumps. Are you cold? I can get your towel. Or would you rather slip back into the water?"

"I'm fine." But then she noticed a couple of the other men looking at her again, so she folded her arms in front of her. "But

I don't know what your father's business has to do with finding Becka."

He smoothed a hand over his wet hair, and Stacie noticed that his other hand rested on the concrete only an inch from her own. "Let me try again, but before I—Would you tell me again about your trip to Chinatown? About the Tangs?"

Hoping to steady her quickening pulse, she took a deep breath and carefully recounted her visit at the emporium, including Manda's reaction when she'd mentioned the missing girl.

"She was nervous and fidgety. That's all, right?"

"So?"

Matt brushed the fingertips of his opposite hand along the rounded edge of the pool. "What if Manda didn't lie to the police? What if she really hadn't seen them before?"

Stacie's fingers started to tremble. "It's the only lead I've got, Matt."

He edged closer to her, pressing the length of his arm against hers, and whispered intensely, "Don't you see? Maybe the reason she, or perhaps neither of them, recognized the pictures is because Becka and the woman hadn't been there. Yet."

His words hit Stacie hard. She gasped.

"And like my father suggested, maybe what we need to do is—"

"—get ahead of the game." Stacie grinned and slapped the concrete on either side of her and pushed off into the pool. "That does it. We're going tomorrow. First thing before rehearsal."

"It's a date," he said.

A light flickered in his eyes, and Stacie, suddenly flustered, dove straight to the bottom of the pool, where she hovered until she needed to breathe. When she came up, she found Zach, wearing a red swimsuit, standing on the edge of the pool next to Matt.

"I always knew you were a fish." Zach smiled mischievously down at her.

Matt stood, nodded dismissively at the two of them, and headed for the diving board.

Zach jumped into the water next to Stacie. He raised his arms over his head, preparing to splash down around her. "Friend or foe?" he asked.

"Foe!" Stacie dove into the water, but he grabbed her foot before she could get away. When he let go and she came back up for air, she plowed him with a wave of water. Back and forth, the two laughed and splashed, just as they had when she and Zach and Janice had spent their last end-of-the-summer week at the campground pool. It had been their final bash before college and homework took over their lives.

"I hope," Zach said when they stopped to catch their breath, "we can spend the rest of our lives like this."

"Drenching each other?"

"No. Enjoying each other. Being friends." He hesitated, and then his expression turned serious. "More than friends."

Stacie's grin disappeared. She let the water drip down her forehead and into her eyes before backing away from him and clenching the poolside. "Please don't, Zach." Not wanting to embarrass him, she glanced over her shoulder to make sure Matt wasn't within earshot. "We're friends. That's all."

"No. It's more than that."

She slowly shook her head, and as she did so, his hopeful smile began to dissolve.

"Please think about it," he said gruffly.

"I have."

"You couldn't have, Stacie. You've been too wrapped up with, well, everything." He nodded to the large round clock on the wall above the green EXIT sign. "Besides, it's midnight." He smiled crookedly. "No one ever thinks clearly after midnight."

Despite herself, Stacie chuckled at the phrase they'd repeated so many times during their teen years, but as soon as the sound left her throat, she wished she'd remained solemn, because Zach suddenly put his forefinger under her chin and asked, "Please?"

Stacie shook her head more decisively this time, but Zach took hold of her hand and gave her a lopsided grin. "You look tired. We'll talk about this later. Ready to go back to your room?"

"That would probably be best," she said tightly.

Zach helped her from the pool, waited as she retrieved her towel and T-shirt, and walked her to the exit. But as she stepped through the doorway, feeling the cool air waft against her wet skin, she glanced back to the pool and saw Matt. Though he was looking straight at her, he raised his arms over his head, preparing to dive.

Flustered again, she turned back to Zach. "Why can't you understand—?"

He lifted his eyebrows, waiting for her to finish her question, but a moment later, when she saw the determination in his eyes, she shook her head. "Never mind." No matter what she said tonight, she knew Zach wouldn't accept it.

"See you guys tomorrow," Matt called.

Zach waved without looking at him.

Stacie waved too, and then Matt, still watching her, leapt into the pool.

At seven o'clock the next morning, Stacie, Janice, and Matt left the motel, climbed into the Garners' Cadillac, and headed for Chinatown. Minutes later, Janice parked in front of the Trading Company. As they'd feared, it was closed, so the three looked for the street entrance to Fan Tan Alley.

"There are shops down there?" Matt asked when they'd found the rectangular, red Fan Tan Alley sign. It contained both English and Chinese characters. "It can't be more than—"

"Four feet wide at its smallest point. We know." Stacie glanced meaningfully at Janice.

Their footsteps clicked hollowly between the redbrick buildings.

Janice nodded. "The 'Baby, I'm Yours' man."

"Is that who you think stole your wallet?" Matt asked Stacie.

"I thought so, but when my aunt said a woman had called . . ." She shrugged.

Tang's Gift Emporium, like the Trading Company, was closed.

"Let's watch from over there," Stacie suggested, pointing to a boarded-over boutique that wasn't quite visible from Tang's front window, "just in case you guys are right about Manda calling the police."

Half smiling, Matt motioned between two empty baskets. "After you."

About half an hour later, eight o'clock by Stacie's watch, the door to Tang's Gift Emporium opened and out stepped—

"Mr. Underwood!"

"Miss Cox!" Glancing down both ends of the alley, he yanked the door closed behind him and then stood there, stiff and ready, like one of the stone lions guarding the Gate of Harmonious Interest. "We're not open yet," he stammered.

"What are you doing here?" Stacie asked.

He glimpsed over his shoulder through the shop's window. "I believe the proper question is, what are *you* doing here?"

"We have an appointment with Elsie Tang."

If a person can blanche and redden at the same time, Mr.

Underwood did, but it was the red that remained. "Impossible." He shooed them from the alley. "I won't allow it."

The door opened again and Manda, carrying the gray cat Stacie and Janice had seen the day before, stepped outside. Her sleek black hair reached far down her back, and she looked only at Mr. Underwood, apparently not seeing the three young people standing nearby.

"Excuse me, Cecil," she said, "Grandmother's asking for you."

Mr. Underwood whirled abruptly and swept passed her into the shop, but what caught Stacie's attention was the doting look on Manda's face as she watched him go.

"He's nothing like Stan," Manda mumbled. Then she saw the three of them.

Janice moved close to Stacie's side. "Is your grandmother better today?"

"Yes." Manda, her eyes darting from side to side, backed against the door.

Stacie took a few steps forward. "We don't want to bother you, Manda. We're only trying to find this woman." She slid the sketch out of her envelope. "She was at the castle two days ago, and she asked about your grandmother."

The girl's eyes flickered to the picture, then up at Stacie's face.

"Please look at it."

"The police already showed it to me," Manda clipped, "and like I told them, I've never seen her before. Neither has my grandmother. Now leave us alone."

"So your grandmother has seen these pictures?"

Manda's expression wavered. "Don't you listen? I haven't seen those people."

"Come on, Stacie, let's leave her alone." Matt's voice was

rough but solicitous, and his hand on her shoulder held her still like a protective vise. "We can still watch the store from a distance," he whispered.

A second later, Mr. Underwood returned. "You're needed inside, Manda." He flipped the CLOSED sign over to OPEN and whisked her into the shop. The door closed crisply behind them.

"You did everything you could," Janice offered quietly. "Like Matt said, we can watch from out here, in case the woman shows up later."

Stacie shook her head. "If Becka's kidnapper is really going to show up, she might recognize us and leave. We've got to hang out inside."

Matt grabbed her arm again. "Don't, Stacie. Maybe we can watch from inside one of the other shops."

Stacie's first instinct was to pull away from him—to tell him to go back to the motel and not worry about her. But the concerned inflection in his voice and the worry in his eyes stopped her. "I've got to try again. I've got to be inside there."

Matt studied her eyes and then sighed. "Okay. Try again if you have to. Janice, that record shop just opened. See if they'll let you watch from there. I'll try that souvenir store when it opens."

"Thanks, guys," Stacie said.

"I don't know what to watch for," Janice protested.

"Neither do I." Matt shrugged. "But you've seen Stacie's pictures. Just pay attention to all the women, especially those with little girls."

Stacie's fingers trembled as she grasped the door handle. "I don't know how I can convince Manda to let me stay." She tried to force courage into her words. "Maybe if I buy something . . . ?"

Matt placed a warm, comforting hand on her shoulder. "You'll find a way."

Stacie smiled gratefully. Then she handed Janice the envelope of photos and stepped inside the store.

Manda stood behind the counter. "Please leave," she said when she saw Stacie.

Examining the display beside her, Stacie hoped to hide her nervousness. "I'd like to buy a trinket or two, if you don't mind. From what I've seen, your shop has the best merchandise."

From the corner of her eye, Stacie saw Manda fold her arms, purse her lips, and stare at her. But that was all right. At least she was in the store.

However, the longer time went on, the more irritating Manda's scrutiny became. In fact, every time Stacie unfolded a rug or took down a wall hanging, Manda's gaze flashed her direction, no matter what other customers were in the room.

And there were many other customers. Not as many as had crowded Fan Tan Alley yesterday, but still a steady stream. Stacie finally realized if she was going to have any chance of seeing and recognizing Becka's kidnapper, but she had to find some other observation point.

Looking around, Stacie decided that the checkout counter provided the best option, so she worked her way to the silk pillow display directly behind the counter. That position not only limited Manda's ability to watch her, it also allowed Stacie a clear view of each person's face as they walked through the door.

Stacie remained there for about ten minutes. She would have stayed longer if a school tour group hadn't filed into the store, prompting Manda to turn to her and say, "Buy something or leave. It's too crowded."

Stacie snatched an ornament, a shining miniature of Craigdarroch Castle, from a Christmas mobile that hung directly above the pillows. She'd been admiring it for several minutes now, especially the way it nestled in white clouds, looking so much like the castle she'd once dreamed of living in with her parents. Standing in front of it was a tiny group of carolers—a family. The father had dark curly hair, and a loose strand fell across his forehead.

"This one's for me," she mused aloud, noticing Matt watching her from the window of the store directly across from her. "Now all I need is something for my aunt and uncle."

Manda scowled. "Move along, then."

Stacie slowly made her way to the next-best position: the colorful Madras rug display beside the back door that led to the stairway.

"This room, boys and girls, has been here since the beginning of the twentieth century," the tour guide announced. "Notice the slit in the ceiling there? That's all that remains of a wall that once separated the main room from a secret chamber. That chamber, it is said, was a hideout for drug dealers."

The tour guide couldn't have been more than twenty-five years old, Stacie guessed, but his false gray beard, black top hat, and silver-rimmed cane made him appear much older. The children obviously agreed with her, because several of them called him "Mister Sir." And one child asked, "Do you know my grandma?"

"Shh!" said a nearby adult.

The tour guide chuckled. "As you can see, there's not a lot of room in this store, but there are many items for sale, just as there were a hundred years ago."

Several children and adults crammed into the aisle next to him, trying to get a closer look at the display of trinkets. One of the adults, a thin woman with shoulder-length black hair and wearing a tailored, pale green pantsuit, patted the top of a red-haired boy's head.

"Watch out. I almost stepped on you," she said.

Stacie leaned over a shelf of delicate glass animals, trying to get a better glimpse of the woman's face. But it seemed the farther Stacie bent, the further the woman turned from her.

"If you break them, you buy them," Manda hissed.

Startled, Stacie nearly knocked over an intricate glass chicken.

"Careful." The man's voice that filled her ear wasn't much louder than a whisper, but his breath was hot on her neck and smelled like rotten hamburger. His hands clasped her waist.

Stacie tried to step away, but the two children at her feet made it impossible, leaving only one other option. Raising the ornament in front of her, shield-like, she turned. The first thing she saw was his "Baby, I'm Yours" necklace.

He winked. "Remember me?"

Stacie recoiled. "Did you, um, get the pictures you wanted yesterday?" she asked, trying not to breathe.

"Yes. I'm flattered you remembered."

"Well, uh, I have shopping to get back to."

He laughed loudly, annihilating all fresh air around her, and she turned away from him. The first thing she noticed was the back of the woman she'd tried to get a closer view of a few moments earlier. She was talking to Manda at the checkout counter.

"Nick?" she heard Manda say.

The man's hands were on Stacie's waist again, and she jumped, knocking a large glass horse from the shelf.

The children shrieked.

"That is fifty dollars!" Manda hollered, pointing at Stacie.

The slender woman half turned. Her thin, pointed features held no expression, but she gazed fully at Stacie from behind brown-rimmed glasses before quickly looking away.

By now, all the customers were aware of Stacie's mishap, and several of them left the store, including the thin woman and the smelly man. Janice and Matt must have noticed that something was wrong too, because they arrived a few moments later.

"That was one of our finest pieces," Manda scolded.

"I'm so sorry." Stacie looked at Janice and Matt as she retrieved a large piece of broken glass before continuing so quietly that only her friends could hear. "There was this man. And he was so close. And his breath . . ."

"Fifty dollars!" Manda demanded again.

Stacie moved to the cash register and placed the miniature castle on the counter. "It looks like I won't be able to buy this after all," she said, taking a thin roll of bills from the front pocket of her jeans.

As Manda took the money, her expression softened a bit. "Who was that man that was bothering you?" she asked.

"You saw him?"

"I see everything." She picked up the telephone receiver and punched only one number. "Cecil? Could you come up here please?" She hung up. "That man came in with that woman."

"You mean that classy one? The woman wearing the green pantsuit?"

"That's her." Manda frowned.

"You're kidding!" Stacie tried to match the two together in her mind, but it was impossible. Ridiculous. "Maybe she can't smell. Or see—" The woman's eyes behind her glasses. They were pale blue. As blue as—

Stacie gasped. She ran out the door and frantically scanned the alley.

Matt and Janice were close behind her. "What's wrong?" Janice asked.

"That woman! She was—I mean—I think she was—" She tried to rush past them, but Matt caught her arm.

"You mean—" Understanding passed over Matt's face. "Was it the kidnapper?"

Janice's eyes widened.

"I think so. But maybe it was because Becka wasn't with her, that I—or maybe it wasn't her. Maybe—how could I have let her get away again?"

Matt pushed into the throng of people. "What do you remember?"

"A green pantsuit."

He nodded and shoved forward. Stacie and Janice took off in different directions, but all three returned to Tangs only a few minutes later.

"No green?" Matt asked when they were together again.

Janice shook her head.

Stacie thought she was going to be sick. "I guess we're back to talking to Manda again. She, at least, spoke to her."

"Sounds reasonable." Matt took hold of Stacie's elbow, leading her back into the store.

"You forgot your change."

Stacie didn't even look at Manda's outstretched hand. "Do you know who that woman was?"

"The one with that creep?"

"Yes." Stacie clenched the edge of the counter. "Did you get her name?"

"Didn't want it."

"Did she use a credit card?" Matt asked.

Manda's lip curled in disgust. "She bought nothing."

"Was this her?" Janice pulled the sketch from the envelope. "Please, look again."

Manda glanced behind them and then stared at the envelope. Finally, she grasped the pictures with her long, well-groomed fingers. Stacie waited while she studied it, watching until the young woman's gaze met hers.

"There are similarities," she finally said.

Stacie pressed her fingertips to her temples, trying to stop her mind from spinning as she remembered how the woman had avoided her gaze, how she'd heard her ask—"Manda! Didn't she ask you about someone named Nick?"

Manda glanced anxiously at the other customers, at the entrance, at the back door. Her gaze held in the direction of the back door, and then she seemed to relax. "Nick's my cousin."

Although she wondered why Manda was suddenly so helpful, Stacie wasn't going to waste time worrying about it. "Was she looking for him?"

A hint of a nod.

Matt leaned on the counter. "What did you tell her?"

"I told her to go to UVic's student center," Manda spat out. "That's where he picks up most of his women."

Matt lowered his gaze to meet Manda's eyes. "Would you be willing to call Nick and see if he'll meet with us?"

Brilliant! Stacie and Janice smiled at each other

"It worked once," he explained. "We got ahead of her, right?"

Manda looked past all of them to the back door, and Stacie, this time following the direction of her eyes, turned and saw Mr. Underwood standing there. From the look on his face, it appeared he'd been there for some time. *So that's why Manda was suddenly willing to help us,* Stacie thought. *Mr. Underwood gave his permission.*

"You don't mind me telling them," Manda said. It wasn't a question or a command, just a statement.

Mr. Underwood moved toward them, his gaze only on Stacie. "For myself, I've never minded. It was only for Elsie." He took a handkerchief from his pocket and wiped his nose. "She's dying of cancer, you see, and stress of any kind is hard on her."

Stacie remembered all too vividly the ravaging effects of

cancer—knew it could drive loved ones to do desperate, foolish things. But she didn't see what that could have to do with any of this, or why he'd lied to her about Elsie's name.

"I've told Elsie about you, Miss Cox," he went on, "and she insists we help you—that we help the child in any way we can. She ran a day-care center for many years, you see." He dabbed his eyes and straightened to his former, lion-like demeanor. "Besides, Nick's got too much of the Yates's blood in him. And if he has anything to do with that child's disappearance, I'll—!"

As he spoke, a look of defiant determination came over Manda's face too. "Grandmother's right. I'll call Nick for you."

Relief washed through Stacie. "Please tell him to meet us around three thirty," she said to Manda, who promptly left the room.

She returned less than five minutes later. "Nick said he'll meet you at six o'clock, after he gets off work, in the Campus Services building. There's an eatery there, near the bookstore."

"We—she—can't make six!" Matt sputtered. "We have a performance then."

Stacie glanced uncomfortably at Matt and Janice. "Mr. Underwood, where exactly is the university?"

"No way," Matt said. "We all have to be at the pageant by five thirty."

"It's several miles from here," Mr. Underwood answered. "Near Cadboro Bay."

"You can't disappoint the Garners," Janice pled. "They've worked too hard to get us here for the pageant. You should hear how they brag about your solo."

Choking back her guilt, Stacie declared quietly, "I'm going. I'm sorry."

Mr. Underwood wiped his nose again. "You're a lot like my Elsie, Miss Cox. She wouldn't have given up either. Proved it by the way she stuck with that no-account Stan all those years." He folded his handkerchief and dabbed it to his eyes. "Let me try my hand at talking to Nick. I used to take Manda and him out for ice cream when they were young. Maybe that will count for something."

"You'd be willing to do that?"

He smiled thinly at her as he started toward the door. "I know I've been difficult. I didn't want Elsie disturbed, you see. Life is very painful for her now, but since she wants us to help you . . ." He was heading up the stairs by then and the door was closing, so Stacie couldn't hear the last of his sentence.

Was this the real Mr. Underwood? she wondered. If so, then she'd never before met anyone like him—a man so devoted to a woman who wasn't his wife—and it made her wonder about life and love and all sorts of mixed-up feelings she didn't have time to think about right then.

When he returned, Mr. Underwood said, "I've set the meeting with Nick at five. It was the best I could get."

"Five might work," Matt offered tentatively.

Stacie reached for Mr. Underwood's hand. "Thank you."

"Anything for Elsie."

Minutes later, Stacie, Janice, and Matt were back in the car. They only had twenty minutes until their practice session began, but if the traffic was good, they'd make it.

"Maybe I should have mentioned this earlier," Janice said when they finally pulled onto the road, "but I can't go with you at five, Stacie. I promised Quinton I'd meet him in the hotel lobby."

"Wow. When did this happen?"

"Last night. I woke up while you were at the pool. Remember how I promised I'd call him? But I'm sure you'll be fine without me. Matt can drive you, if he doesn't mind."

"I think Zach will mind," Matt said hoarsely.

"Ask Zach, then."

Stacie stared at Janice. What was she thinking? Janice knew as well as she did that being alone with Zach, especially in a small space like a car, was not the way to ward off his attentions.

"It's settled, then," Matt said.

"Don't I have a choice in the matter?"

Matt stared stonily out the windshield. "No."

{CHAPTER 17}

eah placed the fragrant, sticky, gingerbread dough on the cookie sheet, set the pan in the preheated oven, and shut the door. Then she clicked on the oven light and peeked through the small window. It was a silly habit, she knew, especially since she'd barely put the pan inside, but she looked anyway.

"I always liked to do this when I was a little girl," Leah had *whispered to Becka.*

Giggling, her daughter pressed her nose against the plastic. "It's hot."

"Be careful! You don't want to get burned."

Becka touched her mother's hand. "I'm sorry."

The doorbell rang. Leah wiped the flour from her hands and pulled out a long sheet of aluminum foil—long enough to cover the cardboard slats Ethan had cut for her last night after she'd told him about Grace. And Stacie Cox.

The doorbell sounded again. *Can't they take a hint?* Leah banged the foil box down on the cupboard next to a stack of Becka's flyers and clomped to the door.

"Hello, Leah."

Grace. She was standing beneath Becka's still-glowing lightbulb. Leah moved to close the door. Grace stopped it.

"I'd like to be alone," Leah said, turning back to the kitchen.

The woman hobbled after her, grabbed her arm, and turned her around to face her.

"Talk to me."

Leah looked at the floor. She tried to swallow away her sudden emotion, but the tears and thoughts she'd fought all morning came anyway. "Last night . . . how could you have left me like that? You know, don't you, that I have to do everything I possibly can, no matter how futile it seems, to help find my daughter?"

"I'm sorry I upset you. I only meant to make you see the truth, so we could move on." Grace moved further into the kitchen where she picked up a stack of wax paper cutouts lying on the counter next to the aluminum foil. "Stencils?"

"Yes." Leah wiped her eyes.

With trembling hands, Grace set the cutouts back on the counter. "I really am sorry."

Leah folded her arms across her waist, lifted her right hand to her mouth to hide her quivering frown, and then paced to the oven. A moment later, she'd regained control. "We're building gingerbread houses tonight," she said with strained cheerfulness. "Would you and your family like to join us?"

"Maybe. I'll see what the boys have going tonight." Grace slowly walked the length of the kitchen, trailing her hand across the counter. Suddenly, she stopped, and red rushed to her cheeks.

"I'm not going to throw them away yet," Leah said, whisking the stack of Becka's flyers, the ones that included the information provided by Stacie Cox, into a drawer. "There are still too many unresolved issues."

Grace slid the cutouts away too. "It's up to you, I suppose. Well, thank you for the gingerbread invitation, Leah, but I don't think we'll be able to make it."

Leah pressed her lips into a thin line, restraining her irritation. *Grace knows I'm not convinced that the Cox lead is a dead-end. How dare she act so offended about it!*

"I do have something I need to tell you, though," Grace went on. "It's the reason I came by this morning." She straightened the fur collar of her black winter coat as if she were about to give an important speech. "I told the police what I knew about Stacie Cox."

Leah pressed her hand against the base of her throat, but felt no pulse.

"They said, 'Her past has nothing to do with this case,'" Grace mimicked. "But I also heard from one of the other officers, unofficially, of course, that they've already checked into Stacie's lead, and it's turned up nothing. So you see, I was right after all. Just another one of Stacie's lies."

Leah stared at Grace, fighting the thoughts and emotions that barraged her, before finally slumping against the counter. "Then we're back to—Delano?" She pressed her hands over her face. "No! Becka can't have fallen into that man's hands!"

"Come here, dear." Grace pulled Leah into her arms, and Leah, unable to restrain her tears, laid her head on the woman's shoulder.

When her sobbing subsided, Leah wiped her face. "I'll have to start praying for someone else to find her now." She'd meant to sound confident, but even to her own ears the words felt hollow and dull.

"Yes." Grace patted her back. "But while the Lord works on answering your prayers, we're going to do everything we can to steer this search in the right direction." She buttoned the top button of her coat. "I have an idea—a good one. I have to stop at the courthouse first, but why don't you come with me to the community club Christmas luncheon? You can get to know more of the business people in town and talk to them about Becka." She smiled. "Seeing the mother always leads to more donations and publicity."

Leah looked back at the floured counter and the baking utensils. The warm scent of still-baking gingerbread. "I—can't. Not today. I have to finish the dough for my family. I promised the kids a break, and they're counting on me."

Grace placed a door-shaped cutout on top of the other stencils and slid the entire stack against the wall. "Can't you do this later?"

Leah hesitated, imagining her sons' disappointment when they came home from school and found that the gingerbread wasn't ready. But then, almost at the same time, she pictured Becka's brown eyes, her lonely arms reaching for her. Grace was right. Leah had to go with her, because Becka was out there somewhere, and she needed help only Grace knew how to give.

Leah turned off the oven. "Wait here," she said. "I'll get my coat."

"All right, dear." Grace opened the drawer and pulled out the stack of flyers. "I'll just get these out of your way," she said, dropping them inside the trash can.

As Becka's pictures, her smiling face, disappeared beneath the lid, Leah felt another wave of desperation rise within her, but even so, she forced herself to turn away and run up the stairs to her room.

If only Stacie's report had been true, she thought. *If only someone really did know where my daughter is!*

And cared enough to find her.

{CHAPTER 18}

tacie and Zach together. It was an image that agitated Matt every time it entered his mind. And it entered it at least once every second or two.

He paused by the podium at the front of the Relief Society room and glanced at the clock on the wall. It was 4:45 p.m. After what seemed like several minutes, he walked to the door, then turned and looked at the clock again. Still 4:45.

"Is it cold in here?" Lara fastened several buttons of the white sweater she wore over her sapphire formal. "I can't seem to get warm."

"I'm too warm." Matt struggled out of his white tux jacket and dropped it into her lap. A button clicked against the metal chair frame. "Maybe you're still sick."

"And maybe you're too worked up about something," Lara retorted. "Sit down, will you? You're driving me crazy."

He sat, but only for a few seconds.

Lara slid her arms into Matt's jacket sleeves then flipped through the orange binder until she found the choir's first song. She set it on the piano.

"Go ahead," Matt said.

Lara raised one eyebrow. "Patience is a virtue."

Frowning, Matt moved to the window and opened it just enough to see that the dark sky was clear of rain clouds. A few stars already dotted the sky, too. Should be safe for driving.

He turned back to Lara who, instead of playing the accompaniment, stared at him, clearly aggravated. He couldn't blame her. He was acting like a jerk, and couldn't seem to fix it, which only made him feel worse. "Would you just play, please? If you're not up to accompanying, I need to practice."

Lara raised her eyebrow again, and a hint of pink touched her otherwise pale cheeks. "Why don't you try the Primary room? Or go over to the park and practice on the choir's keyboard?"

The clock read 4:50.

"It's not set up yet. And, anyway, like you, I have to be here when the rest of the choir arrives." Matt stormed back to the podium, clenched the metal microphone stem, and squeezed. Maybe if he gripped it hard enough he'd regain a bit of his composure. "Come on! Are you going to play tonight or not?"

In answer, Lara placed first one hand then the other on the keyboard and began to play, not quite up to tempo but tolerably well. However, when she finished, her fingers slipped into her lap, and her shoulders slumped forward.

"That was good for a first try," Matt said. "Let's hear the next one."

Lara shook her head. "Can't do it. I'm worn out. Sorry. You're gonna have to accompany again tonight."

"Then move over." He glanced at the clock—it was 4:55. "Please."

Lara didn't move. "I don't know what's eating you," she finally muttered, "but don't take it out on me."

Matt sighed. "Sorry."

Lara reached over to the binder, straightened several skewed pages, and closed it. Then she rubbed her hands up and down the length of her arms before sliding to the edge of the bench, swiveling her legs around, and standing.

Matt slid onto the bench behind her and immediately plowed into the middle of the most challenging piece.

Lara gawked. "What's wrong with you?"

Matt froze, his fingers still on the keys. "What?"

"It's a difficult piece, but you don't have to beat it to death. Lighten up. It's Christmas." She lowered herself into the nearest seat. "And if it's Stacie and Zach you're jealous about, well, from what I can see, that's your fault, so either do something about it or let it go."

He struck a harsh, dissonant chord that wasn't written in the music. *Jealous?* How would Lara know anything about, well, *anything?* She'd been lying around her hotel room for the last three days. "I'm not—jealous. I have a girlfriend."

Lara smirked. "I may have been sick, but I'm not deaf. I've heard what people are saying."

"What's that supposed to mean?"

"It's all right, Matt. Stacie's a great girl. A little quiet, maybe—"

"That's just because she holds a lot of what she feels inside."

"Hmph. I didn't know that. See? I knew you liked her."

He traced along the top of several black keys with his right forefinger. "Of course I like her, but that doesn't mean I—I feel anything more than that."

"Oh, no?"

"No."

"All right, if you say so."

Matt knew it was his cue to keep denying her assumptions, but as he opened his mouth to do so, his mind went blank.

Lara studied his face for several silent seconds before she stood and walked toward the door. "Maybe you've convinced yourself you're not paying a lot of attention to Stacie, but if you ask me, I'd say it's about time you started talking to Stacie, not just staring at her."

Matt shifted uncomfortably and looked at the clock. It was 5:10. "I talk to her."

"Puh-lease!" Lara rolled her eyes. "You go back to St. George soon, right?"

"So?"

"If you wait too long, you'll lose your chance."

She left then, mumbling something about finding out where everyone was.

Matt stared at the music in front of him for a few seconds before flipping the folder over to the first song and gently pressing the keys. It was a tender, dreamy melody. Not the kind Holly liked—it was too sentimental for her taste. But he instinctively knew Stacie would like it just as much as he did. Stacie and Zach.

It was 5:25. He banged a chord. *I'm not jealous!*

The door flew open.

"Good." Brother Fillmore looked at Matt. "You're here." He glanced across the rest of the room and then over his shoulder, scanning the faces of the other choir members who were filing in behind him. "Janice is here too. But where . . ." His head moved from side to side. "Where's Stacie?"

"She's—"

Brother Fillmore didn't wait for Matt's answer. "She's gone again, isn't she?" He bristled to the front of the room, set up his music stand, and shuffled through his stack of music. Finally, he surveyed the group. "Zach's not here either."

"They'll be back for the performance," Janice explained from where she sat on the front row. "We've sung so much today, they should be" —her voice dropped beneath Brother Fillmore's glowering gaze— "warmed up."

Brother Fillmore slapped his black folder on the music stand. "If Stacie thinks she can keep running off, dragging other choir members with her, without suffering any consequences, she's very much mistaken."

"Stacie hasn't run off," Matt said evenly. "She's trying to help—"

"I know what she's trying to do, but she has to stop. *Now.*" He waved his arm as if he were taking in the expanse of the room, the choir, the universe. "It's good that she cares so much, commendable that she wants to help, but there really isn't anything left for her to do. We don't have time for any more wild goose chases."

"Stacie doesn't believe it's a wild goose chase," Matt declared boldly.

Brother Fillmore looked him straight in the eyes for a moment, then cued the choir to silence. "That's her opinion," he said under his breath.

And mine. The thought hit Matt with a clarifying jolt. Lara was right; he was jealous. Not only that, he did care for Stacie more than he'd realized. And though she didn't appear to like him that well . . .

He pictured again the way Stacie had stared at his hand when she'd refused his offer of a truce outside the castle, and how she'd jumped into the pool last night the moment he'd moved close to her. He had to find a way to change how she felt about him. And soon.

CHAPTER 19

A drienne breathed in the smell of cooking hamburgers as she glanced around the eatery. The colors—brown, beige, and splashes of orange—were outdated, but somehow they fit this place. At the back was a small grocery section; at the front was the checkout counter, complete with cappuccino machine, meal options, and a multitude of candy bar selections.

The eating area was small by cafeteria standards, with only about two dozen tables and booths lining the room's perimeter. And it felt almost cozy. Maybe that's why the young cashier knew Nick.

"He's a freak!" the girl had said. Her large, dark blue eyes grew round with indignation. "I mean, he hits on me every day, just before he orders, and then as he takes his food to that table over there, he hits on the very next girl he sees, no matter what she looks like."

"He sits at that table every day?" Adrienne asked.

"Yup! At six o'clock sharp, unless it's taken. Predictable, huh?" The girl's curly blonde ponytail bounced as she turned back to the cappuccino machine. "Wait a minute. Why do you want to know so much about Nick? You're not dating him, are you?"

Adrienne quickly slid her hands down her own slender waistline. She might be older than the cashier, but from what she could see, she was in much better shape. "No. I just need to talk to him. He knows how to find something I'm looking for."

The girl shrugged, and in that tiny action, Adrienne recognized a repulsive shadow of her former self—that dependent, foolish girl who'd pretended she didn't care for the jerk in her life, yet fully believed she needed him and his attentions to make her feel complete. Adrienne pulled Riana closer to her side.

"So, do you want to order something?" the girl asked.

"What do you think, Riana?"

Riana shook her head.

Good. The child was getting used to not eating. So much better for her future figure. "Go ahead, dear."

"Macaroni and cheese?"

Adrienne frowned. "No, dear. Salad." She looked back to the attendant. "Two salads. No dressing."

As the young woman went for their food, Adrienne ran her fingers through her hair and tucked the bottom edge of her form-fitting, pale green blouse back into the waist of her black skirt.

"Is our Paul treasure gonna be here?" Riana asked.

"No, dear. We haven't found him yet. We're going to talk to a friend of his, though. His name's Nick."

"Does Nick know where Paul is?"

Adrienne took lipstick from her purse and dabbed it on her lips. "I believe so, dear. In fact, I think he's hiding him."

"Is he gonna tell us where he is?"

Adrienne filled two plastic cups with water. "Of course he will. Now take these to that seat in the corner over there, Riana. I'll bring the food in a minute."

Riana took the cups, but she didn't move.

"What's wrong?"

Riana jiggled her leg as she looked down at her sandaled feet. "I need to go to the bathroom."

Adrienne knew the closest lavatory was down the hall, away from the eatery. "You'll have to wait."

With her head still bowed, Riana carried the drinks back to their booth, and soon Adrienne picked up their order. But on her way back, she saw a man, dressed in jeans and a dark blue jacket, saunter into the eatery. His dark brown hair fell just below the nape of his neck. He was unshaven, too, in an intentional, rugged way. *Nick! The cashier said he wouldn't be here 'til six!*

Adrienne hurried to their booth. She sat opposite Riana, facing what the cashier had said was Nick's table, and waited for him to move to it.

Stay calm. You're the one in control.

Glancing sideways, she saw Nick wink at the blonde girl then lean his left elbow on the counter. His hand draped over the edge, revealing a gold ring on his middle finger. It glistened in the light when he moved his hand, and Adrienne could see that it was set with three oval-shaped stones, each a paler green than the one preceding it. Jade. Where would a guy like Nick, who worked as a trash collector here at the university, get his hands on such a valuable piece of jewelry?

Riana stood. "Can I go to the bathroom now?"

"Sit down!" Adrienne hissed. "Nick's here. You'll have to keep waiting."

"How long?"

"I don't know. Just eat your lettuce."

Frowning, Riana wiggled back onto the bench.

Adrienne waited until Nick had paid for his food before standing and smoothing her skirt. It was time to make her move.

"Nick Yates?"

Adrienne whirled to the voice. There, standing in the wide

entrance in a blue formal, was Stacie Cox!

The blood drained from Adrienne's face, and her fingers shook in anxious fury. *Not again!* Where was Eric? He was supposed to be following that idiot!

"Trade me places, Riana," she ordered through her teeth.

Riana slid out of her seat. "Can I please, please go to the bathroom now?"

Adrienne moved until her back was to Nick's usual table. "I wish we could, dear." She glanced back at Cox and saw a young man in a white tux guiding her toward Nick. "But it's too late. If we leave now, without eating, someone will notice us."

"Can't we come back and eat it?"

"No. Now sit down and chew slowly." Adrienne pressed her fork into her salad, took a bite, and bit into the prickly stem of a pickled pepper.

"But I have to go bad."

Adrienne spit the unwanted portion into her napkin, paused until her trembling lips had stilled, then slipped Riana's glasses from the front pocket of her backpack and slid them over her daughter's nose "I told you no. Now keep your head down."

Anxiety filled Riana's eyes, but she obediently looked at her plate.

"Do either of you plan on eating?" Adrienne heard Nick ask.

Adrienne nearly choked on a cucumber. This was something she hadn't counted on—to be so close she could hear what they were saying without revealing herself. It was as if Lady Luck had suddenly swooped down and dropped a gift into her lap.

"No. We have to sing soon," Cox said.

"Okay. I'll be back in a minute."

Adrienne heard the grating squeal of chair legs on tile, the brush of bodies lowering onto chairs, and then felt the unsettling sensation of someone moving close behind her.

"Ask him your questions and be done with it," White Tux said. "We only have a half hour, forty-five minutes, tops." He didn't sound happy.

"I warned you we might be late."

Their conversation paused long enough for Adrienne to wonder if they'd left the table, but knowing how close she was to discovery, she didn't dare turn around to find out. Instead, she plunged another forkful of salad into her mouth. And then she froze. Riana was staring at the singers.

"I told you to keep your head down," Adrienne whispered.

Riana's lower lip quivered as she again bowed her head to her food.

Adrienne heard the rustling of cloth and the plunk of a plastic tray on the tabletop.

"This place makes the best vegan burritos," Nick said.

"We hate to be rude," White Tux began, "but we don't have much time."

"Where are you performing?"

"Topaz Park. At a Christmas pageant."

Utensils clanged.

"Soy milk?" Nick asked.

"No, thank you." Cox's voice was quiet but businesslike. "I'll get straight to the point."

"I wish you would."

"Have any strange women contacted you recently? Someone who looks like this, only with black hair?"

Adrienne's hand involuntarily flew to her head, and she bit back the oath that filled her throat. So Cox *had* recognized her at Tang's, even through her disguise and even with Eric's help.

Riana looked up, but only for a second.

"Listen, honey," Nick said. "I talk to women all the time. Some are strange. Most are—"

Not even Adrienne's fury could squelch her image of the too-intimate look she knew he was giving the girl, and she repressed a laugh. From what she'd seen of Cox, she'd have no idea how to handle a guy like Nick. She was much too naive.

"Anyone like this woman?" Cox persisted, a nervous edge to her voice.

"No. But hey, I'm game!"

"Listen, buddy—!" White Tux sounded angry.

Nick laughed. "I was just kidding. What's your interest in this woman, anyway?"

"It's not her we're interested in," White tux snapped. "It's the kid she's got with her."

Adrienne caught her breath. She shifted left in her seat, trying to completely block their view of her daughter. *You've had it now, Cox.*

"A kid?"

Adrienne heard a guilty gulp. What? Was Nick a deadbeat dad like Paul?

"What kind?" Nick went on. "Boy or girl?"

"Girl."

"Well, uh, I gotta go." Squealing chair legs again.

"Wait! Here's my phone number," Cox said.

It sounded like he sat again.

"Please call me if a woman who looks like this, or even sort of looks like this, contacts you, okay?"

"Yeah, sure."

"May I have your number, in case we have any more questions?"

After a long pause, Nick said, "Okay, but I might not answer."

"I can't hold it anymore," Riana whined.

Adrienne glared at her coolly. "You have to."

Riana squeezed her legs together. "Please!"

Adrienne scowled. If Riana wet herself, there was no possible way they'd remain invisible. "All right," she said, trying to figure out the most unobtrusive way to get out of the eating area. "You head for the bathroom, and I'll—no, leave your coat with me. And straighten your scarf. Good. I'll be less than a minute behind you."

"Can I run?"

"No. Walk."

After Riana left the eatery, Adrienne, her face decisively averted from Nick's table, picked up their belongings and strolled nonchalantly from the room.

In the hall, fully outside of the singers' view, she found Eric leaning against the wall with his nose in a newspaper.

"What are you doing?"

Eric lowered the paper. "Adrienne?"

"I'm paying you to watch Cox, right?"

"That's funny. I haven't seen any money yet."

"And maybe you never will if this is what I'm to expect. I had no warning, Eric. I almost got caught in there!" Adrienne started for the bathroom again with Eric tagging along.

"How was I supposed to know you were gonna be here? Cox goes with that choir all over town." He scowled. "In fact, I think you should be reporting to me. It worked at Tang's, didn't it?"

"Get out of here."

"Excuse me?"

"I'll call if I need you," she said coolly.

"Fine!"

Adrienne paused outside the restroom door. She pressed her hand against the cool wall, leaning against it, trying to compose herself before turning to watch Eric storm down the hall and exit through the glass doors at the end of the building. He disappeared into the darkness shortly after he passed the phone booth.

Suddenly, she had an idea. A Plan-B idea mixed with images of Paul, Nick's ring, and Cox's license. "Hurry, Riana," she said, opening the lavatory door. "I have a couple of calls to make."

{CHAPTER 20}

Stacie, you should have just called the police and let them deal with that guy," Zach said after they'd driven several miles in silence. "He was a jerk."

"Like that would have done any good," she answered. "Mr. Underwood told Nick I would meet him."

"Okay, then call them now."

"And tell them what, exactly? Nick didn't know anything."

"Does that mean you're finally gonna end this nonsense?"

Stacie closed her eyes and leaned her head against the back of the seat. "You're starting to sound like Brother Fillmore."

"I'll take that as a compliment, thank you. And while we're on the subject, what's the big idea, sneaking off with Janice and Matt and setting up this crazy meeting?"

She opened her eyes, surprised by the hurt in his voice. "If you were so upset, why didn't you say something earlier?"

"What was the point? You were already set on going through with this scheme. And besides," his tone softened, "I didn't want—someone else—to drive you." He touched the back of her hand.

Not again! Stacie edged away from him and turned her face toward the passenger-side window, hoping he'd take the hint.

He did, or so she thought, until they pulled into the Quadra Street church parking lot.

"You didn't answer my question," he said, helping her from the car.

A cool, damp breeze blew over her and she shivered. "What question?"

Zach motioned her to the church building, where the rest of the choir would be if they hadn't already walked down to the park. "Why did you sneak off with Janice and Matt?" he repeated. "Don't you think you're getting a little, you know, obsessed with this search?"

"If it was your child, wouldn't you want someone to find her, no matter how obsessed his or her actions seemed?"

"If it was *our* child, we wouldn't be here. We'd be out of school."

"That's not what I meant." Stacie stepped sideways, increasing the distance between them.

"I'm sorry." He hurried after her toward the front doors. "I was just worried about you. I didn't mean to get upset." Then, to her complete surprise, he caught hold of her arm, leaned forward, and gently kissed her on the cheek. "Stacie, I've been thinking about this for a long time. Please let me tell you how I feel."

She stepped back slightly. Her throat constricted.

"I love you," he went on, taking her hand. "I've loved you longer than I can remember. That's how the song goes, isn't it?" He grinned, but his eyes were serious.

Somehow, Stacie found her voice. "Please don't, Zach."

"Don't what? Tell you I love you?"

"Yes." She placed her other hand on top of the one he held hers with. "You're very dear to me, Zach. You're one of my best friends."

He lowered his head, about to kiss her on the other cheek.

"You're like the brother I never had."

He hesitated, kissed her quickly, then placed his free hand over their entwined hands. "Family, yes. But not a brother. Someone much more intimate."

Stacie pulled slightly back from him, but he didn't release her. "I'm no good for you, or anyone," she said.

"Of all the crazy . . ." He pulled her closer to him again. "We've always been friends, Stacie, so why don't we just make our relationship more permanent?" His voice became husky. "Think about it. Think about dating—and then marrying me."

"Please listen to what I'm saying, Zach, and try to understand." She swallowed hard. "I'll never marry anyone." Her throat felt as if she'd swallowed dust. "I decided I'd never marry a long time ago, when I found out—about my family."

She tried to remove her hands from his grasp, but again he held tighter. "What about your family?"

"My mother. You know she died of cancer, right?"

He nodded slightly.

"Every woman in my mother's family has died young from breast cancer. It's hereditary. My grandmother died when my mom was ten. My mom's only sister died when she was twenty-four. I've consulted a doctor about it, and while I am taking care of myself, the odds are I will get it too." She pulled away from him again, and this time, he let her go. "I won't leave a family, a child, alone the way my mother left me."

"How come you never told me about any of this before?"

"Some things are hard to talk about, you know?"

Zach stared at her for several long seconds. "Nothing can keep us apart."

"There are lots of things that keep people apart, Zach. But," she took hold of his arm, "we can still be friends. We still have—"

He jerked away from her as if she'd slapped him. "No, Stacie. I'm sorry. I can't do that."

"But why? You said yourself we've always been friends. And we can keep being friends. I know we can."

"No. I can't. Not when I feel as I do. You can understand that, can't you? It would be too hard to be near you and yet know I could never . . ." His eyes filled with moisture, and he turned away, heading toward the park.

"You don't mean that!" Stacie reached after him but he continued on in long strides, his shoulders stooped and tense. Stacie called after him three more times, but he didn't look back. She raced after him and grabbed his arm.

He jerked away. "Let me go, Stacie."

"No."

"Please."

His bicep tensed beneath her grip until she removed her hand, finger by finger from his arm. Then he walked briskly away.

Stacie, her heart aching, folded her arms against her chest and looked at the ground.

"Stacie!"

She glanced up, but Zach was still walking away.

"Stacie."

This time she recognized the voice. He was behind her. She turned, saw the white tux, the dark, wavy hair blowing away from his face, and the one curly strand above his eyebrow. Matt.

"Sergeant Price is looking for you."

"Okay," she said hollowly.

"Are you all right?"

Stacie swallowed hard. "Not really. Um, what does Sergeant Price want?"

"I don't know, but he's over there, on the other side of the parking lot."

Stacie headed in the direction Matt had pointed, and he stepped in beside her.

"When you finish talking to him . . ."

She glanced up, but he quickly looked away, clearing his throat.

"I mean, we need to hurry out to the pageant. Brother Fillmore's getting anxious." His eyes flickered back to her face then away again.

"Thanks for the warning, Matt, but is something wrong?"

"No. Why?" He appeared genuinely surprised, but even so, the longer he looked at her, the quicker her pulse raced.

"Forget about it."

He offered nothing more, and when a sudden wave of grief for Zach pressed over her, she hurried ahead of him so he wouldn't see her tears.

Moments later, they reached Sergeant Price.

Stacie asked the first question that came to her mind. "Have you learned anything more about Becka?"

He motioned toward the church. "Let's go inside, Miss Cox. Out of the cold." His posture was rigid, his voice crisp.

"I know you told me to stay away from the Tangs, but—"

He waved his hand, silencing her. "I've already talked to the Tangs. And anyway, that's of little consequence now that" —he hesitated, then continued on to the doorway— "now that your lead's been eliminated from the investigation for lack of evidence."

"No!"

Matt stepped between her and the officer, then moved so close to her side that she felt his warmth radiate over her like a protective blanket. He pulled open the door. "Is there anything I can do to help?" he whispered so only she could hear.

She stared blankly ahead of her at the officer "I don't know."

When the door closed behind the three of them, Sergeant Price took out his notebook. "Will you please tell me where you were at 5:25 this evening?"

"I was at UVic talking to Elsie's grandson, Nick Yates. But you probably know that, since you—talked to the Tangs."

"Where exactly? In what building?"

"Campus Services."

He studied her face.

Matt stepped closer to Stacie's side, pressing the back of his hand against hers. "What's the problem, Sergeant?"

"At 5:25 p.m., the Saanich police received a 911 emergency call. A woman said a little boy had been run over by someone in the parking lot outside the Campus Services building."

A sickening shiver ran down Stacie's spine as her memory raked over their time on campus—the cafeteria, Nick, the few moments Zach and she had spent in the parking lot. "Is the boy all right?"

"The call was a prank, Miss Cox." He looked her straight in the eyes. "Frankly, I'm surprised you used your real name."

{ CHAPTER 21 }

You can't believe I'd do something like that!"

"Let's just say there are some who doubt your sincerity."

"Who?" Stacie hoped the officer didn't notice the tremble in her lips.

"The authorities at the command center for one, and the girl's parents for another. They're tired of pranks."

Becka's *parents?* Stacie's heart pounded in her throat as she backed away from the officer and tripped over Matt's feet. He caught her and held her upright.

"None of this makes any sense!" Matt said.

Stacie dug inside her purse. "Here, check my phone. You'll see I haven't—"

"The call came from a phone booth outside the Campus Services building," Sergeant Price said evenly.

"But it wasn't me! Maybe the dispatcher heard wrong, or maybe—wait a second!" Her mind was racing now. "The caller used my name." She grabbed Sergeant Price's arm. "Who else in Victoria could do that except the person who stole my wallet and called my aunt?"

Sergeant Price narrowed his eyes. "Why would a thief pretend to be . . . hmm." He carefully removed her hand from his arm.

"Tell me again about your wallet—about how it was stolen."

"I had it when Janice and I first went into Chinatown yesterday, but it wasn't in my pocket after we left Tang's. That's all I know." She thought of Mr. Bad Breath. "For sure."

"Couldn't you have lost or misplaced it?"

Stacie gaped at him. "You believe I lied about my wallet." It wasn't a question. "But what about that call to my aunt?"

"That's right!" Matt cut in. "Stacie definitely didn't do that."

"That may be true," Sergeant Price said, "but on the other hand, you have to admit it's a pretty big coincidence that all these reports—a missing child, a stolen wallet, a questionable call, and a prank—could originate around one person—"

Stacie frowned.

"—or under one person's name within such a short period of time. It sounds a bit like . . . you want attention."

Whether it was the shock of Sergeant Price's allegations or the sudden rush of cold air that blasted her face when Brother Fillmore unexpectedly charged into the building, Stacie didn't know, but either way, she began to shiver.

Sergeant Price motioned her further into the foyer toward a couch. "My questions may take a while."

Brother Fillmore, his hair windblown and his face red, brusquely stepped forward. "I don't know what's going on here," he said, "but can't this wait, Constable? We—Stacie—has a performance right now."

Sergeant Price stiffened. "You obviously don't understand the seriousness of this matter."

Stacie didn't know whether it was the compassionate light that suddenly flickered in the officer's eyes or the steadiness of his expression, but in that quick exchange, Stacie again sensed the trust she'd initially felt for him, and it gave her courage. "You believed me before, didn't you? At the castle?"

Sergeant Price showed no emotion. "Yes."

"Then please give me a chance. Look, Zach Isaacson was with me at UVic. He can verify my story." She quickly turned to Matt. "Will you get him, please?"

Matt nodded, squeezed her arm, and rushed out.

While he was gone and with Brother Fillmore still listening, Sergeant Price repeated his original questions about where Stacie was at 5:25 and what she was doing at the campus. So it was with no little relief that she hurried to Zach's side as soon as Matt and he returned.

"I understand there's a problem here I need to clear up," Zach said detachedly.

Sergeant Price led Zach to the far side of the room where he could talk to him privately, and Stacie strained to hear their conversation, but all she heard were Zach's final, insistent remarks. "I was with her the entire time. She didn't make a call. Besides," he glanced at her then, and the misery she saw in his eyes tore another hole in her heart, "there's no way she'd pull a hoax like that." His voice softened. "She cares about people too much."

Wanting to thank him, Stacie went to him and reached for his arm, but he moved away.

"I've seen that too," Sergeant Price said. He gave Zach the same straight-in-the-eyes look he'd given Stacie only minutes before. "And of course I'll have to talk with Mr. Yates." He turned to Stacie again. "If his story agrees with yours, it should satisfy my commanding officer on this matter. For now."

For now? Stacie wanted to protest, but when she peered up at the officer and saw a reprimand lurking on the edge of his expression, she decided it was best not to push her luck. *For now.*

Brother Fillmore put his hands on his hips. "So this is

settled?"

"Yes," Sergeant Price said.

"Then please excuse us. We have a performance."

Sergeant Price stepped aside, allowing them to pass, and Stacie rushed to the door, but as she passed Brother Fillmore, he whispered, "We'll talk about this later."

{CHAPTER 22}

Adrienne turned off the car's overhead light and leaned against the headrest. Though a few stars lit the sky, she couldn't see the moon. The wall of trees, or perhaps one of the condos that lined the road, probably blocked it from her view, but no matter. Lampposts and several porch lights provided all the light she needed to maintain her surveillance of Nick's home.

"You love me and I love you.There's nothing, baby, we can't do." The singer on the car radio crooned low and raw, and the rhythmic bass pulsed thickly through Adrienne's senses. She reached for the volume button, wanting to nudge it just a little louder, when her phone chimed.

"Hello? Price! Thanks for getting back with me so quickly!"

"Not a problem. Carol said you had more information about that estate robbery?"

"Always right to the point. That's what I like about you, Trent." Adrienne lifted her right, loosely clasped hand and swooped it down and forward as if she were clinking an imaginary wine glass in an exultant toast. A successful, money-making toast.

"So, you found Nick's residence?" he prompted.

"Yes, thanks to you." She opened her purse and flipped through the new bills he'd given her along with Nick's address. It was a

·

moderate reward, since the tips she'd provided about Nick—his record, his being in town, his ring—had only been an educated guess connecting him with the estate thief, but it was enough money to keep her and Riana alive a little longer. "I'm watching it right now, actually, which is why I'm calling. Um, have you checked him out yet?"

"We've done what we can."

"I see. Not enough evidence for a warrant, huh?" The music on the radio changed to a heavier, heart-pounding rhythm, and Adrienne peeked over the seat at Riana. She was still sleeping, still hugging that hard, plastic, gingerbread house Eric had found in Chinatown. "Let's just say I might be able to help you out with that. What's it worth?"

"Depends on what you have."

"How 'bout a connection to the scene of the crime?"

Price inhaled. "You know the drill, Doyle. If it's good, I'll make it worth your while."

Money. What a lovely word. "My sources at the station, whose names will remain anonymous," Adrienne said, "tell me cat hairs were found at the scene." She waited for him to corroborate her information, but as she expected, he remained silent. "Nick, has a cat."

As if on cue, Nick's front door opened, only a crack, but enough to tell her he was home. What she didn't like, however, was that he seemed to be watching for someone.

"Sorry, Price, gotta go."

"Okay. I'll get back with you."

She disconnected just as Nick closed his door. She glanced at her watch. Time to set the trap.

Neighborhood house lights came on. A few turned off. A night jogger with a yellow lab on a leash and a flashlight passed by on the opposite side of the road. When Adrienne saw her coming, she turned off the radio. She left it off even after the woman was long gone.

Finally, five minutes were up. Adrienne phoned Eric. "Now," was all she said. Three minutes later, Eric's FedEx truck turned into Nick's driveway. He got out and then carried the flat, white envelope Adrienne had given him to Nick's front door. It was addressed to Paul Rees.

He knocked. No answer.

Adrienne leaned forward, hardly breathing. *Come on, Nick, open the door!*

Eric knocked again.

The door opened just wide enough for the yellow cat to race out.

Eric started talking.

Adrienne slid further to the front edge of her seat, clenching the steering wheel, watching every move, every gesture, every shake of Nick's head.

Nick opened the door a bit wider. He studied the envelope. Signed for it. *BINGO!* He'd taken the bait.

Eric left the porch, and Nick closed the door. But a moment later, when Adrienne saw Nick peek through his front blinds, watching Eric return to his truck, she felt nothing but appreciation for Eric's expertise. He might have messed up where Cox was concerned, but not here. He looked just like every other FedEx man. No way would Nick suspect him of anything.

Jiggling her foot, her fingers tingling with excitement, Adrienne settled back against her seat and pictured Nick, treasure-seeking Nick, unable to resist opening that envelope from his friend's mother—and Adrienne's client—Mrs. Rees.

Dear Paul,
I've sent this message to every friend I thought might

*know where you are. Please come home. Your wife, your
daughter, and especially I have been looking for you
ever since you left. I know you're angry at your father,
and so am I. He should never have refused to give you
the Ming Ma. But on the other hand, you shouldn't
have taken it. If you would have asked me, I would have
given it to you. But that's water under the bridge. Now
I have a deal for you. Come home, dearest Paul, and
I'll give you the entire Ming collection—all eight, jade
horses—as a Christmas present. You'd like that, wouldn't
you? I know they've always been your favorites.
Love,
Mother*

Adrienne smiled with satisfaction. Clearly, Nick, with his
Chinese relations and his penchant for jade, would immediately
recognize the value of those statues and wouldn't, as both she
and Price fully believed, be able to resist trying to take them from
Paul. And that meant Nick would lead Adrienne straight to her
client's son—and the big payoff.

"Soon, we'll be heading for England," she whispered to the
sleeping Riana.

{CHAPTER 23}

"Where are Ivana and Sharon?" Stacie asked when she finally returned to the motel room after talking with Brother Fillmore.

Janice sat at the small, round dinette table at the far end of the room, writing in a notebook. "Swimming." She wrote a few more words and then looked up. "Are you all right?"

"It was worse than Matt warned me it'd be." Stacie didn't bother to remove her coat, only trudged to one of the two queen-sized beds and sat on the edge. "Brother Fillmore said he'll lower my grade and drop me from the choir if I keep up my," she couldn't keep the sarcasm from her voice, "foolishness. Sometimes he can be so—so—"

Janice sat beside her. "He's only thinking about what's best for the choir. And he's probably worried for your safety."

"I know. That doesn't make things better, though."

The two sat in silence for several long moments until Janice said, "He'll change his mind after you find Becka."

"If I find her."

Janice changed the subject. "So, tell me what happened with Nick."

Stacie plunked backwards and draped her right arm over her

eyes. "Nothing great there, either."

"Well, I have some good news." Janice pulled her legs up onto the bed and sat, cross-legged, in front of Stacie. "The Garners can move back into their house tomorrow."

"Good." She turned silent again.

"Come on, Stacie. It's your turn. What happened with Nick? And why was Sergeant Price at the church?"

"You heard about that?"

"Everyone heard about that."

Stacie sat up and removed her coat. "Basically, it boils down to this: Nick knew nothing, someone used my identity to report a false emergency, and now the police believe I'm a nutcase."

"What?"

Stacie filled in the details as she hung her coat in the closet. Then she took her suitcase down from the shelf, set it on the bed next to Janice, and pulled out sweat pants and a hoodie.

"That doesn't make sense," Janice said when she'd finished. "People don't steal identities just to make a prank call. Do they?"

"I don't know. I have heard of people's names being falsely used in crimes, like speeding or robbery." Stacie bit her lower lip. "I hope this isn't the beginning of something like that."

"I wonder what the reason could be." Janice paled then shook her head. "Let's not get ourselves worked up over nothing. Maybe the thief just wanted a sadistic thrill."

"I don't think it's very thrilling." Stacie slipped off her shoes, then her tights. "Good thing Zach was there to back me up, though. I'd have been stuck talking to Sergeant Price for who knows how long if it weren't for him."

"Zach's always been a good friend."

Hearing the words "Zach" and "friend" in the same sentence re-opened the wound Stacie had been trying to ignore. No longer trusting her emotions, she walked to the window and pulled aside the beige curtains.

"Uh-oh." Janice moved instantly behind her. "What happened?"

It was almost a minute before Stacie could speak, but Janice waited. Finally, Stacie said, "I'm afraid Zach and I aren't even friends anymore."

"That bad, huh?"

"I'd have never guessed how bad it would turn out." She recounted what had transpired between her and Zach, and when she finished, she cleared her throat. "I think I'll change now."

She went into the bathroom, set her sweats on the closed toilet lid, and looked into the mirror. It was the first time she'd seen herself since before she'd left for the University, and her image shocked her. Her hair was blown and tangled, her cheeks streaked with black mascara, and her eyes puffy. "I didn't look this bad while we were performing, did I?" she called through the door.

"No, not entirely. Your mascara hadn't smeared yet."

After removing what was left of her makeup, Stacie slipped out of her formal. She caught a whiff of lemon as it passed over her face, and the fragrance brought a vivid memory of her mother, lying helpless on the couch. She'd been nestled within the quilt Stacie had newly washed for her, and the fabric softener had smelled like lemon.

Is there something like lemon, Stacie wondered, *that reminds Becka of her mother?*

"I heard a sniffle," Janice said outside the door.

Stacie wiped her nose. "It's been a terrible night."

"I know, but you'll get through this."

When Stacie finally opened the bathroom door, she had changed her clothes and now carried a hairbrush in one hand and her formal in the other. "Your turn."

"Not yet." Janice took the hairbrush from her and led her to a chair.

Not having the desire or the will to refuse, Stacie eased into the chair and let Janice gently work the brush through her tangles. "You're definitely going into the right line of work."

"Nursing? What does that have to do with hair?"

"You're a caretaker. I'm kind of surprised you want to work in the ER, though. It seems pretty, you know, gruesome."

"It could be, but think of the adventure. When you work in the ER, you never know from one minute to the next what you're going to face."

"I didn't know you liked adventure this much. Is that why you're still helping me with Becka?"

Janice laughed. "No. I'm helping you because you need help." She paused to untangle the hairbrush from a snarl. "Have I told you my brother wants to be a doctor?"

"Yeah, I think so."

"Well, it's gonna be pretty tough for him to get his schooling. Most of his friends, even his boss, are telling him school's not worth the hassle. So I thought, maybe I could be an example, show him it's all right to reach for something else if he wants. You know, try to make up for being gone so much."

Her last words came out as a whisper, and it was several minutes before either spoke again.

"Janice, why are you so happy?"

"What are you talking about?"

"I mean, it must be terrible being separated from your mother—your entire family—so much."

"You're separated from your parents. Why are you happy?"

"I'm not. That's the point." Stacie reached a hand back to stop the brushing. "And anyway, it's not the same thing. My dad, and then later my—mother—died. I had no choice but to live with someone else. You had, or at least you now have, a choice."

Janice didn't answer, only resumed brushing, and Stacie, beginning to wonder if she'd offended her, recalled what she knew of Janice's life before she'd moved to Rexburg.

Janice's mother had lived with the Garners on the Indian Placement Program and married soon after she left them. Her husband, Janice's father, eventually left her mother with three children. Her mother was poor and couldn't take care of them all, and since she trusted the Garners, she asked them to take care of Janice, the oldest.

Finally, Janice spoke. "My mother did the best she could for me."

"You believe that? I thought you resented her for leaving you. I would have."

"I did at first. All I could think about was finding a way to get home to the reservation so I could help take care of my younger brothers. But in time I understood what my mother meant just before she left me with the Garners." Janice's voice softened. "She hugged me like she would never let me go and then whispered, 'Sometimes you have to choose pain.'" Janice cleared her throat, shifted a little taller, and handed Stacie the brush. "There. Now I need to finish my letter to Quinton."

Stacie stared at her for a long moment. "Oh, yeah." She cleared her throat. "Quinton. How'd that go?"

Janice blushed. "It was nothing like you're thinking. Like he said before, he only wanted to talk to me because I'm Sioux. He works in the Indigenous Studies Department at UVic, and he's writing a thesis on First Nationals. That's why I'm writing this," she motioned to her stack of paper. "So he can get my quotes exactly the way I want them."

There was a click at the door, and the two turned to see Ivana and Sharon enter the room. They both wore shorts and T-shirts over their swimsuits and had white towels wrapped around their waists. With still-perfect makeup and perfectly dry hair, Ivana barely nodded to them before taking her clothes from her suitcase and heading straight for the bathroom.

Sharon carried her suitcase to the bed, took out her clothes, and then sat with her back to Stacie and Janice until Ivana came out a few minutes later dressed in green pajamas.

"Love letters?" Ivana asked.

"No love letters for us." Stacie moved from the table and plunked onto the bed.

"That's your fault, isn't it?" Ivana threw back her own bed covers and sat, cross-legged, watching Stacie with happy eyes. "I mean, rumor has it you've told the best-looking guy in the choir to get lost."

Zach told people about that? Stacie lifted her chin. "You don't know what you're talking about."

"Don't I?" Ivana ran her fingers through her long red hair. "So, what kind of guy are you looking for, since good-looking's out?"

"Mind your own business."

Ivana half smiled. "What about you, Janice?"

To Stacie's surprise, Janice looked up thoughtfully and answered her. "After I graduate, I'm going back to the reservation, so whoever he is, he'll have to be willing to help me take care of my mother."

"I bet you'd have a better chance at finding Stacie's purse snatcher."

"That thief will be caught," Stacie said icily.

"Not by either of you."

"It doesn't matter who catches her as long as she's caught."

"You're one to talk," Ivana sneered. "If *who* doesn't matter, then why are you still playing hero while we're on tour?"

Janice moved next to Stacie. "Because Becka still needs help."

"Becka has the police to help her, and from what I've heard, Stacie's messing them up."

Suddenly, an image flashed through Stacie's mind, and she grabbed Janice's arm. "We were there! At the same time!"

Clearly confused, Janice glanced at Ivana, then positioned herself in such a way that Ivana couldn't see her face. "We were where?"

"Not you and me. The thief and me. At UVic."

"So?"

"So . . . I might have seen her."

Janice shrugged. "Yeah, maybe, but what good does that do?"

"You guys are so rude!" Ivana said, walking away in a huff.

Stacie went back to the window.

Janice came up silently behind her. "What are you thinking?"

"I was mostly wishing."

"For?"

"Janice?" Stacie placed her hand beseechingly on her friend's forearm. "If I prove to the Mounties my wallet was stolen, do you think they'd believe me enough to start looking for Becka here in Victoria again?"

"I don't know. Maybe. But how can you prove that?"

Stacie averted her eyes. "Stop searching for Becka and find the thief."

Janice caught her breath. "Are you crazy?" she said in a low voice. "You have no idea how to find a pickpocket. And that will take too much time. What about Brother Fillmore, and the choir? They might understand why you'd want to search for Becka, but they won't understand this. And Brother Fillmore won't let you mess up the tour any more than you already have."

Stacie closed her eyes. "I don't know what's going to happen. Maybe Brother Fillmore will drop me from the music program. Maybe I won't even graduate. But you understand, don't you? Sometimes you have to sacrifice what's most important to you. You know, choose pain?"

"For someone you don't even know?"

Stacie shrugged, bit her lip, and looked away as unwanted tears welled up in her eyes. "What better thing could I do with— with the time I have?"

Janice gulped. Her eyes filled with tears, too, and a few spilled down her cheeks. "Don't talk like that. You could have years and years ahead of you. And anyway, none of us knows how long we have."

There was knock at the door and Ivana answered it.

"Hi." Matt looked past Ivana and straight at Stacie. "I need to talk to you."

{CHAPTER 24}

Stacie closed the door behind her. She and Matt were alone in the dimly lit hallway.

"Uh, after that incident with Sergeant Price," he began, "and Zach, you know, isn't quite himself, and, well, you looked pretty upset after you finished talking to Brother Fillmore this evening . . ."

She shook her head. "Just tell me, Matt."

"I was" —his dark eyes bored into hers— "worried about you."

Stacie fidgeted with the hem of her hoodie. "I'm fine. Thanks for asking." She turned back to the door.

He briefly touched her arm. "No, don't go. Please."

"Is there something else?" she asked as she turned toward him again.

"I wanted to tell you I" —the corners of his eyes creased into a painfully scrutinizing gaze— "I believe you."

It required several full heartbeats before she could find her voice. "You mean about Becka?"

"Yes. Everything else, too. I wanted you to know."

She stared at him with wide eyes. "Thanks for telling me."

Their eyes locked in an intense gaze that Stacie couldn't break until she heard voices in the stairway at the end of the hall.

Seconds later she saw that the voices belonged to several guys from the choir. They were wearing wet swimsuits and BYU–Idaho T-shirts. Zach brought up the rear.

"How was the swim?" Matt asked when Zach reached them.

Zach glanced briefly at Stacie. "Fine. How was your call to Holly?"

"Good, but she was busy." Matt glanced at Stacie, a little guiltily, she thought, even though he also inched closer to her. "We had to keep it short."

"You're a lucky guy. Not every girl's as devoted as she is."

Stacie turned away from them, trying not to feel the full impact of Zach's insult, but worse than that, hardly able to believe he would act this way. They had been friends for what seemed like forever, and she had never led him on.

"See ya later. Matt." Zach walked away.

"That was, um, interesting," Matt said when he was gone. "What happened between you two?"

Stacie looked away, tucking her hair behind her ears.

After several seconds of silence, Matt touched her arm. "Uh, sorry. You don't have to tell me. I'll go now." But he didn't move.

Stacie didn't move either, only noticed the careful weight of his hand on her arm. Fiery tingles rushed through her body. "Swimming in pea soup," she finally said.

"What?"

She smiled wistfully. "It's the way my mother used to describe uncomfortable silences."

Matt grinned. "It fits."

Still, neither moved nor spoke until several seconds later when Stacie forced herself to step away. Matt's hand slid to her elbow before dropping to his side.

"Well, see ya tomorrow. Bright and early," she said.

"Seven o'clock. That's what Brother Fillmore said, wasn't it?"

"Yes. I think his exact words were, 'I hate to get you up so early, but—'"

"'—*music requires sacrifice.*'" Matt added just the right Brother Fillmore inflection, and Stacie laughed.

He smiled into her eyes. "Well, good night."

Stacie slipped her hand into her pants pocket, reaching for her key. "Uh, Matt?"

"Yes?"

"Wait here a second, will ya?" Her hands trembled slightly as she swiped her key through the lock and opened the door. "Janice? Will you come out here, please?"

A few seconds later, Janice appeared, holding her pen and notebook.

"Just before you got here, Matt," Stacie said, "Janice and I realized the woman who used my name in the prank had to have been at or near the Campus Services Building when Zach and I were there." She watched for his reaction.

"That makes sense."

Stacie looked directly at Janice this time. She hadn't mentioned the next part to her either, and she wasn't sure how she'd take it. "Which means she might have been following me."

Both sets of eyes widened.

"Now what I want to know is, how can I catch her?"

Matt inhaled sharply. "Why would you want to catch her?"

"A equals B equals C," Janice said, frowning. "Stacie thinks if she proves her wallet really was stolen, it'll prove she didn't make the call, which then proves she's not a liar and is telling the truth about Becka."

"If the police don't believe I saw her at the castle," Stacie interjected, "they won't keep looking for Becka after we leave."

"I really think you're better off leaving this to the police, Stacie," Matt said.

"Well, thanks anyway." Stacie seized the door handle.

"Wait a minute!" Matt grabbed her arm before she could slide her key into the lock. "What's the problem?"

"It's obvious you don't want to help me, so . . ."

"I said you'd be better off leaving this to the police, not that I wouldn't help you."

She inhaled, released the door handle, and carefully looked up at him. "So you will help me?"

"That depends."

"On what?"

His eyes warmed wickedly. "On whether or not we really call a truce." He held out his hand. "Friends?"

Stacie stared at it. She couldn't pretend she didn't understand what he wanted—it was the same thing he'd asked for yesterday—but something about him asking for friendship felt inaccurate. Like *friend* wasn't quite what he was to her. Yet there was nothing else he could be.

"Well?"

She hesitantly reached for his hand, and he wrapped it around hers. As she felt the warmth of his skin against hers, tingles shot through her again. "Friends."

"I'm glad that's finally settled." Janice sat on the floor and opened her notebook to a blank sheet of paper. "Okay, so if we're gonna do this, let's start by seeing if we can narrow anything down. What do we know about the thief?"

Stacie released his hand and sat on the floor next to Janice. "She's a woman. At least it was a woman who called my aunt, and 911."

"A woman who was" —Janice pronounced the words slowly

as she wrote— "in Chinatown the day before yesterday and at UVic today. Now, who goes to Chinatown?"

Matt sat across from the two girls. "That question won't get us anywhere. It's too open-ended."

"Okay then, who goes to the University?"

"We can't narrow it down that way, either."

"All right, let's try another route." Janice tapped the back of her pen against the upper margin. "Why would an identity thief use Stacie's name in a prank?"

"Maybe she wanted to, I don't know, try it out, to see if she could get away with using it."

Stacie glanced anxiously at Janice. Matt's suggestion sounded a little too much like their "worse things to come theory."

"Or . . ."

"What?" Stacie asked.

"Maybe, she wanted a good laugh." He lifted one eyebrow teasingly.

"Or maybe she's power hungry," Stacie muttered, "like someone else around here." She propped her right elbow on her knee and lowered her chin on top of her fist. "There are only two things I can think of to do, and neither sounds promising."

"What's the first?" Matt asked.

"Go back to the Campus Services building and ask everyone we see if they were there yesterday afternoon and if they saw someone use the pay phone around 5:25."

"That's insane! We don't have that kind of time."

"What's your other idea?" Janice asked, sounding discouraged.

"Call Nick. Maybe he saw something."

Silence again.

Finally, Janice shrugged. "I know I don't have any ideas, and I doubt Matt does?"

"Sorry."

"So it looks like Nick's the easiest choice." She turned to Stacie. "Where's your cell phone?"

"In my coat pocket."

It didn't take long for Janice to retrieve the phone from the apartment and for Stacie to dial the number.

"The answer's still no," Nick said as soon as he realized who was calling. "I haven't met any strange women." He hung up.

Stacie shut her phone. "He acts like everyone else around here!"

"Not everyone," Matt murmured. "We're still here, still behind you."

"The Garners, too." Janice placed her hand on her shoulder. "Don't look so surprised, Stacie. They've known you almost as long as I have. Remember?"

Quiet warmth bathed over her. "Thanks, you guys." She swallowed. "I guess that leaves the campus?"

Matt looked down at her through lowered eyelids, just as he had that first night he'd acted as her accompanist, but this time, rather than anxiousness, she only felt strength. "Why don't we ask the Garners to help us?" he suggested. "I know they have the pageant to take care of, but maybe they could spare some time, since *we* can't."

Janice's face lit up. "That's a great idea. Stacie, hand me the phone."

Janice dialed, and soon after Brother Garner answered, she asked for their help.

"Well?" both Stacie and Matt said simultaneously. They glanced at each other.

"They'll do it!" Janice mouthed.

It was the best news Stacie'd heard since arriving in Victoria.

4:45 a.m. Adrienne arched her back, flexed her ankles, and peered through the windshield at the misty blackness. It had been hours since she'd stretched her legs or used a restroom, and Nick's duplex had been dark all night. Surely she could risk a twenty-minute break.

She started the engine. The noise woke Riana.

"Stay where you are, dear. We're going for a bathroom. But we'll have to be fast. Understand?"

Riana moaned groggily. "Uh-huh."

"What was that, dear?"

"Yes, uh, Mum."

4:52 a.m. Adrienne parked outside the front doors of a convenience store. "Let's go."

Riana, her hair matted and her glasses askew, stumbled from the floor of the back seat.

"Hurry," Adrienne ordered.

4:54 a.m. They passed a coffee machine counter covered with boxes of assorted "freshly made" donuts. Adrienne's stomach growled, but she smiled through the temptation. She had neither time nor money to waste on food right then, and giving in would only create an unnecessary distraction.

"Restrooms are for customers only," the clerk from behind the checkout counter said.

Adrienne swore under her breath.

4:58 a.m. They left the bathroom.

The clerk eyed her suspiciously, and this time, Adrienne only *thought* the swear word. "Two coffees," she said, putting the money on the counter.

The woman raised a disapproving eyebrow, and Adrienne felt her temper rise. *What? Hadn't she ever seen a kid drink coffee before?*

"The lids are behind the cups." After depositing Adrienne's money in the cash register and motioning toward the coffee machine, the woman took her broom and headed to the aisle at the back of the room.

Swallowing a yawn, Adrienne reached for the first cup, but before her fingertips touched the Styrofoam, she froze. There, on the drab-white wall, kitty-corner from the coffee machine, was a display of Most Wanted and Missing Child posters. Riana's photograph was largest of all. It was the one the police had shown on the television news yesterday, the one that also included Cox's inept depiction of "the woman."

Adrienne glanced back to the clerk, then down at Riana. Thank goodness the girl no longer looked like that kid in the poster. Even her face had narrowed more like her own.

She took the cup, filled it, and pressed on the lid.

She glanced back to the sales clerk again. She was straightening shelves in the back corner. If Adrienne acted now, while all that banging was going on . . . she took two quick steps and ripped the poster from the wall.

Good. The clerk hadn't noticed.

Adrienne crumpled it, tucked it beneath her left arm, and began to fill the second cup, but before the steaming liquid had reached the center mark, her cell phone rang.

Adrienne cursed.

The clerk looked up. "Is there something else I can help you with?"

"No. My phone startled me, that's all."

The woman went back to her work.

Adrienne checked the caller ID, figuring she'd disconnect and return the call later, but when she saw who it was, she answered. "Hello, Mrs. Rees."

"Nick Yates just called me." Mrs. Rees's voice shook with emotion.

"Just called you? Like now?" Adrienne glanced at her watch. "But only minutes ago, his duplex was dark." She covered the half-filled cup and handed it to Riana. "Tell me what he said."

"He said he'd talked to my son, and Paul would be home for Christmas, but—"

"Go on."

"Nick kept telling me how much Paul misses me and how much Paul loved his daughter. But he also asked me a lot of questions."

Mrs. Rees began to weep, and Adrienne, nudging Riana out the door and looking one last time at the clerk to make sure she hadn't noticed the missing poster, rolled her eyes. "Questions like what?"

"Oh, I don't know. Like how big the Ming statues were, and if he could spend the holiday with us too, and" —another, fresh round of tears— "it's hard to explain, but there was something in his voice—Oh, Miss Doyle, I think he was lying. I don't think our trick worked at all. Or that Paul . . . really will be home."

Adrienne pulled out of the parking lot. "Maybe he was lying," Adrienne cooed into the phone, "but don't take it to heart, Mrs. Rees. You will see Paul by Christmas."

Mrs. Rees blew her nose. "How do you know?"

"Simple," Adrienne said. "Our trick did work, don't you see? Nick realizes Paul has the Ming Ma and access to the rest of the jade collection."

"I don't see how that will get my Paul home."

"Think about it. Nick called you, didn't he? A guy like him wouldn't do something like that without a reason, and that reason has to be that he wants to get his hands on that jade. Which means he'll have to get in touch with Paul."

"But how—have you tapped his phones?"

"The police are taking care of that, Mrs. Rees, but I think it's more likely that Nick'll pay Paul a visit, and when he does, I'll be right behind him."

5:10 a.m. Adrienne turned into Nick's neighborhood, but even before she'd finished rounding the corner, she gasped. His pickup was gone.

She made a U-turn, squealing her tires and pleading with the gods that Nick had just gone to work early. Then she headed straight for Esquimalt Road.

5:25 a.m. She saw Nick's pickup waiting in line to cross the Johnson Street drawbridge.

Adrienne released a long, shuddering sigh. "That's the last time I'm letting you out my sight."

5:30 a.m. They were still waiting to cross the bridge. What was the hold-up? If they didn't get a move on soon, she'd—no, she *wouldn't* fall asleep.

She downed the rest of Riana's coffee and turned the temperature control to COLD.

5:35 a.m. The traffic moved.

Adrienne settled comfortably into her seat, stretching her back, resting her head against the support. Strange how she suddenly felt as if she and Nick were the only ones on the road.

She yawned, but it was nothing serious. This drive, the mossy-green rainforest, had always had a calming effect upon her, especially when it rained.

The cool AC brushed across Adrienne's skin like a gentle breeze on a hot day, deceiving her senses. She closed her eyes, only for a second, but it was long enough that she didn't see when Nick stepped on his brakes.

She stomped on hers.

He swerved back and forth.

She swerved, too, mimicking him like a hypnotized puppet. What was wrong with him?

Somewhere in the back of her mind she recognized his actions, knew they meant something as familiar to her as her naked ring finger. But no matter how hard she tried, she couldn't recall what they were.

5:40 a.m. They came to a stoplight.

Several seconds passed.

Adrienne closed her eyes again, listening to the rhythm of the windshield wipers, back and forth, back and forth . . .

Several more seconds passed. The burning sensation behind her eyelids lessened.

Back and forth . . . back and forth . . .

A car horn honked.

She woke up. Where was Nick?

Honk!

"Give me a minute!" she hollered, frantically searching for Nick's 4x4. And then she saw it. He had turned left and pulled slowly into a hotel driveway.

5:42 a.m. Adrienne whipped round the corner after him and took an immediate right.

"Oh, no!" She stomped on the brakes. This was a circular drive—only one way in and one way out. The oldest trick in the book! Now he not only knew that he was being followed, but he also knew that she knew he knew.

Breathe. There has to be some way out of this.

Nick continued around the drive and out the exit, then turned right.

Following the only course left to her, the only thing that might convince Nick she wasn't following him, she turned left.

Did it work?

She watched him through her rearview mirror. He was still

driving away from her. A bit slowly, perhaps, but not enough to—

Metal clashed on metal.

Adrienne's chest plunged into the steering wheel.

Riana screamed.

ven though the choir had been on the tour bus for nearly an hour since leaving Sidney Middle School, Matt still couldn't stop himself from staring sideways at Stacie.

"Is something wrong?" Stacie asked without looking up from her cell phone.

"No, I'm fine." He'd intended to turn from her the very next second, but she glanced up before he had a chance to look away. She seemed both curious about and troubled by his stare.

"Nothing from the Garners yet?" he asked as nonchalantly as he could.

"No. But I haven't had a good signal for a while, either." She repeatedly pushed several buttons.

Matt shifted in his seat, raked his fingers through his hair, and gazed steadily through the corner of his eye at Stacie's downturned face. Why was he so stuck on her? Was it her goodness, her compassion? After all, how many people would risk everything to save a child they didn't even know?

"I'm so tired of this!" Stacie dropped her cell phone into her lap.

Janice, sitting in the seat directly ahead of Stacie, turned to look at her. "It'll be okay, Stacie. The Garners can't have been there very long yet."

Stacie bit her lip and sat taller in her seat. "No matter what I do, I seem to find more dead-ends than helpful information."

Matt instinctively reached out to touch the back of Stacie's clenched hand, but she slid it away.

"Having second thoughts?" he asked.

She shrugged. "Not really." She picked up her phone again and checked for a signal. "I'm just so—"

"Frustrated?" he offered.

Janice turned in her seat again, looking squarely at both of them. "Mostly worried, right?"

"I guess." Stacie shrugged again.

"About what?" Matt asked.

Stacie's lower lip quivered. She turned her gaze to the side window, but not before Matt saw that a fiery blush now colored her cheeks.

"You're doing everything you can," Janice soothed.

"But it's not enough." Stacie clenched both her hands and her teeth. "I've only got one day left!"

Matt resisted his sudden urge to wrap his arm around her shoulders and brush a wayward strand of hair from her cheek. "Janice is right, Stacie. We've done everything we can to this point." He settled back in his seat. "I know. Let's talk about something else for a while. Try not to think about Becka until the Garners call. Okay?"

Stacie bowed her head, then looked up at him again. The red in her face had lightened to a charming pink, and her eyes now held his as if they were two magnets. "Okay."

Matt forced his gaze away and looked at Janice. "So, what are the two of you doing for Christmas?"

"I'm staying here in Victoria with the Garners."

"And you, Stacie?"

She sighed. "I don't know yet."

"What about you, Matt?" Janice interjected. "A big or a small party at your house?"

"Big. Everyone, including all the in-laws and some of the neighbors, comes every year. Dad wouldn't have it any other way."

Stacie raised an eyebrow. "What about the in-laws' parents? Don't they want their family with them too?"

"They must have worked something out."

There was a lull in the conversation, and Stacie, after glancing at her cell phone, leaned against the headrest and gazed out the window.

"Uh, this year I drew my three-year-old niece's name for the gift exchange," Matt said.

"Oh? What did you get her?"

"A stuffed pig. She says 'oink' a lot."

Stacie turned silent and watchful again.

"So," Janice said. "Tell us more about these parents who insist everyone spends Christmas with them."

"It's not like it sounds," Matt said. "They're not selfish people. In fact, they're very supportive. They've encouraged my sisters and I to develop every talent we had. My older sister loved gardening, so they built her a green house. Another sister loved to dance, so every year they enrolled her in a dance class. She now teaches dance at BYU."

"And for you it was music," Stacie said, her gaze holding his again.

He cleared his throat. "Yes. Piano, conducting, voice . . ."

"Then why—"

"Yes?"

Stacie licked her lips. "Then why are you going into the cabinet business instead of music? I'd assumed it was to please your father."

"I used to ask myself that question all the time, but soon after I got home from my mission, I realized Brennon & Son was what I wanted to do. Besides, it's hard to make a living in music."

"I don't buy that," Stacie replied. "Not for you, anyway. You could make a career out of—well, piano, for instance. You're extremely talented."

He felt warmth creep into his cheeks. "You're talented, too," he muttered, again reaching out to briefly touch the back of her left hand with his fingertips.

She didn't move away this time, only watched him, eyebrows raised, clearly waiting for him to say more. And when he touched her skin, he felt as if the air had energized around them. "Okay. There is more to it." He lowered his head, seeking her eyes. "Actually, I love turning a regular piece of wood into something beautiful. It's kind of like, I don't know, turning a blank sheet of paper into a hymn. Can you understand that?"

A tiny smile crept to her lips. "Yes, I think so. It's like the music I feel when I stand on top of a mountain and watch the sunrise."

Matt studied her face, picturing Rexburg's brilliant, white-lit sunrise over the Teton Mountains. "Is that what you think of when you sing 'Silent Night?'" he whispered, leaning carefully toward her.

Stacie's mouth opened slightly, but she didn't speak. Neither, Matt suddenly realized, did anyone else on the bus. He glanced up and down the aisle. For some reason, they were now the center of everyone's attention.

Feeling his cheeks redden, Matt gulped and settled against the back of his chair. He stretched his legs, one under the seat ahead of him and one under Janice's seat, and didn't move again until about ten minutes later when the bus pulled into a small shopping center on the outskirts of Duncan City.

Brother Fillmore stood at the front of the bus. "We have a little over an hour to relax until we have to leave for our next performance," he said. "There are restaurants and a shopping center nearby. Be back by 1:15."

Everyone except Stacie stood. She was looking at her cell phone screen again.

"I'm gonna do some Christmas shopping," Matt said to her. "Would you and Janice like to come with me?"

Stacie didn't look up at him. "Sure." Suddenly, her cell phone rang, and she answered it. "Hello? Sister Garner!"

Matt sat next to her again, listening.

"Well?" Janice asked when she disconnected.

Stacie grinned. "They didn't find anyone who remembered a woman at the pay phone. But guess what? The University has several security cameras around campus."

"Aimed at the pay phone?" Janice put on her coat.

"No, but there are some in that eatery. One points toward the entrance. The owner said we could look at his tapes, so I figured we could watch for when Zach and I leave, and then see if any women happen to follow us out. If someone does, we can search for her and—"

"That's insane!"

Both girls turned to Matt. They looked almost as astonished by his outburst as he was. Before that moment he'd felt misgivings about Stacie's plans to find the thief, but now he felt only dread. He couldn't explain it to her—could hardly understand it himself—but the thought of possibly seeing Stacie followed by a criminal made him crazy. And yet, he wanted it solved, too.

"Why don't we call Sergeant Price instead?" he said. "We really don't have time to go out to the university, and the police are trained in these things . . ." As soon as he said it, Matt realized how lame his excuse sounded. "And while I've said this before, I still believe it. They have a better chance of finding her than we do."

He paused, expecting both girls to retaliate with the fact that the police didn't believe Stacie and probably wouldn't even go out there anyway, but instead, to his astonishment, Janice nodded and said, "This time I have to agree with him."

Stacie flinched, but in the next moment her taut expression relaxed. "I understand," she said quietly. "And you don't need to feel guilty about it. I'm not upset. Don't worry about coming with me to the University. I can check out those tapes on my own." She looked straight in Janice's eyes. Then in Matt's. "You both have too much to lose. And, well, it's not the same for me."

"You have as much to lose as we do." Matt's words came out harsher than he'd intended.

"No, I don't," she whispered hoarsely. "This tape" —she glanced at Janice— "it's all I have." Then she stepped off the bus and disappeared into the crowds of people as easily as a pebble on a rocky beach.

"She's got to be kidding," Janice said before running after her.

Matt only stood there, watching Stacie go, knowing that a second later he would chase after her too. She was wrong. That video might be all she had to help her convince the police to keep looking for Becka, but it wasn't *all* she had. She had him. More fully than he'd realized.

And with only one day left on the tour, he didn't know if or when he could ever tell her.

tacie and Janice stood beneath a store awning, each eating a hot dog and drinking a slushy, banana-mango drink they'd found at a small health-food stand across the street from the shopping center. Stacie's cell phone rang, and she wiped a smear of Dijon mustard from her mouth with her napkin.

"Hello?"

"Stacie! I was so worried I'd interrupt you in the middle of a performance, but—I didn't, did I?"

"No, Aunt Kathy. You're okay. Is something wrong?"

"With us? No, dear. It's just I know you're trying to find that missing girl, and well, I know how hard it's been on you. Almost like before . . ."

Stacie paled. "Mrs. Smythe hasn't done something else now, has she?"

"No. It's—about Becka Hollingsworth. There was a special news report on the television a few minutes ago. Stacie, I'm sorry, but the police have found her . . . her body, that is."

"No!" Stacie dropped the phone.

Janice flung the rest of her food in a nearby trash receptacle, picked up Stacie's phone, and wrapped her arm around Stacie's shoulders, holding her upright. "This is Janice. Are you still there?" she asked into the receiver.

Stacie covered her face with her hands. She didn't want to see, didn't want to feel, didn't want to hear anything more. Had it really *not* been Becka she'd seen at the castle? Or worse, had she been too late?

Just after Janice hung up the phone, Matt rushed forward, carrying a pink pig under his arm. "What's going on?" He tore off his jacket and draped it over Stacie's trembling shoulders.

As Janice filled him in, Stacie stepped away from them, holding her folded arms tight against her waist, wishing there was someplace she could run, someplace where children were never taken from their parents.

When Janice finished, Matt moved next to Stacie and placed his hand on her shoulder. "Stacie," he whispered, "it's not your fault."

She raised her face to his, feeling his steady, unwavering gaze settling her much like Janice's always had. But she couldn't suppress her tears.

{CHAPTER 27}

The rest of the day was a numbing blur of performances and bus rides. Even when Stacie sang her solo at Duncan High School, she felt like she had nothing to give. It was as if she were a marionette—a wooden, unfeeling figure on a string.

Matt undoubtedly heard the deadness in her solo, but he said nothing, only carefully watched her. Even Janice's frequent glances seemed less scrutinizing than his. Zach continued to avoid her whenever they were within speaking distance, but occasionally she thought she glimpsed him glancing at her from across the room.

When she entered the motel room, Stacie sighed, shuddered, and plunged face down onto the bed she and Janice shared. If only she could close her eyes tight enough to squeeze away the nightmare, to make it so she could no longer think of Becka.

Later that evening, Stacie forced herself from the bed and changed out of her white formal into jeans and a burgundy sweater. "I don't see why I have to go to the Garners for dinner," she said dully. "I'd rather stay here." She pulled a brush through her tangled hair.

Janice adjusted the large, silver barrette at the back of her head, "Afraid to drive alone with Matt?"

"'Course not."

"You should be."

Though her pulse quickened, Stacie methodically smoothed blush across her cheekbones. "Matt's nice enough."

"It's not whether he's nice or not that intrigues you," Janice said.

Stacie raised one eyebrow, slowly grasping the meaning of her words. "Don't tell me you think there's something going on between us? That's crazy!"

"I knew it!" Janice grinned. "There is still life inside you."

Stacie scowled with the first flicker of feeling she'd had since hearing about Becka. "You're the one who should be intrigued," she clipped. "About Quinton."

"Quinton's a nice guy too."

"Nice, huh?" Stacie let her insinuation hang in the air for a second. "How can you be so sure? It was pretty obvious at the castle that he was interested in you, but you've only just met him."

Janice shrugged. "It's hard to describe. I just know. And I am being careful." Her smile deepened. "I asked Brother Garner to come with us tonight. Like a chaperone."

"Then why do Matt and I have to come alone in the Garners' car?"

Janice giggled, an action so unlike her that Stacie stopped in mid-swipe of her mascara wand to stare at her. "Okay, let's have it. What's going on?"

"Nothing, really." Janice blushed and looked at her feet. "Quinton just wanted to take me out to see one of the National People's monuments before the Garners' dinner. It's out of the way, and, uh, we didn't think you—or Matt—would want to go."

"Uh-huh. But Brother Garner would, even though we're going to his house?"

Janice blushed even redder. "I'm wanting Quinton and Brother Garner to become—better acquainted."

Uncomfortably surprised by the emotions she saw in her friend's face, Stacie quickly changed the subject. "I'm just shocked Brother Fillmore's letting us go at all."

Janice nodded solemnly. "I bet Sister Fillmore had something to do with that. She seems to know about . . ."

Becka.

Janice put on her long, black suede coat. "But seriously, Stacie, be careful."

"With Matt?"

She hesitated. "Haven't you seen it? You know, how he looks at you?"

Stacie froze. "I hope you're joking."

"Sorry, girlfriend."

This time, Stacie blushed and felt sick. It couldn't be true. *Please, please, Heavenly Father, don't let it be true.* She couldn't handle losing another friend. "Matt has a girlfriend," she said weakly.

Janice laughed. "Oh, don't worry, Stacie! I'm partly teasing. Trying to get you out of this daze you're in, you know?" She grabbed her letter, a full quarter-inch-thick stack of paper, from the dinette table and then grinned. "But if he does confess undying love, at least tell him you'll think about it. For Ivana's sake."

Stacie raised her hairbrush in pretended rage, hoping her performance would mask the fear that suddenly swept through her.

"You know I'm only kidding, right?" she asked. "And anyway,

why would he say something? Like you said, he has a girlfriend." She went to the door. "Well, see ya later. Quinton's waiting."

Not wanting to be alone, Stacie followed her. "So, what do the Garners think of Quinton so far?"

"They like him. A lot. But they want me to be careful since we . . . have different beliefs. Don't you think it's kinda funny how they all work at the castle, and yet until I came along they hardly crossed paths?"

"Life never goes as you think it will." Stacie, trying not to picture her own mother in the hospital, briefly held Janice's gaze.

Janice touched her arm. "Let's just try to have some fun tonight. And try to forget about . . ."

Becka.

When Janice left, Stacie softly closed the door, feeling more than hearing the click of the latch tell her she was alone and that Janice would soon be starting a new life with Quinton. Through her teen years, she'd imagined Janice would always be with her, that the two of them would stand together, side by side, friends through thick and thin. But something about how easily Janice had left just now to be with Quinton made Stacie realize how fragile their relationship really was. Someday Janice, like Zach, would say good-bye, and Stacie hated good-byes. Too many times they meant forever. Even now, when she knew she had to make her heart say good-bye to Becka, Stacie just couldn't.

Suddenly, the room felt stifling, and she had to get out. Even waiting for Matt in the lobby would be better than staying in this room. She put on her coat, turned off the light, and left.

To her surprise, Matt was already sitting in the lobby.

"Hi!" His eyes lit up as he stood and reached for her hand.

Oh, no! Janice is right, Stacie thought with a start. There was more in his gaze than she'd realized. She stuffed her hands in her coat pockets. "Lead the way."

They walked to the car in silence, but after he'd opened the door for her, he again reached for her hand, so she folded her arms.

"Friends," she said.

He nodded dropped his hands to his side. "I hope so," he said before closing the door and walking around to the driver's side.

Good. He understands. But after he sat behind the steering wheel, he kept glancing at her.

"Let's take the fastest route," she said a little squeakily, handing him the Garners' car keys. "Fort Street, right?"

"Yes." Still he watched her.

She shifted uncomfortably. "What's wrong with me? Do I have toothpaste or something on my face?"

"Nothing's wrong. Absolutely nothing."

There was no mistaking his meaning this time, and she blushed. And the more she tried not to blush, the more she was grateful for the darkness. "Shouldn't we leave?"

"There's something I want to do first," he said. There was a hint of a chuckle in his voice. "Close your eyes."

"What?"

"Don't trust me, huh?"

"Not entirely."

He laughed. "Please?"

"Oh, all right." She waited.

He shifted in his seat a bit. "This probably isn't the best time, or maybe it is, if it cheers you up, but anyway, I wanted to give these to you." He placed something in her lap. "I'd actually wanted to give them to you earlier."

She opened her eyes and saw three plastic shopping bags. She looked at him questioningly.

"They're Christmas presents," he lifted his hand, stopping her protest. "From a friend."

Stacie was mortified. "I don't have anything for you."

"I didn't expect you to."

"Well, thank you." The first bag crackled noisily as she reached inside. "Blank DVDs?"

"I almost decided not to give them to you." He cocked his head to one side. "It was supposed to be for tonight, in case we needed to copy the surveillance video."

"Oh." She bit her lip, blinking back the emotion that suddenly warmed her eyes.

"But I then thought, what the heck? You could probably use them for something else." Matt took the empty bag and scrunched it in his fist. "Next."

Stacie couldn't help but smile at his eagerness. It reminded her of a little boy on Christmas morning. She reached into the second bag. "A can of soup?"

"Split pea. Sorry, it has ham."

She laughed. "My mother would have loved it!"

"I hoped you would, too."

Now, even more than before, she wished she had something to give him, to thank him for making her feel lighter than she had for what seemed like ages.

She reached inside the bag for his third gift. A Christmas ornament—a castle nestled in a cloud. It was similar to the ornament she'd wanted to buy at Tang's Emporium.

"It's a souvenir. You know, to remind you of Craigdarroch."

Stacie didn't trust herself to respond, only stared at the castle.

"Do you like it?"

"I—I like it very much." She slipped it into her coat pocket, hoping he didn't see her trembling fingers. "Where'd you get it? I haven't seen one quite like this."

Matt grinned. "Sorry. I never reveal my sources." He turned on the engine and maneuvered the car out of the parking lot. As soon as he pulled into the traffic, he reached over and lightly touched her arm.

"Can I tell you something?" A light flickered in his eyes.

Stacie swallowed hard. "Sure."

"I know I'm a heel to say this," he began, "especially after Zach. And then after what you went through this afternoon . . ." He placed his hand on her forearm. "And you don't even have to respond right now, okay?"

Stacie clenched her palms together and nodded.

"You know what? I'm gonna pull over. I can't talk to you about something this important while I'm driving."

Suddenly, Stacie felt nauseous, and she rubbed her sweaty hands against her jeans.

Matt shifted the car into park, then looked at her with a smoldering yet tender gaze. "I'm starting to care for you, and not just as a friend." He hesitated, searching her face like he was deciding whether or not to continue. "I know I'm being selfish, throwing this at you right now, but this might be my only chance to be alone with you long enough to say it; and I can't handle saying good-bye, knowing I never said it."

Stacie could barely breathe. She watched him, knowing there was more to come, but wishing there wasn't. Yet Matt only looked at her, his eyes boring into hers until she finally broke the silence. "Matt, I—"

In one swift movement, he leaned toward her and placed his index finger gently against her lips. "Stacie, I meant what I said. You don't have to respond unless you want to." A flash of vulnerability crossed his face. "Do you want to?"

No, I don't want to, and even if I did, what would I say? Stacie thought. She *did* have feelings for Matt, but she could never tell him that. And they only had one, maybe two days left together. She could last two days, couldn't she? "No," she whispered.

Matt frowned, and as he slowly leaned away from her again, the warmth in his eyes melted into an ache so strong it surprised her.

Stacie looked sideways, braced herself against the back of the seat. *Resist. Do not comfort him.* Even an action as simple as resting her hand on his forearm and telling him how much she appreciated his midnight-brown eyes—*no, his friendship*—would only confuse matters.

After what felt like minutes later but was only seconds, Matt pulled back into the traffic, and headed towards the Garners' house.

She avoided his face, pretending she didn't notice how frequently the veins on the backs of his hands moved as he clenched and unclenched the steering wheel.

When she saw Sister Garner standing in the driveway. Her umbrella was open, and her rain jacket was zipped to the neck.

Stacie gasped. "Something's wrong,"

Matt nodded crisply, stopped the car, and leapt out.

Stacie reached for the door handle, but Sister Garner yanked it open first. "I just got off the phone with your aunt! I called her when I found out about Becka and—the news came on while we were talking—and—oh, Stacie! The news was wrong."

Stacie barely felt the rain plaster her face. "You mean about Becka?"

Sister Garner nodded. Stacie couldn't tell if it was rain or tears that drizzled down the older woman's cheeks.

"I had a feeling . . ." Matt muttered softly behind Stacie, raising his umbrella over the three of them. His breath tickled the outside of her ear, and Stacie's heart raced. Too bad there could never be anything between them.

"The body they found had similarities to Becka," Sister Garner explained. "So the reporter said without verifying it with the authorities, that it could be her. But now the police say that child's several years older. It couldn't have been—"

"Becka." Stacie almost screamed her name.

"Let's go," Matt said. "We've got work to do."

{CHAPTER 28}

The Garners' copy of the surveillance tape from the eatery was better than Stacie had hoped for. Rather than the one camera view that she'd expected, the screen was divided between four camera angles, including one that captured the entrance. Stacie, Matt, Janice, and Quinton each concentrated on one view.

The first time through the tape, they made a list of every woman who entered the eatery after Stacie, as well as every woman they saw during the time Stacie was there. The second time through, they analyzed each one.

"That woman back by the groceries didn't look our way once," Stacie said before scooping a forkful of mashed potatoes and gravy into her mouth. "I think we can scratch her off the list." She leaned back against the base of the Garners' sofa and stretched her legs straight in front of her across the oriental rug.

Matt drew a line through the words "middle-aged woman near entrance." He sat on the floor too, about two feet from Stacie. "That's three out of eleven down," he said. "Next is 'twenty-something girl standing at counter.'"

Stacie pressed the remote's PLAY button. The television screen flickered into focus. "I had no idea so many people were at the diner that afternoon."

"It's Christmas." Quinton's mouth was half full of turkey. He, Janice, and Brother Garner had arrived less than fifteen minutes before, so water still dripped from his black hair onto his white shirt collar. "The bookstore's having a big sale."

"That explains why there were so many people, but not why I didn't notice them."

"Give yourself a break," Janice said. "You were concentrating on Nick."

Quinton finished off his last bite of potatoes and then rose from the brown leather recliner. "Since it looks like you and Matt have this under control . . ." He looked straight at Janice. "I'm going back for seconds. Anyone want to join me?"

"I'm stuffed." Janice said, easing out of the sofa. "But I'll see if Sister Garner wants help with the dishes."

Sister Garner, followed by Brother Garner, bustled into the room, carrying a freshly made pitcher of hot wassail. "Of course I'd like help if Stacie can spare you."

Janice's dark eyes flashed to Stacie's face, her expression conflicted.

"Go ahead," Stacie said. "We can only focus on one woman at a time, anyway."

Brother Garner laughed. "Well said, well said," and kissed his wife quickly on the mouth.

Quinton, with equal flourish, took Janice's empty plate and led her from the room. Brother and Sister Garner left with them. Matt, however, hardly moved.

Stacie set her plate on the floor between them and rewound the tape a fourth time. "Scratch the last girl off the list too."

Matt nodded. "Next, 'young woman with a baby.'"

"Which screen was she in?"

"Top right."

Stacie pressed FAST-FORWARD and waited for the young woman

to enter the diner. In the meantime, there were dozens of people, most of them young men, speeding in and out of the screen. *Had any of them seen the woman who'd called 911?*

"This seems so useless," she whispered. "Whatever possessed me to do this?"

Matt slowly turned to her, his expression detached, but his voice intense. "You're not talking about finding the thief, are you?"

Stacie's pulse shot into overdrive, and she caught her breath. "Not—entirely."

Thankfully, he didn't press her for an explanation, but it was several long seconds before he spoke again. "Have you ever wondered if it chose you?"

"I—don't understand."

He held her gaze. "Think about it. You were the only one who recognized Becka. The only one with the determination to look for her. The fortitude—"

"Stupidity, you mean."

Matt moved her empty plate out of the way and scooted next to her, his face serious. "Never stupidity, Stacie. No matter what happens, you—we—know you did all you could. Very few people would have done as much. That's partly why I—" He paused. "Are you all right?"

She nodded, closed her eyes, and willed herself not to care about him.

Several seconds passed, and Matt shifted uncomfortably. Finally, Stacie lifted her index finger, letting him know she intended to answer, but to give her another moment.

His countenance turned patient.

Eventually, she trusted herself to speak. "Thank you for—that." She swallowed hard, but her next words still came out slow and quiet. "Every night I've wondered if I'm doing the right thing. It's so confusing. Sometimes when I pray for help it seems like God's answering me, guiding me, and other times . . .," she waved her hand in front of her, ". . . nothing. Like now." She motioned to the paused video screen. "This seems so futile, but what else can we do?" Again she swallowed.

"What does your gut say? You know, your instincts?"

"That's the last thing I can count on."

Matt hesitated a second, looking straight into her eyes. "But they led you to become a lifeguard. A *good* lifeguard."

"So? It didn't change anything."

He pulled back from her then, obviously frustrated. "You're not thinking clearly—No, please, I'm not trying to offend you. It's just—look, you know as well as I do that someone who is good at something, really good at it, has both the training and the talent. The instincts."

She stared at him, suddenly afraid of what he was about to say, yet not wanting to stop him.

"For example," he continued, "I think the reason you noticed Becka in the first place is because of your experience with Jessica. Because your instincts said, 'Something's different here, pay attention.' Do you really think you'd have noticed her otherwise?"

Stacie shrugged. "I don't know. Maybe."

"Come on! You were in a performance! You're much too dedicated to your art to let anything throw you unless . . ."

Stacie's eyes widened and she held her breath. "Unless I knew." Her words were barely audible.

Janice appeared in the doorway. "So, how many women are left?" She was drying a large saucepan with a dish towel.

Stacie could only stare at her friend. She *had* seen Becka, and she knew it.

Matt looked at the list. "Seven. No, six," he answered Janice.

"Is there any way we can speed it up? It's already eight thirty, and Brother Fillmore told us to be back by nine so we'll be well rested before tomorrow." Janice looked at the screen. "How about if we each try watching one section again, or we each concentrate on a different woman this time?"

"It won't work any better this time than it did last time," Quinton said, suddenly behind her, drying a serving dish. "It's too confusing, especially since none of us really knows what we're looking for."

"Well, we've got to do something."

"Janice is right." Stacie's conviction grew stronger as she spoke.

"But what can we do? So far, all we've done is shoot in the dark."

"Not necessarily," Matt stated. Then, so only Stacie could hear, he muttered, "You understood me, I know it." Then he looked at Janice and Quinton again. "We've used deductive reasoning, too. That's how we got this tape in the first place, remember?"

They nodded in agreement, but while Quinton appeared not to have noticed anything extraordinary going on between Matt and Stacie, Janice studied them with narrowed eyes.

"Here, Stacie," Matt continued, "how about if I read the descriptions of the remaining women, and you think about what you know of the thief—"

"—which is practically nothing—"

He gave her a reprimanding look. "—and see if any description appears more promising than another. It seems to me the only way we can catch her is to get ahead of—"

"—the game," Stacie finished.

A small flicker of light flashed into his eyes.

"Go ahead." Stacie shrugged. "It's worth a try."

He found his place on the list. "A girl with a backpack, late teens or early twenties."

"That one's possible."

"Old woman with grocery bag."

"Put her last. I doubt the police would think I had the voice of an old woman. At least, I hope not."

Matt chuckled softly. "Three young teenagers."

"Possible, but I doubt it. Put them just ahead of the old woman. Next."

"Late twenties or early thirties with a backpack and a young girl. And finally, late twenties or early thirties, shopping in the rear aisles."

"Either one of those could—*Oh!*"

Matt grabbed her elbow. "What is it?"

"Say that again."

"What? Shopping the rear aisles?"

"No, before that."

"With a backpack and a—"

"—young girl."

This time, everyone's eyes rounded.

"No way," Matt said.

Stacie crawled closer to the screen. "You're probably right. But it's worth a look isn't it?"

Both Janice and Quinton hurried to Stacie's side.

"Which section is she in?" Quinton asked.

Matt referred to his notes. "Bottom left. The corner booth, close to where" —his words trailed off thoughtfully— "Stacie, Zach, and Nick are."

Stacie rewound to the beginning and pushed PLAY. Brother Garner walked into the room just as the image wavered into focus.

After watching the screen for a few minutes, Quinton said, "The woman I saw at the castle was blonde, not dark like her."

"So was Becka," Stacie agreed. "But at the Tang's, the woman was dark. Look! See how the girl's wearing a scarf indoors? The girl at the castle did, too."

"What about how the woman turned away from Nick's table as soon as Stacie walked in?" Janice asked.

"And how she suddenly traded places with the girl so her back was to you," Matt added. "Go back to when she was leaving. It's the best view we have of her face."

Stacie did as he'd asked and paused the screen. They all stared at the woman.

"She's similar," was all Stacie could say with any certainty.

Quinton moved closer to the screen too. "I wish we could see her eyes better."

"Why don't we focus on the little girl?" Janice suggested. "Stacie has Becka's picture in her pocket, right?"

Stacie tugged it out, pressed it flat below the television screen, rewound the tape to the time just before the girl left, and pushed PAUSE.

"What do you think?" Matt asked.

Stacie leaned as close to the screen as she could while still seeing the image clearly. She scrutinized the sway of the girls arms as she walked, the curve of her face—her chin—her eyes, comparing them to her memory from the castle. "I think it's her."

Janice leaned toward the screen, staring at the child. "Look at the scarf. See how it's fallen off her neck. There's something dark there."

The word *birthmark* hovered in the air around them, but no one said it.

"She does look a lot like Becka." Janice sighed and sat back.

"And that woman does act pretty suspicious," Quinton added.

"I say we call the police," Brother Garner said solemnly.

Stacie turned to him. "Do you really think it's enough to convince them?"

Brother Garner shrugged "You have enough to be suspicious, and if you really want them to continue searching for Becka here in Victoria, you need to keep that woman and child fresh in their minds." He walked between the recliner and couch and lifted the telephone from the lamp table. "Do you want me to call them?"

Stacie nodded gratefully. "Ask for Sergeant Price."

A few minutes later, he hung up. "He's out on patrol. They'll call him, but if he can't come, they'll send someone else."

"I hope he can come. He's the best chance I have that someone will believe me."

Brother Garner patted Stacie's shoulder. "Don't worry. You're not the only one he'd have to discredit."

Stacie sensed the same unity in her friends' demeanors almost as surely as if they'd stepped forward and repeated the same pledge. It was an overpowering feeling.

About a half hour later the doorbell rang, and to Stacie's relief it was Sergeant Price. He watched the video and carefully listened to their conclusions, but when they finished, he shook his head.

"I know it's not a positive identification," Stacie said, "but please. Please check into it."

"You've obviously gone to a lot of work and I'll be sure to report this to my commanding officer. It should have some bearing on the honesty related to your theft case. However," he looked at each of them in turn, "that woman is not the kidnapper."

Brother Garner stepped closer to Stacie. "Are you sure?"

Sergeant Price frowned. "Her name's Adrienne Doyle. She's a PI. Was on our force for a while, but she moved away. She's in town this week working on a case."

"Your knowing her doesn't prove she didn't kidnap that girl,"

Stacie pressed, trying not to panic. "I saw Adrienne when she was pregnant, Miss Cox. I met her daughter two years ago. She had glasses then, too."

"Look closely at this picture, Sergeant," Stacie pled. "Are you sure she's this Doyle woman's daughter?"

Sergeant Price moved closer to the screen. "She was littler then. Very small. Adrienne used to strap her into the most protective car seat I've ever seen. 'I won't take any chances,' she'd say. She was blonde, and Adrienne used to be blonde too."

"What about the birthmark?" Janice asked.

"It looks more like a shadow to me." He stepped back. "Look kids, I know it's hard to hear this kind of news, but unless you have something else, I need to get back to my beat."

Stacie suddenly felt lightheaded. That child was Becka! She knew it. God had helped her know it. "Wait!" She reached for Sergeant Price's sleeve, but before she'd moved even half the required distance, Brother Garner put his big hand on her arm and gently held her back.

"Thank you for your time, Sergeant," he said.

Stacie gaped at Brother Garner. "But I thought—"

Sister Garner wrapped her arm around Stacie's shoulders, hugging her. "It's not over yet," she whispered.

CHAPTER 29

Brother Garner waited at the window, peeking through the wood blinds for several seconds as the officer left before he finally turned around and very slowly, very succinctly said, "I think it's about time you talked to Becka's parents, Stacie. They'll know their daughter better than anyone."

"I agree," Sister Garner said.

Stacie glanced hesitantly from one to the other of them. "But Sergeant Price said the Hollingsworths don't trust me either."

Matt stood resolutely, feet apart, arms crossed over his chest. "They will after they see that video. E-mail it to them."

"That's a great idea," Brother Garner said, "but I don't have that kind of equipment."

"My office at the university does." Quinton took the video from the machine and set it next to their stack of jackets.

Sister Garner patted Stacie's shoulder. "Go ahead, hon, give 'em a call." She must have noticed how nervous Stacie suddenly felt, because she immediately shooed the others into the kitchen. "Let's give her some privacy. I tried a new apple pie recipe today. You kids can test it for me."

"Is that what you want?" Janice turned to look at Stacie.

"I would like to do this alone."

When they were gone, Stacie took a deep breath and dialed. "Hello? Mrs. Hollingsworth?"

"No, I'm sorry. May I ask who's calling?" The voice sounded slightly familiar.

"She doesn't know me, but I really need to talk to her. Is she there? Or, what about Mr. Hollingsworth? Can I talk to him?"

"They're both here." Stacie sensed uncertainty in the woman's voice. "But they're busy. If you leave me your name and number I'll give them the message."

"It's about Becka. Please have them call me as soon as possible. I'm calling from Canada, but my cell number is local. It's 317-2003."

Pause. "Who is this?"

"My name's Stacie Cox." Stacie had meant to answer with confidence and authority, but even to herself, she sounded hesitant.

"Don't you think you've done enough?"

"Excuse me?"

"What are you trying to do? Break another mother's heart?"

Another mother? Stacie caught her breath. Her fingers trembled as realization suffocated her. "Mrs.—Smythe?"

"Do you really think I'd let you get anywhere close to the Hollingsworths?" Her voice was as cool and impenetrable as a glacier.

"Please let me talk to them."

"No."

"Don't do this! . . . Mrs. Smythe? Are you there?"

"Good-bye."

For a horrible moment, Stacie thought Mrs. Smythe had hung up, but then she heard another woman's voice in the background. "Who is it, Grace?"

Mrs. Smythe spoke, but Stacie couldn't make out the words.

And then—

"This is Leah Hollingsworth. My husband and I would appreciate it if you wouldn't call here again."

Click.

Staring at the phone, Stacie sank onto the couch. She held her head in her hands, allowing her thoughts to spiral downward, recalling how she'd failed to recognize Doyle at Tang's. How she'd lost Becka at the castle. How she hadn't noticed. Then she heard Matt's words in her mind. *"You knew."*

Stacie took a deep breath. Yes, she did know. Which meant that she wouldn't let—she refused to even think of that awful woman's name—stop her.

Her cell phone rang and she flipped it open. "Hello?"

"Stacie?"

"Mr. Hollingsworth?"

"No. This is Nick. You told me to call you if someone contacted me?"

"Oh . . . Yes! What happened?"

"A woman in a green sedan followed me to work."

"Did she have a child with her?"

"I don't know, but she had a really thin face, like the one in your picture. Stacie?"

"Yes?"

"I want her off my tail."

Off his tail? "Why is she following you, Nick?"

"Do you want this woman or not?"

"Of course, but—" Stacie's thoughts raced. She had no idea how to get the woman off his tail! And, did she really want to involve herself with Nick? "What did you have in mind?" she stammered.

"Simple. She's following me, right? So I'll lead her to, say, the donut shop out on Portage Road and then you can show up at nine o'clock tomorrow morning. If she follows me inside, confront her there with whatever it is you want from her. If she doesn't, well, you figure it out. Just make sure I get away. And come alone. No cops."

Stacie felt the blood draining from her face. "Okay," she heard herself say. "Tomorrow at nine." She hung up.

It took several minutes before she felt composed enough to return to the others. They looked up expectantly.

"The Hollingsworth's wouldn't even talk to me, but now I at least know why. Grace Smythe answered their phone."

Sister Garner dropped her spatula. "That woman who's suing your campground?"

"Yes. But right after the Hollingsworths hung up on me, Nick Yates called. He says someone's following him."

Matt's eyes narrowed. "Adrienne Doyle?"

"I think so."

Janice brightened. "Remember in the video how she almost walked up to Nick, but turned around as soon as Stacie arrived? Sergeant Price said she was working on a case. Nick must have something to do with it."

"Nick wants the woman to disappear," Stacie added quietly. "'Off his tail,' he said. I told him I'd do it."

Matt looked furious.

Brother Garner rubbed his chin warily. "Did he say why she was following him? We don't want to get involved with anything illegal."

Stacie grimaced upon hearing her own qualms voiced by another. It made the danger feel ten times worse. "He wouldn't tell me."

The Garners' grandfather clock chimed nine o'clock.

"What's the plan?" Janice asked.

"Nick'll lead her to a donut shop, and I'll—"

"You'll what?" Matt demanded.

Surprised by the emotion in his voice, Stacie turned to him. "I'll be there too and, uh, confront Doyle about Becka."

"That woman could be dangerous," he growled.

Stacie nodded, caught his gaze, tried to fake a composure she didn't feel. "Yes, she could be, but unless someone else has a better idea . . ."

After a silent moment, Quinton leaned back in his chair. "Okay, let's say the plan works, and we do get to Becka . . ."

Stacie half smiled, relishing the sound of "we," even though Nick had told her to come alone.

"How do we prove it's her?" Quinton went on. "And worse, how do we get Becka away from Doyle?"

"Her birthmark might have been enough," Stacie answered, avoiding his second question, "if the police had been willing to check it out. But you heard Sergeant Price. He already believes Doyle. And it's likely the other officers will feel the same way. No, I think we're going to need more than the birthmark to convince them to even take a second look."

"Maybe we can get a bit of her hair," Janice suggested, "and have the police test her DNA. I saw that on TV once."

"That woman will be gone with the girl before we could get the results," Matt said impatiently. "That's why we need the police with us right then."

"That's not really an option," Stacie reminded him.

"Why don't we try looking at this from a different angle," Brother Garner cut in. "How about if we try to prove Becka's not Doyle's daughter?"

Stacie and the others stared at him.

"Think about it," he continued. "If she's not her daughter, the police—Stacie, Matt's right, we have no choice but to figure the police into this plan. The police," he repeated, "would have to hold on to the girl, right?"

"And that would give them time to see if she's Becka or not," Janice added excitedly.

Quinton's eyes remained fixed on some unseen point, like he was mulling something over in his mind. "I wonder. What do you think happened to Doyle's daughter?"

Matt banged his hand on the table in front of him. "Don't tell me you think we should start looking for *her* now!"

"Let's not get too hasty." Brother Garner scooted from the table. "Let me make a few phone calls—see what I can find out about Doyle's daughter."

"And in the meantime," Janice said when he was gone, "we've got to get back to the motel." She looked at Sister Garner. "Is it all right if we use your car tomorrow to meet Nick?"

"Of course," Sister Garner replied, "but only if you promise to let the police know about it."

Stacie went to the living room to get her coat. When she returned to the kitchen, she found Janice kissing Sister Garner on the cheek. "Thanks for dinner. It was delicious."

"Thank you, dear." Sister Garner held onto Janice, her eyes glistening, and then pulled Stacie into the embrace too. "Tomorrow's your last concert," she muttered, "and then you, Stacie, go home. Soon after that, Janice will follow."

Stacie noticed Matt's gaze move quickly to her face. To her surprise, there was emotion in *his* eyes too, intense enough that she had to quickly look away. *Only one more day*, she told herself.

CHAPTER 30

The calm before the storm. That's what it felt like to Stacie as Matt held open the car door for her, walked around to the driver's side, and then climbed in and started the engine. "Janice and Quinton seem to be getting along pretty well," he said.

Stacie exhaled. "Yes, they are."

Seconds ticked silently by.

"Everything will work out," Matt said, reaching for her hand.

Stacie tucked her fingers beneath her folded arms. "Tell me more about Christmas at the Brennon house," she said, hoping not only to distract him away from the reason his eyes glowed so warmly, but also to prevent herself from thinking about her rendezvous with Nick the next morning.

Matt glanced curiously at her. "It's pretty normal, really. My sisters and their families all meet at my parents' house on Christmas Eve. We have dinner, and my nieces and nephews put on the Nativity." He smiled. "We never know what to expect. Sometimes it's a play, sometimes a puppet show. One year they took us on a Christmas egg hunt. Whoever found the egg with the baby Jesus inside got to be the wisest Wise Man."

"Who won?"

"I think it was Grandma Winnie. She's a neighbor. She and

her husband used to spend every Christmas Eve with us. They never had children of their own."

"Like the Garners." Like it would be for her.

"Yes, but now Grandma Winnie comes alone."

"Oh." Stacie shifted uncomfortably.

"There is one thing we do differently from other families."

"Yes?"

"At least, I think it's different. We intentionally keep the kids up 'til midnight on Christmas Eve. Then, Father Christmas, my dad, comes to the door and welcomes Christmas Day. After that, it's my turn."

Stacie imagined a living room full of sleepy, excited children pulling on Father Christmas's beard. "What do you do? Dress up as an elf?"

He laughed. "I play a Christmas song, one I've written. I write a new song every year."

"Really?" She couldn't keep the admiration from her voice. "Is that what you were playing the other morning in the Relief Society room?"

He nodded, and even though it was dark, she saw an appreciative gleam in his eyes.

"It was beautiful," she said, looking away. "It reminded me of what my Christmases used to be like."

They turned onto Blanshard Street, a block and a half away from the motel, when Matt abruptly stopped at the side of the road. "You care for me. I can feel it."

Stacie almost choked. "I—like you—I mean, I'm grateful for what you've—like what you said earlier, but I think you're reading more into—whatever it is you're reading—than there is."

"Not possible."

Stacie stiffened.

"I mean," he went on, softer this time, "I've seen it in your face. Not all the time, but enough for me to believe it's there."

Knowing that toughness was a better defense than cowering in the corner, Stacie lifted her chin. "Sorry. This time you're wrong. I like you, yes, as a friend, but I don't love you." Why did her words suddenly feel like a lie?

"Who said anything about love?"

"Uh—I thought—it sounded like—"

"Well, you were right." His eyes laughed at her.

She fumbled with her coat zipper.

"I am talking about love," he continued. "I believe I'm falling in love with you, Stacie Cox, and I want to know your feelings before I go back to St. George."

"The fact is, I—"

He quickly lifted his hand, palm toward her. "Whatever it is," he held her gaze, "let it be the truth."

"You think I'd lie?"

"I don't know what to think. Heck, I can't figure you out from one minute to the next."

"So, you finally admit it."

"I only meant this was important enough—" He clenched his teeth. "Would you please answer the question?"

She looked into his eyes. They seemed more serious, more sincere than she'd ever seen them. "The truth is . . . I won't marry. Ever."

"I don't understand. Won't?"

She swallowed hard and tried again. "Things don't always last."

"Marriages can. They can ever last forever."

This was definitely going to be harder than she'd imagined. "What I mean is, things change."

"Not truth, and the truth is I'm falling in love with you, and I need to know where to go from here."

Stacie shook her head, folded her arms, and pressed herself deep into the seat as he studied her face. Another girl, Stacie was sure, would have died rather than miss a moment like this, but not her. And no matter how strong her feelings for Matt were becoming, they could never be together.

"What's the problem?" he asked guardedly.

Somehow, she found her voice and forced false conviction into it. "It's only been a few days for us, Matt, and—and what about your girlfriend?"

He opened his mouth, about to protest, but she stopped him.

"After you go back to St. George, you'll eventually see I'm right. You only" —she looked down at her hands— "think you love me."

He growled. "I'm not a child, Stacie. I know what I feel."

Stacie squirmed beneath his gaze, and he leaned toward her. "You know I'm telling the truth, don't you?"

She bit her lip and moved closer to the passenger door, fearing that the agonizing moment would go on forever.

At length, his eyes narrowed. "Don't you—trust me?"

"What?"

"That's it, isn't it? You don't trust me."

"Yes. I mean, no. I mean—what are you talking about?"

He turned away from her and raked his hand through his hair. "You know, Stacie, I can't figure you out. You're so caring, so brave, and yet you run whenever someone even hints at—" He stopped. For several seconds, he stared at her, and the longer he didn't speak, the more she fidgeted.

"That's it, isn't it?" he whispered incredulously. "You've chosen not to get too close to anyone. Even your job as a lifeguard keeps you away. Watching them, protecting them, but never getting close enough to become emotionally involved."

"Yes."

That caught him off guard. "Look, I know you've been hurt, maybe more than most people, but you can't stop getting close to others because you're afraid they'll die."

"Yes, I can."

"No you can't. Not when that's not who you are! Look at the way you've sacrificed to help Becka. That's why I—"

His words pierced her heart, and she wished he would get angry and yell at her. Yelling would be so much easier to cope with than anguish.

"It wouldn't solve anything," she interrupted softly, feeling more than hearing the hollowness in her voice. "No matter what I do, there's no hope."

"No hope for what?"

"For a future. Matt, my parents ignored the truth and married anyway, but in the end, it didn't turn out."

"I didn't know about that, but just because their marriage didn't last doesn't mean ours—yours—"

"Not their marriage, Matt. Life. My mother knew she would die young and leave her children—me—alone, but she did it anyway. I know she didn't expect my dad to die first, but still . . . Matt, I couldn't stand it when my mother died! I won't do that to another child."

Matt sat silent for so long that the stoplight at the end of the road turned from green to yellow to red.

"I think we better get back now," Stacie said.

He pulled back into traffic. "Just because your mother—"

"No, Matt. It will likely be the same for me." Stacie stared out the windshield.

When they finally reached the motel, Matt stepped out of the car, and Stacie, not waiting for him to come around to open her door, jumped out too. They walked to the entrance, through the lobby, and straight to the stairwell. Then they stopped.

"Thank you for explaining." He gently tugged a strand of her hair and brushed it behind her shoulder. "It's not what I'd—hoped for, but for you . . ." Then he took her hand, squeezed it, held it as if he couldn't let it go.

Stacie clung to his touch, knowing this could very well be the last time she was ever this close to him.

"I do understand," Matt went on quietly, "so you don't need to worry. I'll never bother you about this again." Hesitantly, he let go of her hand and headed up the stairs.

Stacie waited there, watching him, listening as the sound of his footsteps clicked in time with the rhythm of her breathing and gradually faded into nothing. How could she just stand there, just let him walk away from her like that? Rationally, she knew it was the only choice she had, that she had to let him go, had to choose pain—to sacrifice—as Janice's mother had. Yet every trembling nerve within her body screamed to run after him and tell him how much she cared.

Instead, she climbed one stair then another and another, and though an involuntary sob strangled against the back of her throat, she continued on until she reached her room.

{CHAPTER 31}

Matt pulled the bedcovers up to his chest and willed himself to relax. It didn't work, so he rolled onto his side. Still, sleep wouldn't come. He rolled onto his stomach. That didn't work either. Maybe a drink of water would help.

He climbed from the bed, but as he tromped past the desk he noticed his cell phone lying on top of it. *Oh, yeah. I was supposed to call Holly tonight.*

Inside the bathroom, he found four individually wrapped paper cups. He filled one, drank it, then filled it and drank a second time before crushing the cup and dropping it into the trash.

On his way back to the bed, he glanced again at his phone. Knowing Holly, she was probably still awake, and if he took his phone out into the hall, he could talk to her without disturbing anyone.

Zach snored and rolled over.

Besides, looking logically at their relationship, nothing had actually changed between them. All Stacie and he had ever done together was perform. And search for Becka.

He reached for the phone, but before he could pick it up, he stopped himself.

But beyond logic, there was emotion, and emotionally, his

heart *had* changed. And though Stacie felt they couldn't ever be together, he knew memories of her would remain even when she was gone. *That* was what he needed to tell Holly. But he wouldn't do it now, not on the phone. She deserved better than that.

He walked to the window and peered through the curtains. The city—cars and lights and people—were hurrying below. It had been the same the last time he'd looked out this window, just before he'd left with Stacie and Janice to go to Chinatown. And though he hadn't originally wanted to get involved, he'd helped them—he had *her*. And he'd helped her every day since. Yet now, knowing she needed his help more than ever before, his hands were tied.

He stared at the phone. Or were they?

On and on he stared, letting the idea formulate. Stacie had called the Hollingsworths, seeking their help, but was refused. Not because of herself, but because of a bitter, unforgiving woman. So, what would happen if *he* called? Would they listen to him?

Maybe. It was worth a try.

He took his cell phone into the hall, gathered his thoughts, his emotions, and then dialed the operator. "I need the number for Ethan and Leah Hollingsworth in Rexburg, Idaho. United States."

{CHAPTER 32}

D o you think I did the right thing?" Leah whispered, gazing
through the living room window at the porch light.

"Do you feel it was wrong?" Ethan asked.

She eased onto the couch next to him and leaned against his
shoulder. The boys were quietly sleeping on the floor beneath
the lit Christmas tree, and a CD of their favorite carols played
softly in the background. It wasn't Christmas Eve yet, but the
boys had wanted to sleep there anyway, and Leah, wanting her
family close, had acquiesced.

"I don't know what I feel. It's hard to imagine anyone could
be so cruel, yet Grace was so emphatic."

Ethan gently kissed his wife on the forehead. "I'll call Detective
Boyle tomorrow. First thing. He'll know how to handle Stacie's
phone call." He wrapped his arm around her, and she snuggled
into the crook of his shoulder.

"How's your back feeling?" Leah asked, careful not to lean
on him too heavily. In his attempt to bring a bit of normalcy
back to his family, he'd taken the boys tubing on some snow-
covered sand dunes that morning and hurt his back. He wouldn't
be moving much for a few days.

"Terrible. I'm almost ready for another painkiller."

"Do you want me to get you one?"

"No. Stay here for another minute. It's nice sitting here in the quiet."

They settled into the silence again, listening to the rhythm of the boys' steady breathing mingled with the Christmas lullaby—a lullaby Leah remembered singing with Becka last year.

I hope she's warm. And safe. Leah forced herself not to say the words aloud, not to let her tears fall, not to break the transitory solace of the evening.

"Are the boys' snowsuits dry yet?" Ethan moved his hand to the scrape above his temple. "Since our sledding trip was cut short, I promised them they could spend as long as they wanted outside in the snow tomorrow. I think they're gonna build a snow cave."

"Yes. They put the inner tubes in the shed, too. They did it while we were at the hospital without Grace even telling them to."

Ethan smiled slightly. "They're growing up."

As if he knew they were talking about him, Thomas rolled onto his side, bumping into a tree branch and knocking down an ornament; it was the salt-dough star Becka had made in preschool last year.

Leah squeezed the top of Ethan's hand. "I'll take care of it. I've been meaning to hang it near the top anyway."

She slid from the couch to her knees and crawled to where the boys were sleeping. Thomas's leg now covered the ornament, so she ever so carefully lifted his limb, pulled out the ornament, and—

The telephone rang.

Ethan, keeping his head immobile against the back of the couch, slowly reached to where it rested on the lamp table. "It better not be another reporter. If I have to tell one more person

Becka's not dead, I'll—hello?"

Leah smoothed the quilts around her boys' shoulders and rehung several ornaments that had slipped to the floor.

"It's someone named Matt Brennon." Ethan held the phone receiver in one hand and covered the mouthpiece with the other. "He's in Victoria, British Columbia. With Stacie Cox."

Leah reeled. "What does he want?"

"He says Stacie's spent every spare minute trying to find Becka, and she believes she's found her. He says he's seen the evidence and he agrees, but they need more credible proof."

Leah covered her mouth with her hand.

"They have a video clip of the girl. He wants to send it to us over the internet, let us look at it, and if we think it's her we'll . . ."

"We'll what?" Leah could barely get out the words.

"This is the thing. They've set up sort of a sting for tomorrow morning at nine. They need quick, valid proof it's Becka, because the police won't believe or help them otherwise." His voice filled with emotion. "What do you say?"

"I want to. Everything in me wants to, but if it's a hoax or a mistake—oh, Ethan, I don't think I could bear it!"

"Then let me bear it for you." His gaze reflected a love strengthened and deepened by their ten years together. "Okay?"

"All—all right."

As Ethan listened to Matt and then gave him their e-mail address, his voice became increasingly optimistic, and Leah could hardly wait until he'd hung up.

"When will the clip come?" she was finally able to ask.

"As soon as he can get it ready. Maybe an hour or two. He has to get with a few people first."

"I'll get the laptop."

About two hours later, the video clip arrived, and as soon as

Leah and Ethan saw the girl, they wept.

"Dear, dear Heavenly Father, it's her," Ethan rasped. "It's Becka."

Leah grasped both sides of the screen, yearning to touch her daughter. "Someone's dyed and cut her hair, but they couldn't get rid of the cowlick above her right temple."

"Look at her mouth. She was born with that frown."

"She's lost a lot of weight."

Ethan, supporting his head with both hands, tried to get up, but failed. "Get her file. Maybe there's something there we can scan in and e-mail back to them."

Leah wiped the tears from her face. "Isn't our word enough?"

"Apparently not. Matt said the RCMP have some kind of connection with that woman who has Becka. They already believe her."

Leah ran up the stairs two at a time to their bedroom, pulled their daughter's file from the cabinet, then dashed back. "Should we send more photos?"

"They have her picture, Leah. Matt says it has to be something that will convince the police to hold on to her long enough to get a positive ID." He pulled out a medical certificate. "What about her blood type?"

Leah shook her head. "That's like DNA. It will take too long."

Ethan set the certificate aside and continued searching through their other documents, but when he saw nothing else, he frantically swept through them a second time.

"Send me, Ethan."

"What!"

"One of us obviously has to go, and it can't be you, not in your condition."

He swallowed hard. "Alone?"

"You know it's the only way," she whispered, "and while I'm gone, you can persuade the police at headquarters to get involved. I know we didn't believe those kids before—"

"—because of Grace."

"—but we do now, and we have to convince the authorities to believe them too."

"Why don't we call the police first? They'll send someone with you."

"Or stop me from going."

Ethan stared at her as if every emotion he'd ever known was suddenly swallowed into that moment, then he pulled her close. "Be careful."

"I'll be as careful as I can, but right now I've got to get a flight out of here as soon as possible. Nine o'clock is less than eleven hours away." She pulled away and reached for the laptop.

"There aren't any flights out of Idaho Falls this time of night," Ethan said. "Go and pack, Leah. I'll find some way. Hey! Wasn't there a pilot here the other night, helping with the flyers?"

"I think so. He was a friend of the bishop, wasn't he?"

Ethan released Leah's fingers from around the phone. "I said, go and pack." He kissed her hard on the mouth. "I'll take care of this. You've got to save our daughter."

At six a.m., Stacie silently climbed out of bed. There was hardly time to fumble blindly through her suitcase, so she slipped on the clothes she'd worn the day before, grabbed her purse and the Garners' car keys from the desk, and crept into the hall.

This is an emergency, she told herself. *Anyone else would do the same thing.*

{CHAPTER 33}

Adrienne hit her fist against the steering wheel. "Riana, I told you to stop crying, and I meant it."

"The door's so hard."

"It's better than lying on the seat. Remember how you flew out of it yesterday when I bumped that light pole?"

Riana cried louder, and an early morning walker glanced their way.

"Quiet!" Adrienne hissed.

Riana's noise turned to whimpers, and Adrienne pressed her fist against her forehead. "Stop it! You're giving me a headache."

"My head hurts too."

Adrienne pulled a bottle of Tylenol P.M. out of the glove box of the rental car. Not only had her own car been badly damaged in the accident, but since Nick had caught her following him, a different car was an absolute necessity.

"Do you still have your water bottle?" she asked.

"Yes."

Adrienne handed her one pill. "Swallow this."

"Will it help my head not hurt?"

"Yes." *And it will make you sleep.*

Riana put it in her mouth. "Yuck!"

"I told you to swallow, not chew."

Just then, Nick walked out of his duplex carrying a bag of groceries and the flat, manila envelope. There was only one reason Adrienne could think of that he'd have those two items with him at this time of day: he was going to meet Paul.

"Hold still, Riana."

The girl whimpered, still gagging on the pill's taste.

Twice, Nick cast a fleeting glance over his shoulder, and once, Adrienne thought he looked straight at her, but the movement was so minute, she couldn't be sure. Then he climbed into his pickup.

Adrienne turned on the engine, pressed her phone's speed dial.

Nick pulled out of the driveway.

"Price? Get your boys ready. Yates is on the move. I'll call back as soon as I know more."

She pulled onto the road a short distance behind him.

{CHAPTER 34}

Stacie's phone rang for the fifth time since she'd pulled into the gas station across the street from the donut shop where she would meet Nick. It was 7:30 a.m. She checked the caller ID—*Matt*—and returned it to the passenger seat beside her.

"Okay," she said aloud, clenching her fingers between the ridges of the steering wheel to stop them from shaking. "So that woman follows him into the coffee shop and takes Becka with her. Then what?"

Outside, the mist turned to rain, and Stacie switched on the windshield wipers. "Then I follow them, and I—confront her. That way, with everyone watching, Adrienne won't hurt Becka, right?"

But they won't help me, either.

Stacie rubbed her hands over her face. *I have nothing!* In truth, as far as she could see, there was only one possible scenario in which she had any hope of rescuing Becka. Adrienne would have to follow Nick inside the shop and leave the girl in the car alone.

"If she does that, I might be able to get Becka away before Adrienne returns. Please, Lord, help me!"

The rain intensified, pelting the windshield like bits of wet gravel, but as soon as Stacie switched the wipers on high, her phone rang again. She picked it up and checked the caller ID. It was a Rexburg number she didn't recognize, and one she hadn't programmed into her phone. "Hello?"

"Stacie! Has Matt gotten hold of you?"

"No—uh, who is this?"

"Leah Hollingsworth. I'm in a taxi, and I'm just leaving the Victoria Airport. Where do you need me to go? Stacie? Are you there?"

Stacie blinked. "Y—yes, I'm here, but I thought—"

"I know. Matt called us last night. He sent us that video, but we don't have time to go into that now. The address?"

Matt called her? "Just a second." Stacie grabbed the scrap of paper she'd written Nick's directions on from the passenger seat and read them to Leah twice.

"I'll be there as soon as I can," Leah said, then hung up.

Stacie's grip around the steering wheel tightened, but her shoulders relaxed. *Becka's mother is coming!*

The weather changed from rain to hail, and Adrienne, stopping at the traffic signal, watched as Nick turned right into a donut-shop parking lot and headed inside. Since he didn't take the package with him, she figured Paul must not be there and decided she'd simply sit back and wait until he finished his breakfast.

She turned left into the gas station behind a black pickup. It took the last available parking space, so she drove next to a pump and turned off the engine. Moments later, the hail turned to heavy rain. She took out her binoculars.

The first thing she spotted through the shop's large, picture window was a glass counter covered in pastries. A long line of customers waited near the cash register, and some of the green booths next to the window were occupied. Nick sat next to two young women.

Suddenly, something blocked her view, so Adrienne lowered the binoculars. Standing in front of her driver's side window was a large man in a brown raincoat. He knocked on her window.

She rolled it down an inch, and a blast of icy wind hit her in the face.

"Would you like help with the gas, ma'am?"

Adrienne smiled warmly. "No, thank you. I'll take care of it."

"It's no trouble." He took the pump from its carriage. "How much would you like?"

Adrienne's smile turned cool. She stared at him for the length of time it took the taxi to leave the lot, waiting for him to squirm, but her ploy didn't work.

He pushed the START button. "Tell me when."

Adrienne flung open her door and jumped out. Rain plastered her face. "Stop! I don't need gas."

"Then why'd ya park here?" He gave her a quick once-over.

Remembering she hadn't changed clothes or washed her hair in two days, she raised her jacket hood over her head.

"This space is for paying customers only."

A taxi pulled into the lot.

"Fine, then!" Adrienne grabbed the pump from him. "But I'll do it myself."

"Suit yourself." He watched her start the pump before sauntering back to the station, and she glared back at him. "Jerk!" she muttered.

Then she saw the taxi stop in front of a beige Cadillac that had backed into a parking space just outside the gas station's front door. *The* beige Cadillac she'd seen way too many times before.

Horrified, she yanked the pump from her fuel tank, slammed it back into its carriage, and dove into her car. "Don't move an inch, Riana," she ordered, turning on the engine.

She pulled forward.

The attendant stepped in front of her. He held a cell phone in one hand and a tire iron in the other.

Adrienne slammed on the brakes, glanced back at the Cadillac, and saw the taxi's back door open slightly.

The attendant sidled around the front of Adrienne's car and stopped next to her door. He was so close that one swing with the iron would have left a gaping dent in her hood. "Four dollars and eighty cents," he said.

Adrienne tugged the first bill she saw, a ten, from her wallet and flung it out the window. "Now get out of my way!"

He bent to pick it up as she stepped on the gas.

"Watch out, lady!"

She looked at the Cadillac and the taxi again, then did a double take. Stacie Cox stepped out of the Cadillac, and at the same time, the taxi passenger's door flew wide open, and a woman she didn't recognize ran straight toward them.

"Mommy!" Riana cried.

"Don't be scared, dear. I'm here."

"No." Riana pointed to the running woman. "*Mommy!*"

Dark, cold dread shot through Adrienne's heart. "Get on the floor," she snarled, cranking the steering wheel. "Now!"

The woman pounded Adrienne's hood. "Becka! Becka!" she screamed. "Let her go!"

Adrienne revved the engine and gunned it forward.

Seconds later, it was over, and Adrienne was on the road again.

The Cadillac didn't follow.

eah!" Stacie ran to her, wincing through each of Leah's screams.

"Go, Stacie!" Leah's arms thrashed at her sides as she arched back in pain. "I'm all right."

Stacie knew it wasn't true. Leah's left leg was bent at an odd angle, and the right side of her face was bleeding.

She pressed her hand against Leah's forehead. "Shh, Leah. You'll be okay."

"Get Becka!" Leah's breathing came in great, anguished gasps. "Please, I beg you!"

Stacie looked at the gas attendant who knelt next to her. He held his cell phone to his ear with his shoulder, leaving his hands free to hold a jacket above Leah's face to protect her from the rain. "An ambulance is on the way," he said.

"Go!" Leah pled. "Please don't let her get away with my daughter!"

Stacie jumped to her feet, grabbing the attendant's sleeve. "When the police come, tell them this is Leah Hollingsworth, and Adrienne Doyle is the one who hit her." Then she raced back to the car, shoved it into gear, and headed south as Adrienne had done.

"Heavenly Father, what do I do?" she whispered, scanning both sides of the road. "Where should I go?" She frantically searched left, then right, then peered down the road ahead of her. If ever there was a time she needed an immediate answer, it was now. *Please, Lord!*

Nightmarish images of Leah laying on the ground and a child sobbing, running down stair after stair, searching for her mother, filled her mind. Sometimes, like in her dream, the image was Becka, and other times, it was herself.

Stacie stepped harder on the gas, drove further and further toward the bay, but there was still no sign of Adrienne. It was as if she'd vanished, again.

Calm down. Think. Where would Adrienne go?

Away was the only word that came to her. Adrienne would want to get away. To where? The airport? The ferry? Her hideout, wherever that might be?

"If I were her, I'd want to leave Victoria as soon as possible," Stacie said aloud.

But Adrienne had stuck around for several days, even though she must have suspected Stacie was on to her. So maybe she hadn't left this time, either. Maybe Adrienne still had something here she couldn't leave behind.

Nick!

Stacie whipped into a restaurant parking lot and turned around. As she pulled back into traffic, heading north again, she flipped open her phone and dialed Nick's number. "Where are you?" she demanded when he answered.

"Where are *you*? That woman's still watching me."

Stacie caught her breath. "She is? Where?"

"You don't know? You're supposed to be watching us both."

"I know. But there was an accident. She ran over—"

He cursed. "All I know is she's in the middle of that big

parking lot, kitty-corner from the gas station."

"Okay. Give me a couple minutes."

Stacie pressed harder on the gas pedal, and about two minutes later, she saw Adrienne's red Toyota. No other cars were nearby, and the engine was running.

"Look," Stacie said to Nick, "there's no way I can get close to her there. Not without her seeing me." She turned left at the next intersection and stopped at the side of the road, trying to stay well out of Adrienne's view. "You have to lead her somewhere else."

"Great plan," he sneered. "What makes you think it'll work this time?"

Stacie lifted her chin. "It just has to, that's all. There're no other options."

Nick swore again and hung up.

Less than a minute later, Stacie watched him leave the coffee shop, climb back in his pickup, and head north. Adrienne pulled out behind him, and Stacie, after waiting for several seconds, pulled into traffic behind them both. She weaved around four vehicles before she again caught sight of Adrienne's car.

Stacie stomped on the gas. Her rear wheels fishtailed on a patch of slush, but she didn't slow down, and she didn't loosen her grip on the steering wheel. She only peered straight ahead, her graze locked on the red Toyota.

{CHAPTER 36}

S tacie had left central Victoria and was now driving west along the island's southern coastline. She knew that Adrienne knew she was being followed, since the three of them had been the only ones driving on this snow-covered, forest-lined highway for at least fifteen minutes. Everyone else, it seemed, had taken refuge from the weather.

Stacie's cell phone vibrated on the passenger seat, but she didn't dare pick it up to check the text. That first icy spot at the edge of town had only been the beginning of a long stretch of slippery road. If she unclenched her fingers now, or if she lost control around that next bend, her search would be over.

Her cell phone rang.

"Give up already," she snapped, turning the windshield wipers up a notch.

Eventually, the bend straightened, and Stacie could no longer see Nick or Adrienne.

She slowed . . . slowed . . . peered through the snow and trees. There had to be tire tracks or an unmarked turnoff somewhere.

And then she saw it—a road branching off from the left side of the highway.

Stacie pulled onto the side road and stopped. As she peered

through the trees, she saw both the black pickup and the red Toyota a short distance ahead. *Where are they going*, she thought. Then she grabbed her phone. The text was from Aunt Kathy.

ANSWER John Garner's call. 311.

That was their family emergency code. Stacie quickly clicked to her phone log. The last six calls were from Brother Garner. She hit SEND as she carefully pulled back onto the road.

"Brother Garner?" She gripped the top of the steering wheel with her free hand.

"Stacie! I've been trying to get a hold of you for an hour now. Are you okay?"

"Yes." No need to tell him all the gory details.

"Thank heavens! We're all sick with worry. Even Brother Fillmore. He was on edge throughout the entire performance."

Surely the emergency isn't about the concert! "Aunt Kathy said you called—" She gasped.

"Stacie . . ? Stacie! Are you there?"

Stacie swallowed hard. "Sorry. The roads are bad. Look, Brother Garner, I'm in a bit of trouble right now, and I really need to get off the phone. What's the emergency?"

"What trouble?" He practically screamed.

She pictured Brother Garner standing in the castle, close to the choir, startling them with his outburst, so she answered more quietly this time. "Look, Adrienne has Becka. Leah, her mother, verified that it's Becka. But Adrienne hit Leah with her car. She's probably in the hospital now. Would you check on her?"

"What?"

"And now I'm following Adrienne. Nick, too."

"Stacie, come back *now*. You're in way over your head."

The terror in his voice made the hair on the back of her neck stand up.

"Stacie!"

"I'm here."

"Listen. It took some doing—I even called a private investigator—but I finally found information on Doyle's daughter. She died last August. Adrienne accidentally backed over her with a car."

"Last August? When?"

"The 5th."

One week before Becka was kidnapped.

"But that's not the worst part," he went on rapidly. "As soon as I found out you went alone to meet Nick this morning, I called Cecil. Here, it'll be faster if I let him tell you."

There were now only about fifty feet between Stacie and Adrienne, so Stacie pulled back just a little. Somehow it made her feel safer.

"The police suspected Nick of armed robbery a few years ago," Mr. Underwood told her haltingly.

Stacie forced herself to concentrate on driving, to not think too much about the danger she could be driving straight into.

"But they never found enough evidence to convict him. Nick moved away shortly after that, but when he returned . . . and he was so secretive . . . I'd wondered if he'd got involved in that again. But he never said anything, and I didn't ask." Pause. "I didn't want to upset Elsie."

Breathe, Stacie told herself.

"Stacie!" It was Brother Garner again.

Her pulse pounded wildly in her throat, but somehow she found her voice. "Listen. Will you please call the police and tell them about Adrienne's daughter?"

"Yes, of course. But you've got to get away from there. Now! Nick might be—they both might be—"

"Desperate."

Brother Garner hardly waited for her to fill in the word. "Tell me where you are. I'll inform the police about that, too."

"I don't know exactly where I am, but let me call, okay? They might find me easier if—"

The phone went dead.

"—they can trace my signal." She returned the phone to the passenger seat.

Minutes later, Nick, Adrienne, and Stacie merged back onto the highway, and not long after that, a large body of water loomed ahead of them. Lightning, like fireworks, danced across the sky. A sign said Sooke Basin.

She picked up her phone again, waited until she found a signal, then called 911.

"What's your emergency?"

"This is Stacie Cox . . . hello?" She looked at her signal indicator. It was still strong. "Are you there?"

"I'm here," the woman finally replied.

"I'm following Adrienne Doyle. She has Becka Hollingsworth, a missing child, and she's also the person who hit Leah Hollingsworth near Portage road about a half hour ago. We're headed toward Sooke."

The woman hesitated. "Is there any immediate danger?"

"Didn't you hear me? She kidnapped a little girl!"

"I've got officers on the way, ma'am. Please give me your exact location."

Stacie described it as best she could.

"Please stay on the line and—"

The signal was gone.

Stacie blew out a terrified breath. *Hold on,* she told herself. *The Mounties are coming.*

Even though she fully trusted in the prayers and faith she'd thrown to the heavens, Stacie was still shocked at how quickly the police arrived. It couldn't have been more than two minutes since she'd hung up with the dispatcher. And as she watched the flashing lights through her rearview mirror coming closer and closer, she couldn't help but feel like they were her own private cavalry coming to save the day. Becka would be rescued!

"Hurry!" she said aloud, smacking her palms against her steering wheel.

But as quickly as the police were driving, Adrienne and Nick were disappearing into the distance.

Stacie stomped on the gas. "As long as I can still see Adrienne, I can tell the police where she is."

Faster and faster, they raced through the endless terrain of trees and snow. Sirens reverberated louder and shriller through the forest with each passing second.

Finally, the Mounties caught up with Stacie, so she pulled to the right side of the road to give them room to pass. Then she glanced over her shoulder. One officer was at her bumper, the other beside her.

Why aren't they passing me? She eased further to the roadside and waved her arm. "Up there!" she screamed.

The officer glared at her, signaled her to stop.

"Not me!"

He nudged his vehicle toward her.

"What are they doing?" Stacie stepped on the brakes and jumped out of the car.

"Stop where you are and put your hands in the air."

She froze. "What? You've made a mistake!"

"Now walk backwards to your car."

"But Adrienne's getting away!"

"Slowly. Keep your hands where we can see them. Get out your license and registration."

drienne watched the flashing red and blue lights grow smaller and smaller until they were nothing more than a pin-sized beam in her rearview mirror.

"Doyle, you're brilliant," she said.

When she'd first thought of calling 911 and asking them to stop Cox from following her—"She's endangering my child," she'd told them—she'd only hoped it would give Yates and her enough time to get away. But she'd forgotten how perfectly naive Cox was. Never, never in a million years would she have guessed she'd get *herself* in trouble by trying to outrun the police.

Adrienne laughed shrilly.

This couldn't have turned out any better if she'd planned it. Well, perhaps if Adrienne had known Cox would be following her today she'd have gotten rid of her before that crazy woman started pounding on her car, but no matter. Things were still pretty much on schedule.

Except for the fact that Yates was taking longer to lead her to Paul than she wanted him to. *Hmm.*

"Riana, climb up here."

Yates accelerated, so Adrienne followed suit.

"Riana," she repeated. "Come up here, please."

"My head hurts too much," Riana whimpered.

"That doesn't change the fact that I need you up here."

Adrienne felt a bit of movement behind her.

Just then, Yates swerved to avoid hitting a large tree branch in the middle of the highway and then turned onto another side road.

Adrienne swerved too, and Riana fell back to the floor, screaming.

"Get up, Riana!"

"I'm trying!"

Adrienne slowed the car slightly to negotiate the turn. The forest thickened and the snow deepened.

Riana clambered over the seat.

Stupid kid. She could move faster than that if she wanted to. "There's a notebook on the floor. Get it for me."

With one hand pressed against the side of her head, Riana climbed across the stack of coats and blankets and slid to the floor.

"Hurry up!"

Yates turned hard. Adrienne barely made it around in time.

Riana screamed, jostled to the floor, hit her head again.

"The notebook, Riana!"

Still crying—something Adrienne would have to deal with later—Riana finally handed her the notebook.

Adrienne flipped to the page labeled Nick Yates, then dialed his cell number. "This is Adrienne Doyle," she said when he finally answered. "I'm in the Toyota behind you. No, I wouldn't hang up if I were you."

"What do you want?"

"What do *you* want, Nick?"

"You have the wrong number."

"Do I? Listen, why don't you slow down a bit, give us a chance to work things out?"

"You haven't answered my question," he growled.

The signal disappeared, but a second later, Adrienne had it again. When Nick answered, she continued on as if there had been no interruption. "I want Paul Rees. But I think you've figured that out by now."

"Who's Paul . . . Rees, did you say?"

"Tell me, Nick. What's he doing in return for you hiding him?" She paused then, letting the weight of her words fill the silence. "Guarding your loot?"

A low snarl. "What do you want with him?"

"Treasure," she chuckled. "He's my hidden treasure."

"You're crazy, lady. He doesn't have a dime."

"His parents do, but then, you already know that, too."

The road grew rougher, and they again lost their connection, but Adrienne didn't worry. The stillness gave her power. *He'll be wondering how much I really know.*

"Suppose I do know where Paul is," Yates finally said when she got hold of him again. "Why should I tell you?"

"Because if you don't, I'll tell the police about a certain estate back in Victoria. You know the one. It was burglarized last month. Oh, and there was another one in Seattle. Two months ago, right?"

Silence. Then, "How do I know you'll keep your mouth shut?"

"You'll just have to trust me, hon, since you have no other choice. Like I said, all I have to do is tell the police . . ."

"Paul's in an old shack about a half mile from here," he finally conceded. "You can have Paul and that's it. Nothing else, you understand? If something—*anything*—is missing, I'll know it!"

Adrienne smiled. "You've misunderstood me, Nick. I don't want you to tell me where he is. I want you to take me to him.

Now."

He let out a string of profanities that only ended when she interrupted with, "Nine–one–one is such a simple number to remember."

Nick hung up before she'd finished her threat, but he also slowed, and after giving her a very impolite hand gesture, he turned his truck around.

"Juvenile," Adrienne whispered before hitting speed dial 2. "Price, you and your men need to get up here. Fast."

{CHAPTER 38}

The Mounties stood close to Stacie, one on either side or her, scrutinizing her.

"My license was stolen." Stacie pressed herself against the driver's side of the Cadillac. "But this was an emergency. After Adrienne ran over Leah, and she was hurt" —the words strangled in Stacie's throat— "and I was the only one left, Leah begged me to save her daughter. What else could I do? I had to follow Adrienne."

"What was the woman's full name again? The hit-and-run victim?" the younger officer asked. The older one, Officer Kissel, had stepped to the side, responding to a radio message from dispatch.

"Leah Hollingsworth. Please, we have to go. The longer we wait—" She peered down the road, into the forest, searching for some sign of Adrienne and Nick, but saw nothing but trees and snow. A chill ran down Stacie's spine. "We might never find Becka again!"

Officer Kissel said, "Ten-four," into his radio, glanced down the road, and then took hold of Stacie's elbow. "Come with me, please."

Images of police interrogations and jail time washed over her, smothering all remaining hope. But what about Becka? Would the girl ever be rescued? Ever see her family again? Would Adrienne, or someone else, hurt her? *Oh, Lord, please help that little girl!*

"Stand up, Miss Cox," the younger officer ordered. He too had hold of her arm, and together he and Officer Kissel pulled her to her feet. "Get yourself under control."

Stacie hadn't realized she'd sunk to her knees.

"I know this is out of the ordinary, Miss Cox," Officer Kissel said soothingly, "but just as you had no other choice than to drive that car, we had no other choice than to pull you over. It's what Adrienne Doyle expected, and we didn't want to tip our hand."

Stacie couldn't move, and no matter how hard he urged her forward, she could only stare at him, trying to make sense of what he was saying. "I—don't—understand."

"I'll explain on the way." He opened the rear door of his patrol car. "Again, this is a bit unorthodox, but . . ." He motioned her inside. "Could you?"

Stacie stared into the back seat. "Am I under arrest?"

"No, nothing like that." He again glanced down the still-empty road, more anxious this time. "Like you said, the longer we wait, the more likely they'll get away."

That, at least, did make sense. Stacie dove inside and found herself sitting behind the bulletproof barrier that separated her from the front seat. "Then you believe me?" she asked through the small, square, window-like opening.

The officer quickly settled into the driver's seat. "Yes." He glanced at her through his rearview mirror. "Mrs. Hollingsworth and the gas attendant reported what happened."

"Then Leah's all right?"

"I don't have any information on that." He pulled onto the road behind the other officer. "Right now we need to concentrate on—"

"—rescuing Becka," Stacie interjected.

He frowned. "Our number one priority is to arrest Doyle for the hit and run. But there's a burglary suspect involved too, possibly in possession of stolen goods."

"But didn't—*no*, I'm certain, Leah told you that girl is her daughter! Doesn't kidnapping take precedence over the rest?"

Officer Kissel sighed heavily, but his sigh rang with authority. "Leah Hollingsworth is an injured and distraught woman, Miss Cox. She may have made a mistake about the girl. And besides, as I believe you know, most of our police force, including myself, have met Adrienne's daughter. Adrienne's one of us, you might say." His expression, which Stacie saw through his rearview mirror, told her he considered the subject closed.

"That girl isn't Doyle's daughter!" she sputtered. "Doyle's daughter died last August."

Her words obviously caught Officer Kissel off guard, but all he did was frown again and pick up his radio. "After we apprehend Doyle and Yates, we'll conduct a maternity test. That should take care of the problem." He keyed his microphone. "This is Kissel. I have a 10-12 with me. We're heading north."

"Is it Stacie Cox?"

"Yes. Oh, and have someone check to see if Doyle's daughter died. In August."

Stacie stared at him, wide-eyed, both of them listening to the static until the dispatcher finally said, "Copy that."

Silence again.

Stacie squeezed her fingernails into the vinyl seat. "Do you know where Adrienne is now?" she asked Officer Kissel.

"She called Sergeant Price just after we picked you up. She's at a shack not far from here."

Stacie flopped back in her seat. She was right. It *was* too good to be true. From the tone of his voice, she knew Officer Kissel had done his duty by checking her claim about the child's death, but he hadn't believed her. And yet, all things considered, could she honestly blame him for that? If someone had accused any of her friends—Janice, Zach, or Matt—of such a crime, she wouldn't have believed him either.

She turned her gaze to the window. Trees . . . snow . . . boulders along the river . . . an occasional campsite . . . but the longer she watched them flicker by, the stronger the quiet suffocated her. "Please, I'd really like to know what's going on."

Officer Kissel looked as if he were weighing his answer in his mind. "Sergeant Price," he finally began, "has been investigating Yates in connection with a couple of estate robberies, and because of information Doyle provided, we almost have enough evidence to arrest him."

Stacie reeled. "Adrienne is Sergeant Price's—informant?" *No wonder he wouldn't believe me!*

"Yes, but she's also working on a missing-person case. She came to us with a few suspicions, and when we put our evidence together, we saw, well, too many coincidences to be ignored. In fact, we believe Yates is hiding both Paul Rees—that's her MP's name—and the loot in the same place."

"Which makes Rees an accomplice," Stacie said. A shiver ran through her body.

Officer Kissel nodded solemnly. "Adrienne wanted Paul. We wanted the stolen goods. It seemed like it was the perfect match all the way up until she committed that hit and run, but either some sort of mistake was made there too—"

Stacie glowered at him.

"—or she must not have known we were aware of her involvement with it. But either way, she continued to keep us informed of Yates's whereabouts." He glanced at Stacie again. "We were already on our way out here when you called 911."

Stacie gazed out the window, but saw nothing. "That's how you found me so quickly."

He nodded again. "That, and the fact that Adrienne called 911 several minutes prior to your call and told us you were threatening her." This time, he watched her reaction, but Stacie must have passed his scrutiny, because he added, "It's complicated."

She swallowed hard.

"You're right," Officer Kissel said. "It's also dangerous, which is why you have to stay in this car from here on out."

At first, Stacie felt relieved to hand the search over to them, but the longer she thought about things, the more she realized she couldn't just sit idly by. She'd worked too hard, thought too long, felt too much for Becka. "What if the two of you aren't enough?" she asked, referring to the officer in the other car. "Maybe I could be an extra set of eyes."

"There are at least half a dozen more officers on their way right now. We'll be enough."

"Then why did you bring me along? Couldn't you have left me back there? Told me to go home?"

He lifted one eyebrow. "What would you have done if we had?"

She shrugged. "Gone back . . ."

He shook his head.

"Tried to find Adrienne," she admitted.

"Exactly." He nodded sharply, pulled to the roadside, shifted into park. "The shack's just ahead of us. We'll wait here until the others arrive, but if anyone tries to take the road back to town, we'll stop them. Officer Crandal," he motioned to the other police car, "will be stationed just outside the shack."

Stacie nodded apprehensively as she grasped the enormity of the situation. "So all we do is wait?"

"Yes. And watch."

Officer Crandal's voice crackled over the radio. "They're inside. Doyle signaled through the window. She's seen the goods."

Officer Kissel lifted a pair of binoculars from the seat beside him, put them to his eyes, and slowly swept back and forth across the line of trees, especially toward the west where the river lay.

Stacie's head began to swim, and her heart pounded in her ears. Was this what hysteria felt like? It had been too much, too terrible, too difficult a task for anyone, especially herself, to have taken on. Yet, as Matt had reminded her, she *had* taken it on, and something inside her had urged her to do so.

See, I'm still here.

She felt rather than heard the voice of God in her mind and heart. It was powerful and settling.

"Yates saw me. He's running!" the officer on the other end of the radio called. "South, along the river. I'm going after him."

Officer Kissel aimed his binoculars west, peered through the trees, and waited.

Stacie leaned closer to the barrier between them, yearning for more details, but before she had a chance to ask for them, he shouted into the radio, "He's armed!"

She clenched her seat, counting the seconds, praying that Nick would be caught and the Mounty would be all right. Stacie didn't breathe. Nor, as far as she could tell, did Officer Kissel.

About a minute later, he relaxed noticeably. "Yates in custody." He put the radio back to his mouth. "Any sign of Doyle or Rees? Or the kid?"

Doyle's name sent another wave of hysteria through Stacie. She had to get out of the car—had to get Becka away from that woman! She reached for the door handle.

"They were still in the cabin when I went after Yates," Officer Crandal answered. "Any sign of backup?"

"Not yet."

Stacie returned her hands to her lap, waiting. Waited. There was nothing to do but worry about Becka and anticipate what was coming next.

Suddenly, Officer Kissel straightened, gripped the binoculars with his left hand, and grabbed the radio with his right. "Male suspect running south, close to the road."

He glanced over his shoulder. Stacie did the same but saw nothing.

"I'm going after him."

"Ten-four."

Officer Kissel leapt from the car, leaving the binoculars on the seat, and raced across the road into the woods.

Her teeth chattering and her hands shaking, Stacie reached through the protective barrier and retrieved the binoculars. She peered through them, following Officer Kissel's progress toward the man.

So that was Paul Rees.

He was short and wiry, and he maneuvered through the forest with the agility of an antelope. If Officer Kissel didn't catch him soon, Rees would get a—*wait a second! What was that?*

Stacie whipped the binoculars back north. Trees . . . river . . . snow . . . there! A small figure in a black coat and green scarf.

Becka!

{ CHAPTER 39 }

Stacie couldn't believe what she was seeing. Becka, alone, stepping just outside the trees, running parallel with the road so close to where Stacie sat in the police car.

She yanked on the door handle. It didn't budge. What was going on? Had Officer Kissel locked her inside?

Frantically, she rammed her body against the door, and when it still didn't move, she futilely tried the window. The other door didn't work either. She was trapped.

"Becka!" she screamed, pounding on the window.

The girl didn't hear her, only ran further away.

Stacie banged on the bulletproof barrier. "Becka!"

She poked her right arm through the small opening. It had been wide enough for her to reach through and get the binoculars. Was it wide enough for her entire body to slip through?

It had to be.

"Becka!"

Stacie struggled out of her jacket, then shoved her arms, her head, her shoulders, and then her hips through the opening. She smashed her chin on the steering wheel as she pulled her legs through. She tasted a trickle of blood on her tongue where she'd bit it. Finally, she was out of the car.

"Becka!" She plowed through the four-inch layer of snow. "Come back."

Becka's figure, now almost entirely hidden by the forest, didn't stop.

Stacie yelled again, two more times, until she finally screamed, "I'll take you to Leah!"

Becka slowed.

"It's all right, Becka. Leah, your mother. She's not far away." Becka turned and started toward her. Stacie, her arms outstretched, pushed herself even faster through the trees. Within seconds, Becka was in her arms.

"Becka, Becka." Stacie hugged the reticent child against her breast, smoothing her hair, hardly daring to believe it was really her. "I've found you. Hush, now. Hush. You're safe."

Tears trickled down the girl's cheeks. "Where's Mama?"

"I'll take you to her. But we have to hurry, okay? . . . Becka?"

Becka stiffened. Shook her head. Her lower lip trembled, and she pushed away from Stacie.

The hair on the back of Stacie's neck quivered to attention. Becka, she now realized, wasn't looking at her anymore. She was looking at something, or *someone*, directly behind her.

"I told you, Riana, never to run away from me. You could get lost," said a low, syrupy voice.

Stacie looked over her shoulder, but Adrienne's fist was too quick. Stacie fell to her knees, blood dripping from her nose onto the snow.

"How'd you get away from the police this time?" Adrienne reached inside her coat pocket and pulled out the severed pieces of a small card. She flicked them at Stacie.

Stacie recognized the pieces of her driver's license lying in the snow. "Let Becka go," she rasped.

Adrienne pulled Becka next to her and held her there. "I don't know who you're talking about."

"Yes, you do." Stacie reached out to the girl, her eyes glued to Adrienne's face. "Becka, give me your hand."

Becka nudged her scarf below her chin and wriggled her shoulder, ever so slightly, beneath Adrienne's iron-like grip.

"Her name's Riana, not Becka. See, dear, I told you it was dangerous to run off."

Becka stared at Adrienne, nodded.

Adrienne smiled. "See how this stranger is trying to convince us you're someone else?" She slowly picked up a long, four-inch-diameter splintered log, grasped it with both hands, and waved it back and forth. Back and forth. "Head back to the shack, dear," she said to Becka. "This won't take long." And then she swung.

Stacie dodged the blow and reached for Becka, but on the backward swing the log smashed Stacie in the shoulder. Her cry was loud and low as the excruciating shock seemed to course through every nerve.

Adrienne moved next to her, stared down at her with cool, hypnotic eyes, and lifted the log to her shoulder. "You're too late," she whispered. Then she took Becka's hand and swaggered into the woods toward the river.

Stacie wiped the blood from her nose with the back of her hand, ignoring the throbbing in her shoulder, and slowly pushed herself to her feet. She staggered forward, then stopped. She grabbed hold of a giant hemlock to steady herself, then stumbled forward again.

Soon the forest opened to a clearing where she saw a small, rustic, shack, and behind it, fastened to the riverbank and bobbing up and down with the rush of the current, was a small, gray canoe. Snow lined the upper edges, and Adrienne was urging Becka to climb inside.

Stacie lurched after them. "Stop! Don't do it, Becka!"

Adrienne turned toward her, looking at her as if she were a casual bystander. "She's my daughter," she said without emotion. "She'll do as I say."

Stacie slowed her steps. "It's only a matter of minutes before the Mounties will be here. Becka will only slow you down."

Adrienne pinned Becka against her side so hard that the child grimaced in pain.

"You don't need her anymore," Stacie added, trying to ignore Becka's distress. "Letting Becka go is the only chance you have."

"Riana, get in the canoe."

Becka took one hesitant step into the icy water, and Stacie grabbed for her arm. "No! Don't listen to her. You're Becka! I'll take you to your mother, to Leah!"

The girl looked up at Stacie with confused eyes but said nothing and didn't move.

"Her name's Riana." Adrienne hissed. "My daughter's name is Riana."

Stacie heard a hint of desperation in the woman's voice. "But this isn't your *real* daughter, is it? She's different somehow, isn't she?"

Adrienne stared at her. "No," she said coldly.

"What's different?" Stacie pressed, keeping her gaze glued to Adrienne's, ever aware of the log in the woman's hand. "Is it her hair? Her speech? Her—" She suddenly remembered what Sergeant Price had said about the girl's glasses. "Is it her eyesight?"

Adrienne scowled.

"Is that why Riana died? Because she didn't see you backing the car?"

Adrienne's eyes widened, and she inhaled a great gulp of

air. But just as quickly as it had vanished, her composure had returned. "Riana, get in the boat!"

Becka's lower lip quivered, but she climbed into the canoe. It wobbled back and forth, almost tipping over.

Still on the shore, Adrienne waved the log at Stacie again. "Sit down and don't move," she commanded Becka, her attention still on Stacie. "You don't want to fall in, do you?"

From the corner of her eye, Stacie saw Becka mouth the word *no*. Realizing that any sudden movement could not only dump Becka into the current but also send Adrienne into a log-swinging rage, Stacie fought against her urge to rush after the girl.

Adrienne untied the canoe from the boulder it was fastened to and let it drift slowly, slowly to the end of the rope, taunting Stacie.

Becka wailed in terror.

Stacie lunged after the rope. But as soon as she felt the hemp at her fingertips, Adrienne swung the log. This time, it hit Stacie squarely in the head.

She landed, eyes closed, face down, on a wet boulder. Her ears rang and her eyes watered. Blood dripped from the side of her head, and for a second, all she could feel was a throbbing point of pain.

She moaned, rolled over, and opened her eyes in time to see the log coming at her again. With less than a second to protect herself, she covered her face with her arms and kicked—hard.

Adrienne doubled over, then backed away, tightly clenching the log in one hand and the canoe rope in the other, only now she'd reeled the canoe back to the shore. "It's time for us to go," she said to Becka.

Stacie struggled to her feet.

Adrienne shook her head, smirking slightly, and raised the log for a final blow. Stacie covered her head again, preparing herself for the inevitable rush of pain, but before Adrienne could swing, Stacie heard the sound of men's voices. *The Mounties.*

Adrienne blanched. She stared hard at Stacie for a moment, then methodically kicked the canoe away from the shore. The rope slid along the palm of her hand.

Clenching the side of the canoe, Becka screamed.

Stacie stumbled, charged at Adrienne, straining to catch the rope in time, but just before she got there, Adrienne tossed it into the water. "Distraction," she said. "They'll be so worried about the girl they'll forget about me."

Stacie stared at her then at Becka in horror.

"Don't worry," Adrienne went on, turning upstream as nonchalantly as if she were on a Sunday afternoon stroll, "I told Riana—or, Becka, did you say?—not to stand up."

Stacie whirled. The canoe had already drifted several yards downstream and was so close to the middle of the river that the strength of the current, made worse by the recent storm, was tossing it back and forth against the chopping waves.

"Hold on, Becka!" Stacie screamed. "Stay still. Help's coming!"

But the canoe was so far away by now, and the howl of the wind roared so loudly in her ears, that Stacie doubted Becka could hear her. So she ran, hobbling along the shore, keeping Becka in sight, praying someone would come soon—someone who could help them.

The canoe jammed into a mass of fallen logs. Becka stood.

"No!" Stacie flailed her arms high over her head. "Sit down!"

But it was too late. The canoe tipped, and Becka fell into the water and disappeared beneath the surface.

Terror coursed through Stacie's veins. She scanned the forest behind her. *Where were the Mounties?*

Becka's head bobbed above the water, near the logs, and then went down again.

Stacie rushed to the water's edge, her eyes glued to the spot where Becka had last surfaced. If she didn't go out to her now, Becka would likely drown. But with the water so cold and the winds so high, Stacie knew that if she went in, she too would probably succumb to hyperthermia.

Becka's head surfaced then disappeared again.

No longer thinking, Stacie ran and plunged into the river. The first blast of freezing water punched the air from her lungs. She gasped, but forced herself to fight the panic.

Exhale–gasp. *Calm down.* Exhale–gasp. *Life.* Exhale. *Clear your head.*

By the time she'd regained enough control of her breathing to continue, her limbs felt numb. With each stroke she struggled against the weight of her clothing and the weakness from her injuries.

Keep going. Swim with the current. Focus on Becka.

Stroke after stroke she swam, struggling to keep her head above the chopping waves, thinking only of Becka.

Finally, Stacie reached the overturned canoe. She held onto it long enough to catch her breath, then dove straight down, fighting the current, fighting the numbness in her limbs. She opened her eyes, but the water was so dark she might as well have kept them closed.

She went up for air, searched for some sign of Becka, and finding none, dove again. This time she swam to the bottom of the river.

Seconds later she surfaced. *Oh, Heavenly Father, where is she?*

Back into the blackness.

She felt around the logs, reaching into the current as far and wide as she could without being swept from safety. And that was when she felt something. Something like seaweed. Or hair!

With all her remaining strength, Stacie pulled, felt the child's face, and shoved Becka over her head and into the open air.

She didn't know what happened next. It was as if the girl was gone from her, and Stacie was floating, floating in warmth and quiet and infinite peace. She saw her father leading her along a wooded trail. Matt, his penetrating, watchful eyes, was helping her. Leah, lying hurt and broken on the ground, screamed for the life of her child. And she saw her mother, her own mother, cradling her face against her chest the moment before she'd gone to the hospital for the last time.

Am I dead? Stacie wondered.

Oh, why was it, now that she'd come to the end of her life, that she finally understood how much her mother loved her? That even though her mother had known she would die, she *had* loved her— had chosen to give Stacie life because she'd loved her with everything she had. And had wanted Stacie to live and love, too.

Strong hands pulled her to the light.

Stacie coughed. And wept.

{CHAPTER 40}

Stacie opened her eyes and tried to focus. *Where am I?* she thought. *Did I die?* Then she felt the pain in her head and shoulder and knew that this couldn't possibly be heaven.

"Stacie?"

It was a vaguely familiar voice. Female.

Stacie didn't open her eyes. She only shifted in her bed and moaned again. "Hmm?"

"Thank you. For Becka."

Stacie's eyelids flipped open. "Leah?"

"Yes. I hope you don't mind. I asked the doctors to put you in here. With us." Stacie, her muscles quivering from the strain, pushed herself further up against the pillow so she could look more fully at the woman in the bed next to her. "We're in the hospital?"

Becka lay in her mother's arms, snuggled close. "Is she—all right?" Stacie asked softly.

"Yes. But a bit malnourished. Dehydrated, too. And terrified." Leah smoothed her right hand over Becka's hair, stopping momentarily against a tear-stained cheek. "She won't let go of me, you know. But then I can't bear to part with her, either."

Stacie's throat and eyes burned with fresh emotion, and when, a moment later, she saw tears running softly down Leah's cheeks, she gulped.

"I'm sorry," she said finally.

Leah wiped her face with the back of her hand. "You have nothing to apologize for. It's me. I'm the one to blame."

Stacie stared at her. "You? None of this is your fault. When I think how close I was, twice, how I could have saved Becka if I'd only known, I—"

"I'm the one who let her leave my sight." Leah's voice was both flat and raw and held the same words that had sliced through Stacie's thoughts since Jessica had died.

"And when I think," Leah went on with sudden vehemence, "that I let Grace have so much power over my decisions, that if Matt wouldn't have called, we might never have found my Becka . . ." She shuddered and wiped fresh tears from her face.

"You couldn't have known what would happen," Stacie whispered.

"I'm trying to accept that excuse." Leah reached with her free hand for a tissue and dabbed it to her face. "The same goes for you, now that I've met you. And knowing what you did, well, Grace is wrong about you."

Stacie tried and failed to keep her lips from trembling.

Leah continued, "Don't let Grace's bitterness destroy you."

Stacie stared back at the woman, then lowered her eyes to the sheet folded neatly over the blanket across her lap. "I was angry, you know."

Leah tilted her head quizzically.

"At Mrs. Smythe," she clarified. "I wasn't supposed to babysit her kids, but she left them at the pool with me anyway. And when the boys started fighting, and I couldn't get them to stop . . . and then, well, afterwards, I told myself it was Mrs. Smythe's fault. But only part of me believed it."

New tears came to Leah's eyes. "Becka was mad at me, too, and I—it wasn't your fault. It wasn't my fault. It was"—she haphazardly swept her arm in front of her, taking in the whole of the room—"Adrienne Doyle's fault."

The two looked at each other, neither breathing, and when Leah smiled an unhappy, aged sort of smile, Stacie laughed. Not loudly, for she felt no mirth, but her entire body shook, and tears she could no longer contain spilled from her eyes. And when the cry was over, she felt lighter and at peace.

Leah sighed, closed her eyes, and snuggled closer to her daughter. Watching her, Stacie exhaled long and deep, and then closed her eyes. She must have fallen asleep, for when she opened her eyes again, she found Janice standing over her with her hand pressed against her forehead.

"You're awake," she said.

Stacie smiled and glanced over at Leah. Both she and Becka were still sleeping. "Shh. They really need the rest."

Janice moved closer to Stacie. "It's good to hear your voice. The doctor said you'd be fine, but when you didn't wake up sooner, we were worried."

"I actually woke up a while ago," she whispered, nodding toward the other bed. "We talked, and everything, you know, it's all right."

"I'm so glad." Janice grinned, but then her expression turned solemn. "But what did you think you were doing, running off like that? Alone! Do you have any idea how dangerous that was? How worried we all were? Brother Fillmore nearly called off the concert so we could look for you. It was only when he learned the police were involved that he consented to go ahead with it." She scrunched her eyebrows disapprovingly. "Information he found out on his own, by the way, from Sergeant Price. Not you!"

Stacie grimaced. "Sorry."

"And Matt! Pacing, fuming, yelling at everyone. It was a good thing Lara was feeling better, because he wouldn't have been any use to us at all. He didn't even calm down after we found out Adrienne Doyle was in custody."

Stacie tried to sit up again. "They caught her?"

"Just after you jumped in the river." Janice grasped her firmly by the shoulders and gently urged her back against the pillows. "Yes, Sergeant Price told us all about it. Said he saw, from a distance, Adrienne set Becka adrift. It was then he knew Leah was the real mother." She smiled. "Actually, he said if he hadn't known better, he'd have thought *you* were the real mother."

Stacie shifted uncomfortably. "I'm not Becka's mother. I'm not anyone's—mother." *Yet.*

The unspoken word jolted through her senses, but more than that, the memory of Matt standing at the bottom of the hotel stairs, his dark eyes telling her good-bye, flashed through her mind. "So—um—you stayed?"

Janice nodded. "Some of the others wanted to stay too, to make sure you were okay, but it was too expensive. And, well, they had their families to get back to."

Matt among them, Stacie thought, staring stoically in front of her, hoping Janice couldn't see her disappointment.

"Oh, yeah!" Janice moved to the nearby closet and retrieved Stacie's cell phone from her purse. "You left it in the Garners' car. You have a few messages from your aunt."

"Oh, no!"

Leah's eyelashes fluttered.

Is she awake? Stacie wondered. Then she looked at her phone. She had two new messages, so she clicked on the first.

Glad you're okay. Don't ever do that again!

The second message read:

Heard you need to recuperate. Garners invited us for Christmas. Be there around 4.

So her aunt and uncle were coming to Victoria for Christmas. That was good news, yet Stacie couldn't help but gape at the phone, feeling as if her old life was settling over her again— as if nothing had changed. Yet something deep inside her *had* changed. While she'd always believed that remaining alone was best, searching for Becka had changed her mind. Life and love were risky, and the only way to have them was to face them, to fight for them. But, Stacie thought with a sigh, the problem was she'd learned that lesson too late

She reached out to set her phone on the nearby nightstand, and there, sparkling as if it were resting in full sunlight, was the miniature castle Matt had given her. She blinked back the tears that suddenly burned hot behind her eyes. "Sorry," she said, not looking at her friend. "I don't know what's gotten into me."

"I do," Janice whispered. "You really should give him a chance."

With shaking fingers, Stacie pulled a tissue from the box next to the castle and blew her nose. "It's too late. He's gone and—"

Janice shook her head and motioned to the door. "He's out there. Like me, he hasn't left this place since the paramedics brought you in."

Stacie stared at her, mouthing Matt's name, afraid if she said it out loud it wouldn't be true.

"Yes, Matt. I'll tell him he can see you now."

"Wait a second!" She glanced at Leah. Her eyes were open now—Becka's too—and both of them were smiling at her.

"Pretend we're not here," Leah said. "I'll close my eyes. See?

And Becka, she'll hardly know what's happening anyway."

"No, wait, Janice! Maybe later—"

Janice laughed. "I'll leave. After I call him in."

A strange kind of panic—or was it hope?—washed through her. "How's my—I mean, I don't have mascara smeared all over my face again, do I?"

Laughing louder now, Janice walked out of the room.

Before the door closed behind her, Matt stood in the doorway, looking at Stacie with those earnest brown eyes. He wore jeans and a long-sleeved T-shirt.

"How do you feel?" he asked.

"Okay, considering . . ." His tenderness and the intensity of his gaze pushed all but one coherent thought from her mind: *I love him.* "Uh—how are you?"

"Fine." His eyes were guarded, his voice careful.

"And, uh, Holly?"

"I don't know, but I'm sure she'll be fine." He stepped toward her, his gaze riveted to her face.

Stacie blinked, trying to reclaim her senses. "Did something happen to her?"

Slowly, cautiously, Matt took Stacie's hand in both of his, and she marveled at how comforting it was—how warm his skin felt against hers, how crazy she must have been to have ever pulled away from him.

"I'd wanted to tell her in person, but" —he shrugged— "I realized it couldn't wait."

Stacie bit her lip to keep it from quivering, to stop her heart from hoping too much. "For what?"

Still holding onto her with one hand, he placed the other carefully along the side of her neck just below her ear and leaned toward her. "We broke up, and I—uh—decided I don't want to live in St. George."

Stacie couldn't believe it. "What about your father's business?"

Matt smiled. "All I'll have to do is tell him how well the construction industry is doing in Rexburg, and he'll agree to let me start it up there." His thumb caressed her jawbone.

She caught her breath. "You'll be in—"

"Rexburg, yes. Near you, if that's all right."

Through the corner of her eye, she saw Leah trying not to smile.

"That's perfect," Stacie whispered.

Matt started to let go of her hand, trying to adjust her blankets, but she clung to his hand, and when he grinned, his smile warmed his eyes. "After you told me how you felt about marriage and having children, I decided to let you have your way. But the harder I tried to forget you, the harder you held on."

"That's not true! I told you to leave."

He laughed roundly, and the sound rumbled through her being. "Maybe not intentionally, but you did hold on. Everywhere I looked, you were there. The castle, the piano, the swimming pool. But especially in my heart. I had no chance to escape—not that I really wanted one."

"But—"

He lifted her hand to his lips and kissed her fingertips.

She cleared her throat. "But we were only together for a week. Less than that."

"Actually, last night, after I called Leah, I realized I was interested in you all fall semester. I just hadn't let myself believe it." He moved his face close to hers. "But even so, we'll spend as much time as you need for us to get to know each other." He pressed his index finger against her lower lip. "I believe I'll enjoy that."

"What—" She swallowed, trying to think logically. "What

about—I'm still my mother's daughter."

"And your father's. You inherited his genes too, right?"

His voice captivated her, and the longer she gazed into his eyes, the stronger her hope grew.

"Anyway, we'll cross that road *if* it comes," he added. "That is . . . *if* you love me?"

Stacie tenderly kissed the back of the hand she held in both her own. "I do love you," she said. "But what if it's *when* it comes?"

"Then we'll deal with it." He pulled her into his arms.

"Are you sure?"

"Oh, yeah."

And the kiss that followed pressed so sweetly, so dizzily, so exultantly upon her heart that she finally felt peace.

ABOUT THE AUTHOR

Ronda Gibb Hinrichsen studied writing at Ricks College, Weber State University, and Utah State University. Her magazine credits include stories and articles published in *The Friend*, *New Era*, *Ensign*, *Guideposts for Kids*, and *Class Act*. Ronda currently writes feature articles for yourLDSneighborhood.com.

Ronda first knew she wanted to be a writer when she was in the sixth grade. Her English teacher read S.E. Hinton's *The Outsiders* to the class, and when she reached the section where Johnny urges Ponyboy to stay "gold," Ronda realized she wanted to write "golden" words just as Hinton had. More than that, she wanted those words to encourage the "golden" in others. That remains one of her goals.

Ronda, her husband, and their three children live in northern Utah. She loves to hear from her readers and can be contacted through her website at www.rondahinrichsen.com or by e-mail at storywriter@rondahinrichsen.com.